"Yes?" she whispered.

"Yes," Ford ground out. He couldn't get the word out fast enough.

Then she gave him what was undoubtedly the most tender, reverent kiss of his life. Just a gentle brush of her perfect lips, and Ford was consumed with a kind of yearning he'd never known before.

More. The blood in his veins pumped hard and fast. *More. More. More.*

She pulled back just far enough to smile into his eyes. "Thank you."

"For?" he asked, incapable of forming more than a single, strangled syllable.

"For telling me that story about Percy and the puppies. It might be the best gift anyone has ever given me."

Ford really hoped that wasn't true. Maple deserved better than that. She deserved a lifetime of birthdays with cake piled high with pink frosting and blazing candles, Easters with baskets full of chocolate bunnies and painted eggs, a puppy with a red satin ribbon tied in a bow around its furry little neck on Christmas morning. She deserved the perfect kind of love she seemed so hungry for. Yesterday, today...always.

He reached out and tucked a lock of dark hair behind her ear. "There are more stories where that one came from."

But to hear them all, you'd have to stay.

Dear Reader,

Surprise, and welcome to Bluebonnet, Texas! Would you believe that I've lived in Texas my entire life, and this is the very first time I've written a miniseries set in my home state? *Dog Days of Summer* is officially my twenty-seventh book for Harlequin, so I figured it was time. Also, I had a ball writing my last book, *Fortune's Lone Star Twins*, which is part of the legendary Fortunes of Texas series and obviously set right here in the Lone Star State. So I decided to create my own town in the Texas Hill Country. Bluebonnet is full of small-town charm, swoony heroes and dogs.

Lots and *lots* of dogs.

Dog Days of Summer is the first book in my new Comfort Paws series, featuring stories about therapy dogs and the relationships that spring up around them. This series is really meaningful to me, personally, because I do volunteer pet therapy with my dog Charm. I've been involved with this sort of volunteer work for many years. In fact, my first therapy dog was a golden retriever named Nellie, and she was my inspiration for Lady Bird in *Dog Days of Summer*.

I hope you enjoy this romantic journey with Maple and Ford! Look for the next book in the Comfort Paws series, coming later this year.

Happy reading,

Teri

DOG DAYS
OF SUMMER

TERI WILSON

Harlequin

SPECIAL EDITION

 **Harlequin®**
SPECIAL
EDITION™

Recycling programs for this product may not exist in your area.

ISBN-13: 978-1-335-59471-6

Dog Days of Summer
Copyright © 2024 by Teri Wilson

Sit Stay Heal
Copyright © 2024 by Teri Wilson

 Harlequin Enterprises ULC
22 Adelaide St. West, 41st Floor
Toronto, Ontario M5H 4E3, Canada
www.Harlequin.com

Printed in Lithuania

 MIX
Paper | Supporting responsible forestry
FSC® C021394

USA TODAY bestselling author **Teri Wilson** writes heartwarming romance for Harlequin Special Edition. Three of Teri's books have been adapted into Hallmark Channel original movies, most notably *Unleashing Mr. Darcy*. She is also a recipient of the prestigious RITA® Award for excellence in romantic fiction and a recent inductee into the San Antonio Women's Hall of Fame.

Teri has a special fondness for cute dogs and pretty dresses, and she loves following the British royal family. Visit her at www.teriwilson.net.

Visit the Author Profile page
at Harlequin.com for more titles.

For our special friends
at Juniper Village Lincoln Heights
and Northwood Elementary School

xoxo Teri and Charm

CONTENTS

DOG DAYS OF SUMMER

Chapter One

So this was Texas.

Maple Leighton wobbled in her Kate Spade stilettos as she stood on a patch of gravel across the street from the Bluebonnet Pet Clinic and fought the urge to hot-foot it straight back to New York City. What was she even doing here?

You're here because you sold your soul to pay for veterinary school.

A doctor-of-veterinary-medicine degree from a top-rated university in Manhattan didn't come cheap, especially when it was accompanied by a board-certified specialty in veterinary cardiology. Maple's parents—who were both high-powered divorce attorneys at competing uptown law firms—had presented a rare, united front and refused to fund Maple's advanced degree unless she followed in their footsteps and enrolled in law school. Considering that her mom and dad were two of the most miserable humans she'd ever encountered, Maple would've rather died. Also, she loved animals. She loved them even more than she loathed the idea of law school. Case in point: Maple had never once heard of animals clawing each other's eyes out over visitation rights or who got to keep the good wedding china.

Especially dogs. Dogs were always faithful. Always loyal. And unlike people, dogs loved unconditionally.

Consequently, Maple had been all set to plunge herself into tens of thousands of dollars of student-loan debt to fulfill her dream of becoming a canine heart surgeon. But then, like a miracle, she'd been offered a full-ride grant from a tiny veterinary practice in Bluebonnet, Texas. Maple had never heard of the clinic. She'd never heard of Bluebonnet, either. A lifelong Manhattanite, she'd barely heard of Texas.

The only catch? Upon graduation, she'd have to work at the pet clinic for a term of twelve months before moving on to do whatever her little puppy-loving heart desired. That was it. No actual financial repayment required.

Accepting the grant had seemed like a no-brainer at the time. Now, it felt more like a prison sentence.

One year.

She inhaled a lungful of barbecue-scented air, which she assumed was coming from the silver, Airstream-style food truck parked on the town square—a *literal* square, just like the one in *Gilmore Girls*, complete with a gazebo right smack in its center. Although Bluebonnet's gazebo was in serious need of a paint job. And possibly a good scrubbing.

I can do anything for a year, right?

Maple didn't even *like* barbecue, but surely there were other things to eat around here. Everything was going to be fine.

She squared her shoulders, pulled her wheeled suitcase behind her and headed straight toward the pet clinic. The sooner she got this extended exercise in humiliation started, the sooner it would be over with.

Her new place of employment was located in an old house decorated with swirly gingerbread trim. It looked like a wedding cake. Cute, but definitely not the same vibe as the sleek glass-and-steel building that housed the prestigious veterinary cardiology practice where Maple was *supposed* to be working, on the Upper West Side.

She swung the door open, heaved her bag over the threshold and took a glance around. There wasn't a single person, dog, cat, or gerbil sitting in the waiting room. The seats lining the walls were all mismatched dining chairs, like the ones in Monica Geller's apartment on *Friends*, but somehow a lot less cute without the lilac walls and quirky knickknacks, and Joey Tribbiani shoveling lasagna into his mouth nearby. The celebrity gossip magazines littering the oversize coffee table in the center of the room were so old that Maple was certain the couple on the cover of one of them had been divorced for almost a year. Her mother had represented the wife in the high-profile split.

I turned down my dream job to come here. A knot lodged in Maple's throat. *Could this* be *any more of a disaster?*

"Howdy, there."

Maple glanced up with a start. A woman with gray corkscrew curls piled on her head and a pair of reading glasses hanging from a long pearl chain around her neck eyed Maple from behind the half door of the receptionist area.

"Can I help you, sweetheart?" the woman said, gaze snagging on Maple's shoes. A furrow formed in her brow, as if the sight of a patron in patent-leather stilettos was somehow more out of place than the woefully outdated copies of *People*.

Maple charged ahead, offering her hand for a shake. "I'm Dr. Maple Leighton."

A golden retriever's tawny head popped up on the other side of the half door, tongue lolling out of the side of its mouth.

"Down, Lady Bird," the woman said, and the dog reluctantly dropped back down to all fours. "Don't mind her. She thinks she's the welcome committee."

The golden panted and wagged her thick tail until it beat a happy rhythm against the reception desk on the other side of the counter. She gazed up at Maple with melting brown eyes. Her coat was a deep, rich gold, as shiny as a copper penny, with the feathering on her legs and underside of her body that goldens were so famous for.

Maple relaxed ever so slightly. She could do this. Dogs were dogs, everywhere.

"I'm June. What can I do for you, Maple?" the receptionist asked, smiling as benignly as if she'd never heard Maple's name before.

It threw Maple for a moment. She hadn't exactly expected a welcome parade, but she'd assumed the staff would at least be aware of her existence.

"Dr. Leighton," she corrected and pasted on a polite smile. "I'm here for my first day of work."

"I don't understand." June looked her up and down again, and the furrow in her brow deepened.

Lady Bird's gold head swiveled back and forth between them.

"Just one second." Maple held up a finger and then dug through the vast confines of her favorite leather tote—a novelty bag designed to look like the outside of a New York pizza parlor, complete with pigeons pecking at the sidewalk—for her cell phone. While June and Lady Bird cocked their heads in unison to study the purse, Maple scrolled quickly through her email app until she found the most recent communication from the grant committee.

"See?" She thrust the phone toward the older woman. The message was dated just over a week ago and, like every other bit of paperwork she'd received about her grant, it had been signed by Dr. Percy Walker, DVM. "Right here. Technically, my start date is tomorrow. But I'd love to start seeing patients right away."

What else was she going to do in this one-horse town?

June squinted at Maple's cell phone until she slid her reading glasses in place. Then her eyes went wide. "Oh, my."

This was getting weird. Then again, what wasn't? She'd been in Bluebonnet for all of ten minutes, and already Maple felt like she'd landed on a distant planet. A wave of homesickness washed over her in the form of a sudden craving for a street pretzel with extra mustard.

She sighed and slid her phone back into her bag. "Perhaps I should speak with Dr. Walker. Is he here?"

June went pale. "No, actually. I'm afraid Dr. Walker is…unavailable."

"What about the other veterinarian?" Maple asked, gaze shifting to the old-fashioned felt letter board hanging on the wall to her right. Two veterinarians were listed, names situated side by side—the familiar Dr. Percy Walker and someone named Dr. Grover Hayes. "Dr. Hayes? Is he here?"

"Grover?" June shook her head. "He's not in yet. He should be here right shortly, but he's already got a patient waiting in one of the exam rooms. And I really think you need to talk to—"

Maple cut her off. "Wait a minute. We've got a client and their pet just sitting in an exam room, and there's no one here to see them. How long have they been waiting?"

June glanced at an ancient-looking clock that hung next to the letter board.

"You know what. Never mind," Maple said. If June had to look at the clock, the patient had already been waiting too long. Besides, there was a vet in the building now. No need to extend the delay. "I'll do it."

"Oh, I don't think—" June began, but then just stood slack-jawed as Maple swung open the half door and wheeled her luggage behind the counter.

Lady Bird reacted with far more enthusiasm, wagging her tail so hard that her entire back end swung from side to side. She hip-checked June and nearly wiped the older woman out.

Someone needs to train this dog, Maple thought. But, hey, at least that wasn't her problem, was it? Goldens were sweet as pie, but they typically acted like puppies until they were fully grown adult dogs.

"Where's the exam room?" Maple glanced around.

June remained mum, but her gaze flitted to a door at the far end of the hall.

Aha!

Maple strode toward the door, stilettos clicking on the tile floor as Lady Bird followed hot on her heels.

June sidestepped the rolling suitcase and chased after them. "Maple, this really isn't such a good idea."

"Dr. Leighton," Maple corrected. Again. She grabbed a manila folder from the file rack hanging on the back of the exam-room door.

Paper files? Really? Maybe she really could make a difference here. There were loads of digital office-management systems specifically designed for veterinary medicine. Maybe by the time her year was up, she could successfully drag this practice into the current century.

She glanced at the note written beside today's date on the chart. *Dog seems tired.* Well, that really narrowed things down, didn't it?

There were countless reasons why a dog might be lethargic. Some serious, some not so worrisome at all. She'd need more information to know where to begin, but she wasn't going to stand there in the hall and read the entire file folder when she could simply go inside, look at the dog in question and talk to the client face-to-face.

A ripple of anxiety skittered through her. She had zero problem with the dog part of the equation. The part about talking to the human pet owner, on the other hand…

"Dr. Leighton, it would really be best if we wait until Grover gets here. This particular patient is—" June lowered her voice to a near whisper "—rather unusual."

During her surgical course at her veterinary college in Manhattan, Maple had once operated on a two-headed diamondback terrapin turtle. She truly doubted that whatever lay behind the exam-room door was something that could shock her. How "unusual" could the dog possibly be? At minimum, she could get the appointment started until one of the other vets decided to roll in to work.

"Trust me, June. I've got this." Maple tucked the file folder under her arm and grabbed hold of the doorknob. "In the meantime, would you mind looking into my accommodations? Dr. Walker said they'd be taken care of, but I didn't see a hotel on my way in from the airport."

She hadn't seen much of anything from the back seat of her hired car during the ride to Bluebonnet from the airport in Austin, other than wide-open spaces dotted with bales of hay.

And cows.

Lots and *lots* of cows.

"Dr. Walker…" June echoed, looking slightly green around the gills. She opened her mouth, as if to say more, but it was too late.

Maple was already swinging the door open and barreling into the exam room. Lady Bird strutted alongside her like a four-legged veterinary assistant.

"Hi there, I'm Dr. Leighton," Maple said, gaze shifting from an elderly woman sitting in one of the exam-room chairs with an aluminum walker parked in front of her to a much younger, shockingly handsome man wearing a faded denim work shirt with the sleeves rolled up to his elbows. Her attention snagged on his forearms for a beat. So muscular. How did that even happen? Swinging a lasso around? Roping cattle?

Maple's stomach gave an annoying flutter.

She forced her gaze away from the forearms and focused on his eyes instead. So blue. So *intense*. She swallowed hard. "I hear your dog isn't feeling well this morning."

There. Human introductions out of the way, Maple could do what she did best and turn her attention to her doggy patient. She breathed a little easier and glanced down at the animal, lying as still as stone on the exam table and, thus far, visible only in Maple's periphery.

She blinked.

And blinked again.

Even Lady Bird, who'd muscled her way into the exam room behind Maple, cocked her head and knit her furry brow.

"I, um, don't understand," Maple said.

Was this a joke? Had her entire interaction at this hole-in-the-wall practice been some sort of weird initiation prank? Is this how they welcomed outsiders in a small town?

Maybe she should've listened to June. How had she put it, exactly?

This particular patient is rather unusual.

A giant, Texas-size understatement, if Maple had ever heard one. The dog on the exam table wasn't just a little odd. It wasn't even a dog. It was a stuffed animal—a child's plush toy.

And Cowboy Blue Eyes was looming over it, arms crossed and expression dead-serious while he waited for Maple to examine it as if it was real.

Don't say it.

Ford Bishop glared at the new veterinarian and did his best to send her a telepathic message, even though telepathy wasn't exactly his specialty. Nor did it rank anywhere on his list of abilities.

Do not *say it.*

Dr. Maple Leighton—she'd been sure to throw that *doctor* title around—was definitely going to say it. Ford could practically see the words forming on her bow-shaped, cherry-red lips.

"I don't understand," she repeated. "This is a—"

And there it was.

Ford held up a hand to stop her from uttering the words *stuffed animal*. "My grandmother and I prefer to see Grover. Is he here?"

"No." She lifted her chin a fraction, and her cheeks went as pink as the blossoms on the dogwood trees that surrounded the gazebo in Bluebonnet's town square. "Unfortunately for both of us, Grover is out of the office at the moment."

"That's okay. We'll wait," Ford said through gritted teeth and tipped his head toward the door, indicating she should leave, whoever she was.

Instead, she narrowed her eyes at him and didn't budge. "I'm the new veterinarian here. I'm happy to help." She cleared her throat. "*If* there's an actual animal that needs—"

"Coco isn't eating," Ford's grandmother blurted from the chair situated behind where he stood at the exam table. "And she sleeps all day long."

As if on cue, the battery-operated stuffed animal opened its mouth and then froze, exposing a lone green bean sitting on its fluffy pink tongue. There was zero doubt in Ford's mind that the bean had come straight off his grandmother's plate during lunch at her retirement home.

Dr. Maple Leighton's eyes widened at the sight of the vegetable.

Lady Bird rose up onto her back legs and planted her paws on the exam table, clearly angling to snatch the green bean for herself.

"Down, Lady Bird," Ford and Maple both said in unison.

The corners of Maple's mouth twitched, almost like she wanted to smile…until she thought better of it and pursed her lips again, as if Ford was something she wanted to scrape off the bottom of one of those ridiculous high-heeled shoes she was wearing. She'd best not try walking across the cobblestone town square in those things.

Her forehead crinkled. "You know Lady Bird?"

"Everyone in town knows Lady Bird," Ford countered.

Delighted to be the topic of conversation, the golden retriever opened her mouth in a wide doggy grin. This time, Maple genuinely relaxed for a beat. The tension in her shoulders appeared to loosen as she rested her hand on top of Lady Bird's head.

She was clearly a dog lover, which made perfect sense. She was a vet. Still, Ford couldn't help but wonder what it would take for a human being to get her to light up like that.

Not that he cared, he reminded himself. Ford was just curious, that's all. Newcomers were somewhat of a rarity in Bluebonnet.

"Can I speak to you in private?" he said quietly.

Maple lifted her gaze to meet his and her flush immediately intensified. She stiffened. Yeah, Maple Leighton definitely preferred the company of dogs to people. For a second, Ford thought she was going to say no.

"Fine," she answered flatly.

Where on earth had Grover found this woman? She had the bedside manner of a serial killer.

Ford scooped Coco in his arms and laid the toy dog into his grandmother's lap. She cradled it as gently as if it was a newborn baby, and Ford's chest went tight.

"I'm going to go talk to the vet for just a minute, Gram. I'll be right back. You take good care of Coco while I'm gone," he said.

"I will." Gram stroked the top of the dog's head with shaky fingertips.

"This will only take a second." Ford's jaw clenched. *Just long enough to tell the new vet to either get on board or get lost.*

He turned, and Maple had already vacated the exam room. Lady Bird, on the other hand, was still waiting politely for him.

"Thanks, girl," Ford muttered and gave the dog a scratch behind the ears. "Keep an eye on Gram for me, okay?"

Lady Bird woofed. Then the dog shuffled over to Ford's grandmother and collapsed into a huge pile of golden fur at her feet.

"Good girl." Ford shot the dog a wink and then stepped out into the hall, where Maple stood waiting for him, looking as tense as a cat in a roomful of rocking chairs.

It was almost cute—her odd combination of confidence mixed with an aching vulnerability that Ford could somehow feel deep inside his chest. A ripple of… something wound its way through him. If Ford hadn't known better, he might have mistaken it for attraction.

He crossed his arms. "You okay, Doc?"

"What?" She blinked again, as if someone asking after her was even more shocking than finding a fake dog in one of her exam rooms. Her eyes met his and then she gave her head a little shake. "I'm perfectly fine, Mr...."

"Ford."

She nodded. "Mr. Ford, your dog—"

"Just Ford," he corrected.

Her gaze strayed to his faded denim work shirt, a stark contrast to the prim black dress she was wearing, complete with a matching black bow that held her dark hair in a thick ponytail. "As in the truck?"

He arched an eyebrow. "Dr. *Maple* Leighton, as in the syrup?"

Her nose crinkled, as if being named after something sweet left a bad taste in her mouth. "Back to your 'dog'..."

Ford took a step closer to her and lowered his voice so Gram wouldn't hear. "The dog isn't real. Obviously, I'm aware of that fact. Coco belongs to my grandmother. She's a robotic companion animal."

Maple took a few steps backward, teetering on her fancy shoes in her haste to maintain the invisible barrier between them. "You brought a robot dog to the vet because it seems tired. Got it."

"No." Ford's temples ached. She didn't get it, because of course she didn't. That hint of vulnerability he'd spied in her soulful eyes didn't mean squat. "I brought my grandmother's robotic companion animal here because my gram asked me to make the dog an appointment."

"So you're saying your gram thinks Coco is real?"

"I'm not one-hundred-percent sure whether she truly believes or if she just *wants* to believe. Either way, I'm going with it. Pets reduce feelings of isolation and loneliness in older adults. You're a vet. Surely you know all about that." Ford raked a hand through his hair, tugging at the ends. He couldn't believe he had to explain all of this to a medical professional.

"But Coco isn't a pet." Maple's gaze darted to the exam-room door. "She's battery-operated."

At least she'd had the decency to speak in a hushed tone this time.

"Right, which is why Grover usually tells Gram he needs to take Coco to the back room for a quick exam and a blood test and then he brings the dog back with fresh batteries." He threw up his hands. "And we all live happily ever after."

"Until the batteries run out of juice again." Maple rolled her eyes.

Ford just stared at her, incredulous. "Tell me—does this pass as compassion wherever you're from?"

"I'm from New York City," she said, enunciating each syllable as if the place was a foreign land Ford had never heard of before. "But I live here now. *Temporarily.*"

Ford's annoyance flared. He wasn't in the mood to play country mouse to her city mouse. "As much as I'd love to take a deep dive into your backstory, I need to get back to Gram. Can you just play along, or do we need to wait for Grover?"

"Why can't you just replace the batteries when she's not looking? Like, say, sometime before the dog gets its mouth stuck open with a green bean inside of it?"

"Because Gram has been a big dog lover her entire

life and it makes her feel good to bring her pet into the vet. She wants to take good care of Coco, and I'm not going to deny her that." He let out a harsh breath. "No one is."

Maple just looked at him as if he was some sort of puzzle she was trying to assemble in her head.

"Are you going to help us or not?" he finally asked.

"I'll do it, but you should know that I'm really not great at this sort of thing." She pulled a face, and Ford had to stop himself from asking what she meant. Batteries weren't all that complicated. "I'm not what you would call a people person."

He bit back a smile. Her brutal honesty was refreshing, he'd give her that. "Could've fooled me."

"There are generally two types of doctors in this world—general practice physicians, who are driven by their innate need to help people, and specialists, who relate more to the scientific part of medicine," Maple said, again sounding an awful lot like she was talking to someone who'd just fallen off a turnip truck.

If she only knew.

"Let me guess. You're the latter," Ford said.

Maple nodded. "I have a specialty in veterinary cardiology."

"Got it. You love dogs." It was a statement, not a question. "People, not so much."

She tilted her head. "Are we talking about actual dogs or the robot kind?"

Ford ignored her question. He suspected it was rhetorical, and anyway, he was done with this conversation. "June can show you where Grover keeps the batteries. I'll go get Coco."

"Fine," Maple said.

"I think the words you're looking for are *thank* and *you*." He flashed her a fake smile, and there it was again— that flush that reminded Ford of pink dogwood blossoms swirling against a clear, blue Texas sky.

"Thank you." She swallowed, and something about the look in her big, brown doe eyes made Ford think she actually meant it.

Maple and her big-city attitude may have gotten themselves clear across the country from New York to Texas, but when she looked at him, *really* looked, he could see the truth. She was lost. And he suspected it didn't have much to do with geography.

She turned and click-clacked toward the lobby on her high heels.

"One more thing, Doc," Ford called after her.

Maple swiveled back toward him. "Yes? Is there a teeny tiny robotic mouse in your pocket that also needs new batteries?"

Cute. Aggravating as hell, but cute.

"Welcome to Bluebonnet."

Chapter Two

If Maple had been the type to get teary-eyed, the way Ford's Gram reacted once Coco was back up and running might've made her crack. The older woman was as thrilled as if Maple had breathed literal life into her ailing little dog, and she promptly ordered Ford to get Maple a pie from someplace called Cherry on Top as a thank-you gift.

But Maple wasn't the type to cry at work, not even when his gram called her "an angel sent straight from heaven." So she averted her gaze and focused on the jar of dog treats sitting on the counter in the exam room until her eyes stopped stinging. All the while, Lady Bird nudged her big head under Maple's right hand, insisting on a pat. The dog was relentless.

As for the pie, Maple wasn't holding her breath.

"So long, Doc." Ford held the door open for his grandmother and escorted her out of the clinic without so much as a backward glance.

Maple sagged with relief once they were gone. She wasn't sure why the pang in her chest felt so much like disappointment.

She rubbed the heel of her hand against her breastbone, ignoring the way Lady Bird's soft gaze bore into her as if the dog could hear Maple's thoughts. Still, it was unsettling.

She turned her back on the dog to home in on June, still stationed behind the reception desk. "Do we have any more patients waiting to be seen? *Live* ones, that is?"

"I tried to warn you," June insisted as she replaced a jumbo-size pack of size C batteries in one of the overhead cabinets above her desk. "And no, we don't have any more patients waiting. But it looks like someone is here to see you."

June's gaze darted over Maple's left shoulder, toward the tempered glass window in the front door. Maple's heart thumped in her chest as visions of pie danced in her head.

Stop it, she told herself. *What is wrong with you?*

Bluebonnet was small, but not small enough for Ford to have already procured a baked good and made his way back to the clinic. Also, she didn't want to see him again. Ever, if she could help it.

She followed June's gaze and caught sight of a red-faced man marching up the front step of the building's quaint covered porch. Again, no animal in sight—just a middle-aged human with salt-and-pepper hair and an angry frown that Maple felt all the way down to her toes.

Before she could ask June who the man was, he burst through the door and stalked toward Maple. He looked her up and down, jammed his hands on his hips and glanced at June. "Is this her?"

"Yes, sir," June said.

Lady Bird, clearly unable to read the room, wagged

her tail and panted as she danced circles around the cranky visitor.

Actually, he wasn't technically a visitor, as Maple realized when she spotted the monogrammed initials stitched onto his shirt collar—*GH*, as in Grover Hayes. Oh, joy.

"You must be Dr. Hayes." Maple stuck her hand out for a shake. "I'm Dr. Leighton."

"So I gathered." He narrowed his gaze at her. "Unfortunately, the first I'd heard of you was when June called me a little while ago to tell me that a complete and total stranger had insisted on treating Coco in my absence."

In Maple's defense, the only reason she'd taken over the appointment was because he'd been late. Still, this didn't seem like the time to point out his breach in professional etiquette.

She'd come all this way. Today had been *years* in the making. How was it possible that Percy Walker, DVM, hadn't informed a single other person at this practice that she was starting work this week? It just didn't make sense. The practice had paid tens of thousands of dollars for her education, and not a single other person here knew who she was?

"I don't understand." Maple shook her head.

"That makes two of us," Grover huffed.

"I have years' worth of emails, some as recent as a week ago. If we could just talk to Dr. Walker, I'm sure we can clear all of this up." Maple took a deep breath. The sooner Percy Walker materialized, the better. "Do you know when he's going to be in? Technically, my start date isn't until tomorrow. I came by the office because I just got to town, and I was ready to hit the ground running."

She glanced toward her suitcase, still sitting behind the reception desk like a fly floating belly-up in someone's soup. "Plus, I'm not sure where I'm staying. Dr. Walker said my accommodations in Bluebonnet would be taken care of by my grant."

Now that Maple was saying all of this out loud, she realized it sounded a little off. She'd just flown across the country to a strange town in a strange state with no idea where she might be staying. For all she knew, Percy Walker was an internet catfish.

Except catfish didn't ordinarily fund someone's higher education, did they? Didn't catfishing usually work the other way around? Even so, either of Maple's lawyer parents probably would've been delighted to point out a dozen red flags after looking over the simple one-page contract she'd signed when she'd accepted the grant.

Which was precisely why she'd never shown it to them.

"I'm afraid Dr. Walker won't be coming in." Grover went even stonier faced, a feat that Maple wouldn't have thought possible if she hadn't witnessed his near transformation into an actual gargoyle with her own two eyes. "Ever."

Maple blinked, even more alarmed than when she'd walked into the exam room to find a fake dog on the table. "Ever?"

"Ever," Grover repeated.

What was going on? Had her one and only contact at Bluebonnet Pet Clinic gotten fired? Resigned?

In either case, did this she mean she could go back to

New York now? Could she really be that lucky? Maple felt a smile tugging at the corners of her lips.

"Dr. Percy Walker passed away eight days ago. The funeral was yesterday morning," Grover said.

And just like that, the smile wobbled off Maple's face. "What?"

Passed away, as in *dead*. Now what? Was she free to grab her suitcase and get on the next plane back to New York? As heavenly as that sounded, it just didn't seem right.

Of course. June chose that moment to oh-so-helpfully chime in, "For the record, I tried to tell you that too, Maple."

Dr. Leighton. Maple swallowed. She didn't bother correcting the receptionist this time. What was the point?

"Wait a minute." Every last drop of color drained from Grover's face as he regarded her with a new wariness. "Your first name is Maple?"

She nodded. "Yes. Maple Leighton, DVM."

"Why didn't you tell me this?" Grover's gaze flitted toward June. Lady Bird's followed, as if the golden was trying to keep up with the conversation.

Good luck, Maple thought. She could barely keep up with it herself.

"She *really* prefers to be called Dr. Leighton," June said, peering at Maple over the top of her reading glasses.

Maple had worked long and hard for that degree. Of course, she wanted to be called "Doctor," although perhaps she shouldn't have been so eager to correct June. Clearly, no one here cared a whit about her veterinary degree. Inexplicably, all Grover seemed interested in was her first name.

"Does my first name really matter all that much?" Maple asked. This day was getting more bizarre by the minute. Had she traveled to Texas, or fallen down a rabbit hole, Alice in Wonderland-style?

"In this case, it just might," Grover said, looking distinctly unhappy about it. "We need to talk. Follow me."

He swept past her without waiting for a response.

Maple glanced at June, who simply shrugged. Clearly, she didn't know what was going on any more than Maple did.

Lady Bird trotted gleefully after Grover, which frankly, felt like an enormous betrayal. Completely unreasonable, since Maple had known the dog for all of twenty minutes. Still, it was nice having someone on her side in the middle of all this chaos. Even if that someone was a dog.

Then, just as Maple's heart began to sink to new depths, Lady Bird stopped in her tracks and turned around. The golden fixed her soft brown eyes on Maple and cocked her head, as if to say, "What are you waiting for?"

Hope fluttered inside Maple, like a butterfly searching for a safe place to land.

"I'm coming."

Dr. Grover Hayes's office was located just off the reception area, behind the very first door on the right. By the time Lady Bird led Maple there, Grover was already seated at his desk and shuffling through a pile of papers.

"It's around here somewhere. Just give me a second," he said. Then he nodded toward a chair on the other side of his desk, piled high with file folders. "Sit."

Maple assumed he was talking to her rather than Lady Bird, although in all honesty, it was difficult to tell.

She had a feeling if he'd been addressing the dog, he would've been more polite. So she scooped the stack of patient files into her arms, deposited them on a nearby end table and sat down. Once Maple was settled, Lady Bird plopped on the ground and planted her chin on the tip of one of her stilettos.

Perhaps it was that tiny show of affection that gave Maple the confidence to assume she was actually employed at the clinic, despite all current evidence to the contrary.

"I was thinking that while I'm here, I could help us get started on a digital office system. Having patient files on a cloud-based platform would save loads of time."

Grover glanced up from the stack of papers in front of him and snorted. "Our system works just fine."

Maple's gaze swiveled from the mountain of files she'd just removed from her chair to the mishmash of documents on Grover's desk. "I can see that. Efficiency at its finest."

"And let's not forget that you don't even work here, missy," Grover added, although he seemed to have lost a fair bit of his bluster.

What *was* the man looking for, anyway? Had the mention of her first name somehow reminded him that he did, indeed, have a copy of her grant paperwork lying around somewhere?

"Ah, here it is." He grabbed hold of a slim manila envelope and frowned at the words written neatly across the front of it before shoving it toward Maple.

Last Will and Testament of Percy Walker

"Take it." Grover shook the envelope until Maple begrudgingly accepted it.

She placed it in her lap, unopened, where it sat like a bomb waiting to detonate. Her mouth went dry. *Something about this feels woefully inappropriate.* Maple didn't really know Percy Walker. They'd exchanged little more than a handful of emails over the past four years. Why would his business partner just hand her his last will and testament?

Maple shook her head. "I'm sorry? Why do you want me to have this?"

"Go on." Grover waved a hand at her. First impressions were rarely one-hundred-percent accurate, but he didn't seem at all like the type of person who'd have the patience to deal with an elderly woman and her beloved robotic companion animal. Wonders never ceased, apparently. "Open it."

She lifted the flap of the envelope and slid the legal document from inside.

The pages of the will were slightly yellowed with age. Maple's eyes scanned the legalese, and familiar words popped out at her—phrases that had been part of her parents' vocabulary for as long as she could remember. She still had no idea what any of it had to do with her.

"Would you care to give me a hint as to what I'm looking…for?" she asked, but her voice drifted off as her gaze snagged on the first paragraph of the second page.

I have never been married. As of the date of this will, the following child has been born to me:
   Maple Maribelle Walker

Maple's heart immediately began to pound so hard and fast that Lady Bird lifted her head and whined in alarm.

"This isn't me." Maple shook her head. If she shook it any harder, it probably would've snapped right off and tumbled to the floor. "It can't be. My last name is Leighton."

But her first name was obviously Maple, and her middle name, which she'd hadn't mentioned to anyone in Bluebonnet, was indeed Maribelle.

What were the odds this was all some crazy coincidence? Maple had never met another living soul who shared her first name. In Manhattan, she'd grown up among a sea of Blairs, Serenas, and Waverlys, acutely aware that she hadn't fit in. Maybe it was a more common name down here in Texas?

"My parents are both divorce lawyers," she said, as if that fact was relevant in any way. "In *Manhattan*. I'm not even from here."

"Clearly." Grover let out a laugh.

Finally, they agreed on something.

"What's your middle name?" he asked, frowning like he already knew the answer.

Maple reached down to rest a hand on Lady Bird's head. The dog licked her with a swipe of her warm pink tongue. Maple took a deep breath. "It's Maribelle."

If the furrow in Grover's forehead grew any deeper, Maple could've crawled inside of it and disappeared.

"Surely there's another Maple Maribelle who lives right here in Bluebonnet," she said, but she was grasping at straws, and she knew it. If there'd been anyone else who remotely fit the bill, Grover wouldn't have gone pale the moment he'd heard her first name.

"I'm afraid not," Grover said. "I think it might be time for you to call your lawyer parents up in New York to try and get to the bottom of this. In the meantime, I'll give Percy's attorney a call and see if he can come right over."

"But why?" The last thing Maple wanted to do was call her mother and father. When she'd told them she was starting a new job this week, she'd conveniently left out the part about the practice being located in Texas. They didn't know about the grant, either. For all they knew, she was still living in her little studio apartment in the city, ready to launch her new career as a veterinary cardiologist.

As she *should* be.

In hindsight, Maple clearly should've gotten their advice before signing on the dotted line.

"With all due respect, Percy Walker is dead. Why would I need to get my family involved?" She picked up the last will and testament by the very tip of the corner of its stapled pages. Maple hadn't wanted to rid herself of an item so badly since the last time she'd played a game of hot potato. She would've thrown the document across the desk if she hadn't suspected that Grover would toss it right back at her. "What difference does any of this make?"

Couldn't they simply pretend none of this had happened? No one else needed to know that her first and middle name matched the one listed on Percy's will. Maple wasn't his daughter, full stop. She knew it, and now Grover knew it. Case closed.

Maple didn't know why there was a voice screaming in the back of her head that things couldn't possibly be that simple. She almost wanted to clamp her hands over her ears to try and drown it out. Even the comforting weight of Lady Bird's warm body as the dog heaved herself into a sit position and leaned against Maple's legs failed to calm the frantic beating of her heart.

"I'm afraid it makes a very big difference, young lady." Grover sighed, and Maple was so thrown by this entire conversation that she forgot to get offended at being referred to in such a condescending manner. "If you're the Maple Maribelle listed in that document, that means you're Percy's sole beneficiary and you've inherited everything—his house, his half of this veterinary practice…"

Lady Bird let out a sharp bark.

Grover's gaze drifted toward the golden retriever. "*And* his dog."

Chapter Three

Maple tried her mother first, but the call rolled straight to voice mail, so she left a message that was as vague and chipper as possible. Other than a brief mention of Texas, she in no way hinted at her current existential crisis. No need to panic anyone. This was all just some huge misunderstanding. As soon as she met with Percy's attorney—the only one in town, apparently—Maple could get on with her new life in Bluebonnet.

She was assuming Grover would let her stay, of course. Whether or not Percy left behind any paperwork documenting her grant didn't really matter. Maple owed the clinic a year of work and, as unpleasant as it seemed, she intended to fulfill that obligation. If Grover wouldn't let her stay…

Well, she'd simply deal with that later. Right after she managed to convince Grover she was in no way related to his recently deceased business partner.

"It's not true," she said aloud, as if the crammed bookshelves and clutter scattered atop Percy Walker's desk could hear her. Grover had banished her to Percy's office to make her phone calls, against Maple's fervent protests.

Lady Bird, who'd sauntered into the office on Maple's

heels and promptly arranged herself on a faded flannel dog bed in a corner by the window, lifted her head from her paws. She cocked her head and eyed Maple with obvious skepticism. Or maybe Maple was just anthropomorphizing. She had a tendency to do that on occasion.

"I'm not his daughter." Maple fixed her gaze on the dog. "Seriously, I'm not. I don't belong here."

Lady Bird's tail *thump-thumped* against her dog bed. The golden clearly wasn't listening.

"A simple phone call will prove it." Maple turned her cell phone over in her palm and scrolled through her contacts for her dad's information. If her mom wasn't answering, maybe he could help. She couldn't keep sitting here in a strange man's office in a strange town, trying to convince a strange dog that she really was who she said she was—Maple Maribelle Leighton of New York City.

Before she could tap her father's number, her phone rang with an incoming call and Maple jumped. She really needed to get a grip.

It's Mom. She pressed a hand to her abdomen as her mother's name scrolled across the top of the phone's small screen. *Thank goodness.*

"Hi, Mom," she said as she answered, going for bright and confident, but managing to sound slightly manic instead.

"Hi, honey."

Wait. That wasn't her mother's voice. It almost sounded like her father.

Maple frowned down at her phone. "Dad?"

"It's both of us, Maple," her mother said.

"*Both* of you?" Maple glanced at Lady Bird in a panic. The last time her parents had joined forces, it had been to try and talk her into going to law school. If they were willing to put aside their many, *many* differences to join forces, things must be far more dire than Maple imagined.

But wait—Maple hadn't even mentioned Percy or his will in her voice mail. How could they possibly know she'd been calling about something as delicate as her parentage?

"You mother said you're calling from Texas," Dad said.

And there it was.

Maple's heart sank all the way to her stilettos, which seemed to be covered in a layer of barbecue-scented dust. One brief mention of Texas had been enough to get her parents back on speaking terms?

This couldn't be good.

"I'm here for work. Remember when I told you about my vet school scholarship?" Maple swallowed. Lady Bird, sensing her distress, came to stand and lean against her legs, and Maple felt a sudden swell of affection for Percy Walker. Whoever he'd really been, he'd raised a lovely, lovely dog, and that alone spoke volumes about his character. "There was a small technicality I might not have mentioned."

"What kind of technicality?" her dad asked. Maple could hear the frown in his voice clear across the country.

"In exchange for a full ride, I agreed to spend a year working at a pet clinic here in Texas." Maple took a deep breath. "I guess you could say I live here now. *Temporarily.* Something strange has come up, though, so I wanted to call and—"

"Where in Texas?" Mom asked in a voice so high and thin that Maple barely recognized it.

"It's just a small town. You've probably never heard of it." Maple bit down so hard on her bottom lip that she tasted blood.

Maybe if she didn't say it, she could stop this conversation before it really started. She could keep on believing that she knew exactly who she was and where she'd come from. She could swallow the name of this crazy place and pretend she'd never set eyes on Percy Walker's last will and testament.

In the end, it was her dad who broke the silence. And the moment he did, Maple couldn't pretend anymore. There was more to her educational grant than she'd thought. Had there ever even *been* a grant? Or had it simply been Percy's way of getting Maple to Texas? To *home*?

Maple shook her head. She'd never felt farther from home in her entire life.

Dad cleared his throat. "Tell us the truth. You're in Bluebonnet, aren't you?"

An hour later, Maple stared in disbelief at a version of her birth certificate she'd never set eyes on before.

It had been sent via fax from her mother's office in Manhattan, straight to the dinosaur of a fax machine at June's workstation in the pet clinic's reception area. Maple wouldn't have believed it if she hadn't seen it herself—not even after her mom and dad had calmly explained they weren't actually her birth parents. Maple had been adopted at only two days old. Charles and Meredith Leighton had flown down to Bluebonnet and collected her themselves.

It had been an open adoption, arranged by one of their attorney friends. Maple's birth mother had only been seventeen years old, and she'd died in childbirth. The grief-stricken father had been so overwhelmed that he'd agreed to give the baby up, under one condition: the adoptive parents had to promise to keep the baby's first and middle names. Maple Maribelle. Once Maple held the faxed birth certificate in her trembling hands, she understood why.

Mother's Name: Maple Maribelle Walker

The words went blurry as Maple's eyes swam with tears. She'd been named after her birth mother. Everything she'd read in Percy's last will and testament had been true. The man who'd paid for her education and brought her to Bluebonnet had been her *father*.

And now he was gone.

They both were.

"Let's see that, missy." Grover snatched the birth certificate from her hands.

At some point, Maple was going to have to school this man on how to speak to his female colleagues. But, alas, that moment wasn't now. She was far too tired to argue with the likes of Grover Hayes. All she wanted to do right now was crawl into bed and pull the covers over her head. Too bad she still had no idea where she was staying.

"Believe me, no one is as surprised by this crazy turn of events as I am," Maple said as Grover studied the document.

Grover made a noise somewhere between a huff and a growl. Lady Bird's ears pricked forward and she cocked her head.

"We need to talk," Maple said, even though she had no idea what she was going to say. Up was down, down was up and nothing make sense anymore.

"Just come home," her mother had said.

"I've booked you on the first flight out of Austin tomorrow morning," her dad had added. "First class."

It had been decided. Maple had never belonged in Bluebonnet. As far as her parents were concerned, she should just come back to New York and forget her ill-fated trip to Texas had ever taken place. They'd fallen all over themselves apologizing for never telling her the truth about her birth. Maple couldn't remember either of her parents ever uttering the word *sorry* before. It was almost as disorienting as learning she'd been born right here in Bluebonnet.

"Indeed, we do." Grover stalked toward his office, fully expecting Maple to follow.

What choice did she have?

At least June shot her a sympathetic glance this time. Maple gave the receptionist a wan smile and fell in step behind Grover as Lady Bird nudged her gold head beneath Maple's hand.

The dog was growing on Maple. Technically, the golden was hers now, right? She could pack the dog up and sweep her off to New York if she wanted to. Not that Maple would do such a thing. New York City was made for purse dogs. Life in Manhattan would be a major adjustment for a dog accustomed to living in the wide-open spaces of Texas. It wouldn't be fair.

But that didn't stop Maple from dreaming about it.

"I've been thinking things over, and I've decided to

let you off the hook," Grover said as soon as the office door shut behind them.

Maple heaved another pile of file folders out of the office chair she'd occupied earlier and plopped down on the worn leather. "I'm not following."

"For the grant. You and Percy had an agreement, did you not? A fully funded veterinary education in exchange for one year of employment here at Bluebonnet Pet Clinic?" Grover leaned back in his chair.

Maple nodded. "Yes, but…"

"But I'm letting you off the hook. Percy's gone now. I think we both know the real reason he wanted you to come here." Grover shrugged. "I see no reason to make you fulfill your obligation. I think this morning proved you're not a good fit here. Wouldn't you agree?"

Ooof. He was one-hundred-percent right. There was no reason why his words should've felt like a blow to the chest, but they did.

"Agreed." Maple gave a curt nod and tried her best not to think about the way she'd spoken to Ford Bishop earlier. The appointment had been a total disaster. Yet another reason to put this town in her rearview mirror as quickly as possible.

Lady Bird sighed and dropped her chin onto Maple's knee.

"So." Grover shrugged. "You're free to go."

Maple gripped the arms of her chair so hard that her knuckles turned white. The effort it took not to sprint out of the building, roadrunner-style, was almost too much to bear. "I'm leaving on the six a.m. flight out of Austin tomorrow morning. My ticket is already booked."

Her dad had even managed to pull some strings and

gotten Maple another shot at her dream job. The veterinary cardiology practice that had made her such a generous offer after graduation still wanted her to come to work for them. When Maple had asked how that was possible, since she knew for a fact that the position had been filled after she'd turned it down, her father had simply said that veterinary cardiologists got divorced, just like everyone else did. He'd apparently represented Maple's new boss in a nasty split and was now calling in a favor.

"Good." Grover nodded. *"Excellent."*

Maple knew she should ask about Percy's estate. Didn't she need to sign some papers or something? There was the veterinary practice to think about…Percy's personal effects…and his dog.

She could deal with all of that from New York, though. Her parents were lawyers. Maple probably wouldn't have to lift a finger. They could make it all disappear, just like they'd promised on the phone.

None of this is really your responsibility. You can walk away. Grover just said so himself. Maple buried her hand in the warm scruff of Lady Bird's neck.

Charles and Meredith Leighton had been divorced since Maple was in first grade. The separation had been monumentally ugly—ugly enough that she could remember hiding in her closet with her stuffed dog, Rover, clamping her hands over her ears to try and muffle the sound of dishes smashing against the marble floors. They were two of the city's highest paid divorce attorneys, after all. Fighting dirty practically came naturally to them.

The fact that they seemed to have to put aside their

many, *many* differences to help Maple deal with Percy's estate and get her back to New York was nothing short of surreal. In the ultimate irony of ironies, she'd managed to fulfill her childhood dream of stitching her broken family back together. All it had taken was the accidental discovery of a whole *other* family that she never knew existed.

"Where am I supposed to stay tonight?" Maple said, willing her voice not to crack.

Grover opened the top drawer of his desk and pulled out an old-fashioned skeleton key, tied with a red string. He set it down and slid it toward Maple.

She eyed it dubiously. "What is that for?"

"It's the key to Percy's place." Grover paused, and the lines on his face seemed to grow deeper. "Although technically it's your house now."

Not for long.

She reached for the strange key and balled it into her fist. Percy's house was the absolute last place she wanted to go for her few remaining hours in Bluebonnet. She longed for a sterile beige hotel room—somewhere she could hide herself away and feel absolutely nothing. Unfortunately, the closest place that fit the bill was nearly fifty miles away. Maple had already done a search on her cell phone.

She slapped the key back down on the desk.

"I'm not sure staying at Percy's house is the best idea. I don't even know how I'd get there. I don't have a car." With any luck, Uber hadn't made it all the way to rural Texas. "Didn't I see a sign for a bed-and-breakfast near the town square? I'm sure that's much closer."

"Closer than next door?" Grover stood, reached for

his white vet coat and slid his arms into its sleeves. "I think not."

"Percy's house is right next door?" Maple squeaked.

Of course, it was. The population of this place was probably in the double digits.

"Yes, he lived in one of the Sunday houses. He owned this one, too, until he sold it to the practice." Grover cast a sentimental glance at their surroundings. Then his gaze landed on Maple and his expression hardened again.

"What's a Sunday house?" she asked before she could stop herself. Why spend any more time in Grover's presence than absolutely necessary? The wording made her curious, though. She'd never heard of such a thing in New York.

"A Sunday house is a small home that was once used by ranchers or farmers who lived in the outlying area when they came into town on the weekends for social events and church. Sunday houses date back to the 1800s. There are still quite a few standing in the Texas Hill Country. A lot of them are historical landmarks." He glowered. "You might want to brush up on some local history before you think about selling the place."

"I'll get right on that," she muttered under her breath.

"Percy's home is the pink house just to the right of this one." He fumbled around in the pocket of his white coat and pulled out a banged-up pocket watch that looked like something from an antique store. He squinted at it, nodded and slid it out of view again. "I'd walk you over there, but I've got an appointment with a turtle who has a head cold."

Sure he did.

Maple didn't believe him for a minute. Grover just

wanted her gone. At least they'd finally agreed on something.

"You can leave the key under the front mat when you head out in the morning. Have a safe trip back home," Grover said, and then he strode out of his office with a tight smile.

Nice to meet you, too, Maple thought wryly.

Lady Bird peered up at her with a softness in her warm brown eyes that made Maple's heart feel like it was being squeezed in a vise. Was she moving too fast? Maybe she should slow down a take a breath.

She closed her eyes, leaned forward and rested her cheek against Lady Bird's head. A voice in the back of her head assured her she was doing the right thing.

This was never what you wanted. Now you have an out. You'd be a fool not to take it.

Maple sat up and blew out a breath. Lady Bird's tail beat against the hard wood floor. *Thump, thump, thump.*

"Come on." Maple said, and the dog's big pink tongue lolled out of the side of her mouth. "Let's get out of here."

She sure as heck wasn't going to spend the night in Percy's house alone, and Lady Bird seemed more than willing to accompany her.

June was clearly more conflicted about Maple's decision to fly back to Manhattan. She at least had the decency to look somewhat sorry to see Maple go.

"You don't have to be in such a hurry, you know," the older woman said as Maple took hold of her wheeled suitcase. "Don't mind Grover. I know he seems madder than an old wet hen, but he's not that bad once you get to know him. He and Percy were really close. He's taking the loss hard."

So hard that he basically ordered his dead friend's long-lost daughter to leave town immediately. Do not pass GO. Do not collect 200 dollars.

Maple fought back an eye roll. "I'm going to have to take your word on that, June."

June nodded and fidgeted with her hands. "You let me know if you need anything tonight, Dr. Leighton. I'll be 'round to collect Lady Bird first thing in the morning. She's been staying with me since Percy's passing, but you take her tonight. That dog has a way with people who need a little TLC. She's actually sort of famous for it around these parts."

Maple suspected there might be more to that story, but before she could ask June to elaborate, a client walked into the clinic holding a cat carrier containing a fluffy black cat howling at the top of its lungs.

"I think that's my cue to go." Maple tightened her grip on the handle of her suitcase. "Thanks for everything. And June…?"

June regarded her over the top of her reading glasses. "Yes, Dr. Leighton?"

"You can call me Maple." Maple's throat went thick. She *really* needed to make herself scarce. It wasn't like her to get emotional around strangers. Then again, it wasn't every day that she learned something about herself that made her question her place in the world.

June's face split into a wide grin, and before Maple knew what was happening, the older woman threw her arms around Maple's shoulders and wrapped her in a tight hug.

It had been a long time since someone had embraced

Maple with that sort of enthusiasm. As much as she hated to admit it, it felt nice.

"I really should go now," she mumbled into June's shoulder.

June released her and gave her shoulders a gentle squeeze. "Goodbye now, Maple Maribelle Walker."

Leighton, Maple wanted to say. *My name is Maple Leighton*. But the words stuck in her throat.

She dipped her head and dragged her luggage toward the door, carefully sidestepping the cat who was now meowing loud enough to peel the paint off the walls. Lady Bird trotted alongside Maple as if the cat didn't exist. Golden retrievers were known for their unflappable temperament, but this really took the cake.

If Grover hadn't told Maple which house in the neat row of half-dozen homes with gingerbread trim had been Percy's, she still would've located it easily. Lady Bird led the way, trotting straight toward the little pink house with her tail wagging to and fro.

A nonsensical lump lodged in Maple's throat at the sight of it. It looked like a dollhouse and was painted a pale blush-pink that reminded her of ballet slippers. Everything about the structure oozed charm, from the twin rocking chairs on the porch to the white picket fence that surrounded the small front yard. Maple couldn't help but wonder what it might've been like growing up in this sort of home, tailor-made for a little girl.

Tears pricked the backs of her eyes. There must be something in the water in this town. Maple never cried, and this was the third time today that she'd found herself on the verge of weeping.

She took a deep inhale and pushed open the gabled

gate in the white picket fence. Lady Bird zipped past her, bounding toward the tiny covered porch. The dog nudged at something sitting on the welcome mat while Maple hauled her bag up the front step.

"What have you got there, Lady Bird?" Maple muttered as she rummaged around her NYC pizza-parlor handbag for the ridiculous skeleton key Grover had given her earlier. Was there *anything* in Bluebonnet that didn't look like it had come straight out of a time capsule?

The key felt heavy in her hand, weighted down by yesteryear. Maple's fingers wrapped around it, and she held it tight as she bent down to see what had captured Lady Bird's attention.

Once she managed to nudge the golden out of the way, Maple saw it—a large pink bakery box with the words *Cherry on Top* printed across it in a whimsical font.

Her breath caught in her throat. Ford Bishop had really done it. He'd done as his grandmother had asked and brought her a pie. Maple had been so busy with her identity crisis that she hadn't eaten a bite all day. She hadn't even thought about food. But the heavenly smell drifting up from the bakery box made her mouth water.

She picked it up, closed her eyes and took a long inhale. The heady aroma of sugar, cinnamon and buttery pastry crust nearly caused her knees to buckle. Then her eyelashes fluttered open, and she spotted the brief note Ford had scrawled on the cardboard in thick strokes from a magic marker.

The man had terrible handwriting—nearly as indecipherable as that of a doctor. Maple had to read it a few times to make out what it said.

Doc,

I wasn't sure what kind of pie you liked, so I went
with Texas peach. The peaches were homegrown
here in Bluebonnet. There's more to love about this
place than just dogs, although our canines are ad-
mittedly stellar. Just ask Lady Bird.

Regards,

Ford Bishop

Maple's heart gave a little twist. She couldn't even
say why, except that she'd spent the entire day trying to
hold herself together while her life—past, present, and
future—had been fracturing apart. She didn't belong
here in Texas. That much was clear.

But the secret truth that Maple kept buried deep down
inside was that she'd never fully felt like she'd belonged
anywhere. Not even New York. She'd always felt like
she was on the outside looking in, with her face pressed
against the tempered glass of her own life.

Maple had always blamed her social anxiety on her
parents' divorce and a lifetime of learning that love was
never permanent, and marriages were meant to be broken. Her mom and dad had never said as much aloud,
but they didn't have to. It had happened in their very
own family. Then Maple had quietly watched as her
parents battled on behalf of other heartbroken husbands
and wives.

She'd avoided dating all through high school, afraid
to lose her head and her heart to someone who might
crush it to pieces. Then in vet school, she'd decided to
prove her parents wrong. She'd thrown herself into love
with all the naivete of a girl who hadn't actually learned

what the words *prenuptial agreement* meant before her tenth birthday. When she fell, she fell hard.

Justin had been a student in her study group. He was fiercely competitive, just like Maple. She'd foolishly believed that meant they had other things in common, too. Two peas in the pressure cooker of a pod that was veterinary school.

For an entire semester they did everything together. Then, near the end of the term, on the night before they both had a final research project due in their animal pathology class, he disappeared…

Along with Maple's term paper.

At first, she'd thought it had to be some weird coincidence. He'd been in an accident or something, and she'd simply misplaced her research paper or left it at the copy place, where she'd had all one hundred pages of it bound like a book for a professional aesthetic. But Maple knew she'd never make a mistake like that. Instead, she'd made one far more heartbreaking. She'd trusted a boy who'd used her for months, biding his time until he could swoop in and steal her research project so he could turn it in as his own.

By the time Maple flew into her professor's office the following morning to report the theft, Justin had already switched out the cover page and presented the work as his own. The professor insisted there was no way to tell who'd copied whom, and Maple had been left with nothing to turn in. It had been the one and only time in her life she'd received an F on a report card.

Lesson learned. Her parents had been right all along.

But maybe there was more to the detached feeling inside of Maple than her messed up childhood and her ill-fated attempt at romance. Maybe the reason she'd never felt like she fit in was because she'd been in the wrong place. The wrong *life*.

If Maple hadn't known better, she would've thought the wistful feeling that tugged at her heart as she read and reread Ford's note might have been homesickness. Nostalgia for a place she'd never really been but longed for, all the same.

Homegrown here in Bluebonnet. Her gaze kept straying back to that phrase, over and over again, as she stood on the threshold of Percy Walker's home, clutching a pie that had been a reluctant thank-you gift from a perfect stranger. Somewhere in the distance, a horse whinnied. Lady Bird whimpered, angling for a bite of peach pie.

It wasn't until Maple felt the wetness on her face that she realized she'd finally given up the fight and let herself cry.

Chapter Four

Percy's landline rang in the dead of night, jolting Maple from a deep sleep.

At first, she thought she must be dreaming. It had been years since she'd even *heard* the shrill ring of a landline. She scarcely recognized the sound. Then, once she dragged her eyes open, she realized she was in a strange bed in a strange house with a strange dog sprawled next to her.

Yep. She plopped her head back down on her pillow and threw her arm over her face. *Definitely a dream.*

But then she caught a whiff of cinnamon on her forearm, and everything came flooding back to her at once. She was in Bluebonnet, Texas. Percy Walker, DVM, was her father, and Maple had found out the truth too late to do anything about it. No wonder she'd eaten an entire peach pie straight from the box for dinner while Lady Bird chowed down on a bowl of premium dog food.

That pie had also been *delicious*. Hands down, the best she'd ever tasted. Maybe Ford had been right about the virtues of homegrown produce. In any case, Maple had zero regrets about the pie.

She let her swollen eyes drift shut again. She'd wept

throughout the entire peach-pie episode, and subsequently had the puffy face and blotchy skin to show for it. Lovely. Her mother would no doubt book Maple a facial the second she deplaned at JFK.

At least the landline had stopped ringing. A quick glance at her cell phone told her it was after two in the morning. If she fell back asleep in the next fifteen minutes, she could still get a good three hours of shut-eye before her hired car showed up to take her to the airport in Austin. As she'd suspected, Uber wasn't a thing in Bluebonnet. It was going to cost her an arm and a leg to get to the airport on time because she'd had to book a service all the way from the city.

Worth every freaking penny, she told herself while Lady Bird snuffled and wheezed beside her. The dog snored louder than a freight train. Alas, not quite loud enough to drown out the landline as it began to ring again.

Maple sat up and tossed the covers aside. "Seriously?"

Who called a dead man's house at this hour?

She stumbled toward the kitchen, where the phone—a vintage rotary classic with a cord approximately ten thousand feet long—hung just to the left of the refrigerator.

Maple plucked the handset from its hook. "Whoever this is, you've got the wrong number."

"Oh." The woman on the other end sounded startled. Again, *seriously*? Couldn't people in Bluebonnet tell time? "I was looking for Lady Bird. Is she not there?"

Maple felt herself frown. "Lady Bird is a dog."

"Of course, she is. Is she available?"

Maybe Maple really *was* dreaming. "You want to speak to Lady Bird on the phone?"

She glanced around, but for once, the golden wasn't glued to her side. No doubt she was still splayed diagonally across the bed, belly-up.

"That's cute, but no. This is Pam Hudson. You can call me Nurse Pam. Everyone does. I work at County General Hospital, and we were hoping Lady Bird could come in to visit with a patient."

Maple blinked as something June said in passing earlier came back to her.

That dog has a way with people who need a little TLC. She's actually sort of famous for it around these parts.

Lady Bird must be a therapy dog. Therapy dogs were specially trained to provide comfort, support, and affection to people in health-care settings. Why hadn't anyone said anything?

Probably because it was none of Maple's business, considering she already had one stylishly clad foot out the door and she hadn't planned on taking the golden with her.

"I apologize for the late hour, but we have a little boy here who's had quite a difficult night, and he's been asking for Lady Bird for the past half hour. It would mean the world to him if she could come visit, even for a few minutes," Nurse Pam said.

"Right now?" Maple asked in a panic.

No. Just…no.

Therapy dogs didn't visit patients all on their own. They worked as a team in conjunction with their owners. And as of today, Lady Bird's owner was Maple.

But Maple wasn't cut out for that type of work, as evidenced by the epic disaster at the pet clinic. She was the absolute last person who should be visiting someone sick and vulnerable. Therapy dog handlers were compassionate. They were active listeners and knew how to engage with people experiencing all sorts of challenges or trauma. They were confident in social situations.

Maple was none of those things.

"I know it's late. I'm so sorry for the interruption, but Oliver always lights up when Lady Bird is here. Percy was always so good about bringing the dog around whenever we called, no matter the hour. I know this is none of my business, but I heard you're his daughter." Pam's voice cracked. "We're really going to miss him around here."

Maple's throat clogged.

Not again. She was done with crying. She'd had her pie-fueled moment of weakness. There was no reason whatsoever to get emotional over a person she'd never met before.

"Do you think you'll be able to bring Lady Bird by?"

The nurse was relentless. Fortunately, Maple had the perfect excuse. "I'm sorry, but even if I wanted to—" *which I don't* "—I can't. I don't have any way to get there. I don't have a car. In fact, I'm leaving early in the morning, and—"

"That's an easy fix!" Pam gushed. "Don't you worry. Someone will be by Percy's house to pick you up shortly."

Maple froze, a deer in headlights. This couldn't be happening. "Wait, no. That's really not—"

Pam interjected, cutting her off. "No need to thank me. We help one another out here. It's the Bluebonnet way."

Of course, it was. Maple couldn't wait to get out of

this place and back to New York, where she was hemmed in by people on every side and none of them knew her name or cared a whit about her.

She opened her mouth to protest again, but it was too late. There was a click on the other end of the line as Pam hung up the phone.

Maple gaped at the receiver. She tried pressing the silver hook where the handset usually rested, but no amount of jabbing at the ancient device would make Pam reappear.

"Nope," Maple said aloud. "Nope, nope, nope."

She wasn't going to do it. Pam couldn't make her. Maple would just call the hospital back and refuse.

But Maple had been half-asleep when she'd taken the call and couldn't remember the name of the hospital the nurse had mentioned. Nor did she know what floor or department Pam had been calling from. All she remembered was that the patient was a little boy named Oliver and that Oliver was having a tough night.

Join the club, Oliver.

Maple dropped her forehead to the phone and concentrated on taking deep breaths. As out of it as she'd been a few minutes ago, she was wide-awake now. Any minute, a stranger intent on dragging her to the hospital was going to knock on the door and they were going to find Maple on the verge of a panic attack, dressed in her favorite cupcake-themed pajamas with pie crumbs in her hair.

This town was the *worst.* How did introverts survive here?

The dreaded knock at the door came in just under twenty minutes. Maple had barely had time to pull on her softest pair of jeans and a J.Crew T-shirt with sketches of dogs of various breeds drinking cocktails from martini glasses. Comfort clothes. Clothes that said she was staying in for the night, no matter what Nurse Pam had to say about it.

She swung Percy's front door open, ready to dig in her heels.

"Look, I—" Maple's tongue tripped over itself as she took in the sight of the man standing on her porch dressed in hospital scrubs. She swallowed hard. "It's you."

Ford Bishop.

Just how small was the population of this town? The man was everywhere—bringing his grandmother into the pet clinic, buying pies, delivering therapy dogs to the hospital in the dead of night. Maple apparently couldn't swing a stick in Bluebonnet without it smacking into one of his nicely toned forearms.

Oh, no. She was staring at his forearms again, wasn't she?

She blinked hard and refocused on his face…on those eyes of his that somehow made Maple want to close her eyes and fall backward onto a soft featherbed.

Something was very clearly wrong with her. She was suffering from some sort of pie-induced hysteria. Maybe even a full nervous breakdown.

Ford tilted his head, studied her for a beat and gave her a smile that almost seemed genuine.

"Hey there, Doc."

Ford squinted at Maple's T-shirt.

Were those dogs? Drinking *martinis*? Interesting choice for a late-night visit to the children's wing of a hospital, but Ford wasn't judging. He was honestly shocked that Pam had managed to twist Maple's arm into bringing Lady Bird to visit Oliver at all.

Shocked, but relieved—so relieved that he'd have happily chauffeured Maple to the hospital in her PJs, if necessary.

"What are you doing here?" Maple asked, blinking rapidly, and Ford's relief took a serious hit.

"I'm giving you and Lady Bird a ride to County General," Ford said. Why else would he be on her doorstep in the middle of the night, dressed in scrubs with his truck still running at the curb?

He wasn't sure why she couldn't drive herself. Percy's truck was newer than his, and as far as Ford knew, it remained parked right in the garage, where he'd left it. But Ford was happy to give Maple and the dog a ride, if needed. He just wanted to get Lady Bird to the hospital by any means necessary.

"There's been a misunderstanding." Maple shook her head. "Lady Bird isn't feeling up to it."

At the mention of her name, Lady Bird made herself visible by nudging the front door open wider with her snout. The dog wiggled past Maple to offer Ford a proper golden-retriever greeting, complete with tail wags and copious amounts of drool.

Ford dropped to a knee to let Lady Bird plant her paws on his shoulders and lick the side of his face. The dog's wagging tail crashed into Maple's shins. When Ford looked up at her, a deep flush was making its way up her neck.

Liar, liar, pants on fire, he thought.

"I'm no vet, but it seems to me if this dog was feeling under the weather earlier, she's suddenly made a miraculous recovery." Ford stood, and Lady Bird added an exclamation point to his observation by continuing to prance around him like he was hiding bacon in the pockets of his scrubs.

For the record, he was not. The only thing in Ford's pocket was his cell phone, which pinged at least once an hour with a text from Gram. The last missive had been a photo of Coco lying at the foot of her bed watching *Jeopardy* on the small television in Gram's room at the senior center.

"Thank you for the pie. It was heavenly," Maple said, and Ford was pretty sure he spotted a crumb from the crust of said pie in her hair, but he thought it best not to mention it. "But this day has been a real doozie. Pam kind of strong-armed me into the whole pet-visit thing, and I just…can't."

Ford crossed his arms. After this morning, he shouldn't have been surprised. This was a kid they were talking about, though. Was she really saying no?

"Don't look at me like that." Maple scowled.

"How am I looking at you?"

"Like I'm evil incarnate." She gave her chin a jaunty upward tilt. "I told you I wasn't a people person."

Ford narrowed his gaze at her. "Is that what I should say to the eight-year-old little kid who's been puking all night after his most recent chemo treatment when he asks why he can't see Lady Bird?"

She recoiled as if she'd been hit.

"Sorry. That was probably too harsh." Ford held up his hands. He wasn't in the business of guilting people into doing good deeds, all evidence to the contrary.

And he certainly didn't think Maple was evil incarnate. Lost, maybe. Overwhelmed, certainly. Bluebonnet was a small town, and, of course, Ford had heard about Percy's last will and testament. As hard as it was to believe, Maple was Percy Walker's daughter.

The way she wrapped her arms around herself told Ford that no one found it more impossible to believe than she did.

Time to start over. "Look, Oliver is a sweet kid. His mom works nights. He's tired, and he's very sick, or else I wouldn't be standing here on your porch at two in the morning asking for this small favor."

It wasn't small to the average person—especially a person who seemed to have at least a dash of social anxiety. Ford knew this. He just really, *really* wanted Oliver to get a few minutes with Lady Bird. Once the kid set eyes on that dog, he'd sleep like a baby for the rest of the night. Happened every time.

"Lady Bird will do all the work. Oliver will hardly even look at you, I promise. The dog is the star of the show. I'd take her there myself, but I can't. I could get called away, and hospital rules say I can't leave a patient alone with a therapy dog." Ford shifted from one foot to the other. He needed to get back to work. "Please?"

"You can't leave a patient alone with a therapy dog, but you *can* leave them with someone you don't really know? Someone who isn't even the therapy dog's owner?" She chewed on her bottom lip.

"Aren't you, though?" Ford glanced down at Lady Bird, who'd planted herself directly between them with one big paw resting on Maple's toe. Her impractical stilettos had been replaced with an oversize pair of house slippers. Brown corduroy and large enough to look like they'd come from the men's department. Ford realized he hardly knew Maple, but the shoes definitely seemed out of character.

Then it hit him: the shoes belonged to Percy.

"I'm not staying," Maple said with a shake of her head. She gestured to the house, the dog, and the town in general. "I'll figure out what to do with all of this later, but I can't stay here. I'm going back to New York in the morning."

Ford bristled, even though he couldn't help but think the slippers told a different story. Maple Walker Leighton was more curious about her birth father than she wanted to admit.

But that wasn't any of Ford's business. As for why the sight of her in those slippers filled his chest with warmth, he really couldn't say.

"Please," Ford said again and then reached to pluck the crumb from her hair. He just couldn't help it. Maple's lips parted ever so slightly at his closeness, but she didn't move a muscle. He held up the crumb between his thumb and forefinger. "What if I promised you more pie?"

Her expression softened. Just a bit—just enough for the warmth in Ford's chest to bloom and expand into something that felt far too much like longing.

No, he told himself. *Don't even think about it.*

This was a business transaction, not a flirtation. He was offering pie in exchange for her dog-handling services. That was it. Come tomorrow, Ford would never set eyes on Maple again.

He swiveled his gaze toward Lady Bird. "Tell Maple there's nothing to be afraid of. She might even have fun."

"I'm not afraid," she sputtered.

"I beg your pardon, I'm not talking to you. This is a conversation between me and the dog." Ford flashed her a wink, and then fixed his gaze with Lady Bird's again. "Go on, tell her."

Lady Bird tossed back her head and let out a *woo-woo* noise somewhere between a howl and a whine.

Maple laughed, and the sound was as light and lovely as church bells. She should really let her guard down more often. "This is *craziness*. Have you two practiced this routine?"

No, but Lady Bird had a wide array of tricks in her repertoire. Percy had trained the dog well, and Ford had seen the golden in action enough times to have committed some of her commands to memory.

Ford didn't tell Maple that, though. He just waggled his eyebrows and shot her one last questioning glance.

"Okay, fine. I'll do it." She thrust two fingers in the air. "Under two conditions."

"Done." Ford nodded, turned toward his truck and whistled at Lady Bird to follow.

"Wait!" Maple shuffled after them in her too-big slippers. "You don't know what the conditions are."

Ford swung open the passenger-side door of his truck and Lady Bird hopped inside. "I'm guessing the first one is pie."

She crossed her arms, all business. "Accurate."

Ford wondered what, if anything, could make this woman relax. Not that it mattered since she was so dead set on leaving, but it might have been fun to try and find out. "And the second?"

"You've got to promise to get me home in plenty of

time to meet my car service for my ride to the airport in the morning."

"No problem, Doc," he said and gave her a curious look, which Maple either didn't notice or chose to ignore.

"I'll be right back. I need to put on some shoes and grab my purse," she said.

"We'll be waiting right here." Ford banged his hand on the hood of his truck and felt his mouth hitch into a grin as she disappeared back into the house.

You've got to promise to get me home, she'd said. Not *back here* or *back to Percy's house*.

Whether or not she'd realized it, Maple had just called this place home.

Chapter Five

After they'd arrived at the hospital, Maple tried to hang back and linger in the doorway to Oliver's room so Ford could check and make sure the little boy wasn't asleep, but Lady Bird had other ideas. The golden hustled right inside, dragging Maple behind her as if they'd been issued a personal invitation. Which she supposed they had, basically.

If the child was disappointed to find Maple on the other end of Lady Bird's leash instead of Percy, he didn't show it. His entire face lit up the second he spotted the dog.

"Lady Bird. You're here!" Oliver scrambled to push himself up in his hospital bed for a better view.

"Hold up, there. I've got you," Ford said as he reached for the call-button remote and pressed the appropriate arrow to raise the head of Oliver's bed.

Maple wondered if the mechanical sounds or the moving piece of furniture might spook Lady Bird, but she handled it like a pro. She shimmied right up to the edge of the bed and gently planted her chin on the edge of the mattress, easily within Oliver's reach.

The boy laid a hand on the golden retriever's head and moved his thumb in gentle circles over Lady Bird's soft, cold fur. "I knew you'd come."

If Maple had still been harboring any doubts about caving and letting Ford take her to County General, they melted away right then and there. A lump formed in her throat. *I knew you'd come.* Even at his young age, Oliver already knew what made dogs so special. They were loyalty and unconditional love, all wrapped up in a warm, furry package. The very idea of Lady Bird failing to show up to comfort him in the dead of night was inconceivable.

The ball of tension in Maple's chest loosened a bit. Even if Oliver ended up despising the sight of her, like everyone else in this town, at least she'd done one thing right. She'd gotten the dog here and managed to help preserve the child's belief in the goodness and loyalty of man's best friend. It felt good, despite the fact that she was still doing her best to blend into the beige hospital walls.

"Oliver, bud. I want you to meet a friend of mine." Ford smiled at her, and for reasons she really didn't want to think about, her heart went pitter-patter. "This is Maple. She's taking care of Lady Bird for now."

Maple held up a hand and took a step closer to Oliver's bed. "Hi."

"Hey," Oliver said without tearing his gaze away from the dog. Lady Bird had nudged her head so it fully rested in the boy's lap, and her eyes were trained on his pale face.

"I've got to go check on something, okay?" Ford glanced at the smart watch on his wrist. "I'll be back in about fifteen minutes. Twenty, max."

He was leaving? Already?

Ford shot her a reassuring wink. "Oliver, take it easy on Maple, okay? She's shy."

Maple's face went warm. "I'm sure we'll be fine."

She was sure of nothing of the sort. So far, the people she'd met in Bluebonnet weren't at all like the people she knew back home. She'd been in town for a day, and already everyone seemed to know more about her personal business than she typically shared with friends, much less strangers. There were no walls here. No barriers to hide behind. No *crowds*. She felt wholly exposed, which was especially nerve-racking considering she was trying to adjust to a whole new version of herself as a person.

You're still Maple Leighton. Absolutely nothing about your life has to change.

But what if she wanted it to?

She didn't, though. Of course not. Maple had a plan—a plan that she'd worked long and hard for. Grover had given her full permission to skip the first wasted year of that plan and move full steam ahead toward her dreams. Her dad had already paved the way for her to walk right into her perfectly planned future. Now wasn't the time to entertain change.

Something about the quiet intimacy of a hospital room in the middle of the night was making her question everything, though. Time seemed to stand still in places like this. The outside world felt very far away.

Maple took a deep breath and moved to sit in the chair that Ford had dragged too close to Oliver's bedside for her. This was crazy. She had no clue what to say or do, and panic was already blossoming in her chest as Ford sauntered out of the room in his blue hospital scrubs.

"You like dogs, huh?" she said quietly after Ford was gone.

Oliver nodded but didn't say anything. He just kept

toying with Lady's Bird's ears, running them through his small fingers. The dog's eyes slowly drifted closed.

"She really likes that." Maple smiled. "I love dogs, too."

"My mom says when I'm better, I can get a dog of my own." Oliver's gaze finally swiveled in her direction. The dark circles under his eyes made her heart twist. *When I'm better...* She prayed that would happen and it would be soon. "When I do, I want one just like Lady Bird."

"She's quite special." Maple's throat went thick, and she wondered what would happen to the dog once she'd gone. She'd been staying with June since Percy's passing, but the older woman hadn't said anything about keeping Lady Bird and giving her a permanent home.

Why would she? This dog is supposed to be yours *now.*

Maple's grip on the leash tightened.

"Do you want to see some pictures I drew of her?" Oliver asked with a yawn.

Maple nodded. "I'd love to."

Oliver pointed at his bedside table. "They're in the top drawer. You can get them out if you want to."

"Are you sure?" Maple hesitated. She wasn't sure rummaging through a patient's nightstand was proper protocol.

But Oliver seemed determined. He nodded. "There's a whole bunch of drawings in there, right on top of the chocolate bars I'm not supposed to know about. My mom keeps them for me. She's going to make a whole book out of my drawings for me when I leave the hospital."

"That's a great idea," Maple said, biting back a smile at the mention of secret chocolate. Something told her nothing got past Oliver.

She pulled open the drawer and sure enough, there

was a neat stack of papers covered in bold strokes of crayon nestled inside.

"These are amazing, Oliver." Maple slowly flipped through the drawings, which seemed to chronicle Oliver's stay in the hospital.

In the first few, the little boy in the pictures had a mop of curly brown hair. Soon, the child in the drawings had a smooth, bald head, just like Oliver's.

"That's Ford," Oliver said when her gaze landed on a rendering of a man in familiar-looking blue scrubs with a stethoscope slung around his neck.

Maple grinned. "It looks just like him."

Except the kid had forgotten to add a yellow halo above Ford's head. Maple still wasn't sure what, exactly, Ford did around here, but she had a feeling that escorting therapy dogs and their handlers to the hospital wasn't part of his official job description.

He was almost too wholesome to be real—like the humble, flannel-wearing, small-town love interest in a Hallmark movie. Whereas Maple was the big-city villainess who always ended up getting dumped for a cupcake baker in those sticky-sweet movies. It happened every time. How many cupcake bakers did the world *actually* need, anyway?

"And here's Lady Bird." Maple held up the next drawing, which featured a big yellow dog sprawled across Oliver's hospital bed, definitely a case of art imitating life. "I'd know that big golden anywhere. I really love your artwork, Oliver."

The child gave her a sleepy grin. "There's lots more."

"There sure is." Maple sifted through page after page of colorful renderings of Lady Bird, and she felt herself going all gooey inside. Not full-on cupcake-baker-gooey, but definitely softer than she normally allowed herself to feel around people she'd only just met.

Then she flipped to the next page, and her entire body tensed.

"That's Lady Bird with Mr. Percy." Oliver lifted one hand from the dog's ear just long enough to point to a crayon-sketched figure with gray hair and an oversize pair of glasses perched on his round face.

Mr. Percy. Maple's *father*.

She wasn't sure why his likeness caught her so off guard. She knew good and well that Lady Bird was Percy's dog, and he'd been the one to take the dog on her pet-therapy visits. But something about seeing him drawn in Oliver's young hand brought back the feeling she'd had just hours ago when she'd toed off her stilettos and slid her feet into his slippers.

She still wasn't quite sure why she'd done it. The shoes had been placed right next to the bed in the small home's master bedroom, as if Percy was expected to climb out of bed and slip them on just like any other day. Before she'd known what she was doing, she'd put them on and tried to imagine what it might be like to follow in her birth father's footsteps. Was it just a coincidence that she'd become a veterinarian, just like him, or was there a part of him still living inside her? Perhaps there had been, all along.

Maple wasn't sure what to believe anymore. All she knew was that somewhere deep down, she was beginning to feel a flicker of connection to a man she'd never met before.

And it scared the life out of her.

"Ford said Mr. Percy is in heaven now," Oliver said.

Maple's heart squeezed into a tight fist. She knew next to nothing about her birth father, but heaven seemed like just the right place for the kind man in Oliver's drawing.

"Ford's right," she heard herself say.

Oliver's eyes drifted shut, then he blinked hard, jolting himself awake.

"Oliver, it's okay if you fall asleep. Lady Bird and I will be here when you wake up. I promise," Maple said.

"Really?" the little boy asked, eyes wide as he buried a small hand in the ruff of fur around the dog's thick neck.

"Really." Maple nodded.

What was she saying? She had a plane to catch and a whole life waiting for her back in New York. Her *real* life, as opposed to the one here in Bluebonnet that was rapidly beginning to feel like some kind of alternate universe.

But try as she might, Maple couldn't think of a more important place she needed to be at the moment than this hospital room. For once in her life, she was right where she belonged.

"You *do* realize what time it is, don't you?" Ford narrowed his gaze at Maple, still sitting at Oliver's bedside mere minutes before the deadline she'd given him when he'd picked her up earlier and all but dragged her to the hospital against her will.

"Not precisely, but I have a good idea," she said, gaze flitting toward the window, where the first rays of sun bathed the room in a soft golden glow.

Ford crossed his arms. "You made me promise to

get you home in time for your rideshare to Austin. That means we need to go now, or all bets are off."

"I guess all bets are off, then." Maple reached over the guardrail of the hospital bed and rested a hand on Lady Bird's back. The big dog was stretched out alongside Oliver, paws twitching in her sleep.

Ford didn't know what to make of this unexpected turn of events. The dog's part in the impromptu sleepover was no surprise whatsoever. He'd seen Lady Bird sleep anywhere and everywhere, and the golden seemed especially fond of Oliver.

Maple, on the other hand…

Ford felt himself frown. Every time he thought he had this woman figured out, she threw him for a loop. It almost made her fun to be around.

"Why are you looking at me like that?" she asked.

"How am I looking at you?" Ford crossed the room to drag the other armchair closer to the recliner, where Maple had her feet tucked up under her legs. He raked a hand through his hair and sat down.

She gave him a sidelong glance. "Like you don't believe me when I say all bets are off."

"Probably because I don't. You seemed awfully sure about catching that rideshare."

She shrugged, but the way she averted her gaze told him her decision hadn't been as casual as she wanted him to believe. "I promised Oliver that Lady Bird would be here when he woke up."

Ford nudged her knee with his. "Careful there, Doc. You almost sound like a people person."

She turned to glare at him, but he could tell her heart

wasn't in it. "I'm sure it's just a phase. I'll get it over it soon enough."

"If you say so." He bit back a smile.

"Can I ask you a question?" she asked, deftly changing the subject.

He leaned back in the chair and stretched his legs out in front of him. "Shoot. I'm an open book."

"What exactly do you do here?" She eyed his scrubs, and a cute little furrow formed in her brow. "Are you a nurse?"

"I'm a pediatrician. I have a solo practice in Bluebonnet, but I've got privileges here at County General. Oliver is one of my patients." Ford had, in fact, been Oliver's doctor since the day he'd been born. He loved that kid. Sometimes being a small-town doctor meant you got a little too close to your patients, although Ford usually didn't consider that a problem.

Oliver's case was different, though. *Special.* He would've moved heaven and earth to see that child healthy again.

The furrow in Maple's brow deepened, and Ford had the nonsensical urge to smooth it out with a brush of his fingertips. "Please tell me you're joking. You can't be a doctor."

"Not a joke. I assure you." A smile tugged at his lips. He was enjoying her befuddlement a little too much. "What's wrong, Doc? Have you got a thing against physicians like you do against robotic animals?"

She regarded him with what could only be described as abject horror. "I do when said physician intentionally let me believe he wasn't a doctor."

Ford shook his head. "I never intentionally misled you. Name one time I did that."

"How about every single time you've called me Doc?" She was blushing again, and Ford wasn't sure if it was embarrassment or rage. Probably some combination of the two, if he had to guess.

"But you *are* a doctor—a doctor of veterinary medicine. As I recall, you seem especially proud of the title." Okay, so maybe the nickname had been somewhat of a taunt. Ford hadn't been able to resist.

She gasped as if she'd just remembered something, and then she covered her face with her hands. "Oh, my gosh. You let me go on and on about the two types of doctors, didn't you?"

"You mean general-practice physicians who are driven by their innate need to help people and specialists who relate more to the scientific part of medicine?" Ford said with his tongue firmly planted in his cheek as he parroted her own words back to her.

"I guess we know which one you are, Mr. Hometown Hero." She snorted.

She had him pegged, that was for sure. Ford had made it his mission to become a pediatrician back in the fifth grade when his best friend, Bobby Jackson, had died from acute myelogenous leukemia. Over the course of a single little league season, Bobby had gone from being the star pitcher for the Bluebonnet Bears to being bedridden with the disease. By Christmas, he was gone. Ford's small world had crumbled down around him, and in a way, he'd been trying to put it back together ever since.

So, yeah, he'd gone into medicine to help people. Was that really such a bad thing?

Lately, he'd begun to wonder. If he'd become a specialist instead of a pediatrician, he could've done more for Oliver and other children like him.

Children like Bobby, he thought as the memory of his best friend floated to the forefront of his mind. It had been years since Ford had spent the night at Bobby's ranch, tucked into their matching Spider-Man sleeping bags in the treehouse in Bobby's shady backyard. Two and a half decades, in fact. But he still remembered those nights like they'd happened yesterday—the shimmering stars overhead, the swishing of the horses' tails as they grazed in the pasture just beyond the barbed-wire fence, the feeling that Bluebonnet was the safest place in the world and nothing bad could ever happen there...

Ford knew better now, obviously. But that didn't stop him from doing his level best to make it true. He'd moved away once, and that had been a terrible mistake. Now, he was home for good and still trying to hold things together, as if it was possible to carry the entire town on his back. At least that's what his sister always said.

Maple resumed glaring at Ford, a welcome distraction from his spiraling thoughts. Why did things always seem so much more hopeless in the dead of night?

"You're impossible. I can't believe you didn't tell me," Maple said.

Ford arched an eyebrow. "You didn't ask."

She sure as heck hadn't. She'd barreled into town like a tornado, all too ready to flatten everything and everyone in her wake.

That had certainly backfired.

Ford had heard all about Percy's last will and testament. There were no secrets in Bluebonnet. By now, everyone in town knew that Maple Leighton was Percy Walker's long-lost daughter.

She'd had quite a day. Ford should probably go easy on her, but where was the fun in that? Besides, Maple didn't seem like the type who wanted to be treated with kid gloves. Everything Ford knew about her thus far screamed the opposite.

He slid his attention away from Oliver and Lady Bird, still sleeping soundly in the hospital bed, and found Maple watching him, eyes glittering in the darkened room. Their gazes met and held, until her bow-shaped lips curved into a knowing smile.

A delicious heat coursed through Ford, like wildflower honey warmed by the summer sun. "What's the grin for? I thought I was impossible."

"Oh, you definitely are." Her eyes narrowed, ever so slightly. "And that just made me realize something."

"What's that, Doc?"

She looked away, focusing on the boy and the dog. But Ford could still spy a ghost of a smile dancing on her lips. "You're not quite as nice as you seem, Ford Bishop."

Chapter Six

"What are we doing here?" Maple peered out the windshield of Ford's pickup as he pulled into one of the prime parking spots along Bluebonnet's town square.

He shifted the truck into Park and nodded at Cherry on Top Bakery, situated directly in front of them. "I promised you pie. Or have you decided to forgo that condition, too?"

Maple's heart thumped at the mention of her conditions. Missing her rideshare had seemed like a perfectly logical decision an hour ago, when she'd been sitting at Oliver's bedside with Lady Bird. Now, not so much.

She swallowed. Oliver had woken up shortly after she'd learned Ford was the boy's doctor. Maple had seen his eyes flutter open and then slam shut when he realized the adults were still there. Oliver made a valiant attempt at faking it, no doubt to prolong saying goodbye to Lady Bird. But as soon as Ford told Maple in a loud whisper that the hospital breakfast for the day would include sweet-potato, hash-brown egg nests—Oliver's favorite, apparently—the child sat up, bright-eyed and bushy-tailed.

Ford had escorted Maple and Lady Bird out of Oliver's

room just as his breakfast arrived. Approximately two seconds later, panic settled in the pit of Maple's stomach.

What was she *doing*? She was supposed to be half-way to Austin right now, not sitting in close proximity to an actual gazebo beside Ford in his charming, vintage pickup truck. He had one of those classic turquoise Fords from the 1960s, and naturally, it was in perfect, shiny mint condition. What else would Dr. Small Town Charm drive?

"The condition absolutely still stands." Maple was starving. She hadn't eaten a thing since diving head-first into the peach pie Ford had left on her front porch the night before. "But look, they're not open yet."

She waved toward the Sorry, We're Closed sign hanging in the bakery's front window. The rest of the town square was deserted, as well. Maple wasn't sure what time sleepy small towns like this typically woke up, but apparently it was sometime after 6:42 a.m.

Ford shrugged and flashed her a smile worthy of a toothpaste commercial. "I know the owner."

"Of course you do." Maple rolled her eyes.

Ford climbed down from the driver's seat and Lady Bird, who'd been nestled between them on the bench seat during the ride back to Bluebonnet from County General, bounded after him.

Maple paused, wondering how fast she could get to Austin if she went straight back to Percy's house to pack her things and summon another hired car. Why was this state so darn big?

Lady Bird gazed up at her with an expectant wag of her fluffy gold tail. *Are you coming or what?*

Maple's stomach growled, right on cue. There had to

be other flights from Austin to New York today, right? They were both huge, metropolitan cities. Just because she'd missed the early morning flight didn't mean she was stuck here indefinitely. Surely, there was time for a tiny bite of pie.

She slid out of the passenger seat and headed toward the bakery, where Ford swung the door open like he owned the place. Lady Bird pranced straight inside while Maple lingered on the threshold.

She glanced at Ford as he held the door open for her. "Are dogs allowed in here?"

"What dog?" A woman with a high blond ponytail juggled pies in each hand and winked at them from behind the counter. "I don't see any dog, just my sweet nurse friend Lady Bird."

Lady Bird immediately got an extra spring in her step at the sound of her name. She trotted toward the counter, nose twitching in the general direction of the pies, which smelled like they'd just come straight from the oven.

"Hi, there. I'm Adaline." She slid the pies onto the counter and waved at Maple with an oven mitt decorated with the same whimsical cherry print as her ruffle-trimmed apron.

"I'm Maple."

"Maple is new in town," Ford said as he lowered himself onto one of the barstools at the counter. He gave the stool next to him a pat. "Come on, scaredy cat."

Adaline lifted an eyebrow.

"Maple is a tad shy," Ford said. "Right, Lady Bird?"

Maple *really* wished he'd stop staying that, although she supposed it was preferable to Ford broadcasting the fact that she'd told him she wasn't a people person. Did he have to say anything at all, though? Why did it feel like the entire town was populated by oversharers?

Lady Bird woofed her agreement before collapsing in a heap at Ford's feet. Great. Even the dog had an opinion about her social skills.

"Oh, wait." Adaline's eyes lit up. "You must be the peach pie from yesterday."

"That was me." Maple took the seat next to Ford. "It was delicious, by the way."

"So delicious that she insisted I bring her in for more." Ford pointed at one of the pies in front of Adaline. "Do I smell cherries?"

Adaline jammed her hands on her hips. "Ford Bishop, are you seriously waltzing in here less than an hour before we open, expecting to eat my inventory?"

"Yes." He nodded. "Yes, I am."

Maple glanced back and forth between them, wondering how they knew each other. The vibe between them was playful, but it didn't have a flirtatious edge.

Maple breathed a senseless sigh of relief. Lady Bird lifted her face from her paws and gave Maple a little head tilt, as if the dog could read her mind. Intuition was a valuable quality in a therapy dog, but in this case, it just seemed nosy.

And way off base. Maple didn't have a jealous bone in her body where Ford was concerned. In fact, a small-town baker was exactly the sort of person he should be with. Maple should be rooting for these two crazy kids.

Then why aren't you?

"Fine," Adaline said, relenting, then she reached for a silver cake server. "But only because Maple is new in town, like you said. She deserves a proper welcome."

"I'm not really, though—new in town, I mean." Maple protested as Adaline served up an enormous slice of cherry pie and slid the plate toward her. Her mouth was already watering. "I'm not staying in Bluebonnet. I'm leaving today, actually."

Probably, anyway. She still needed to get that figured out.

"Oh." Adaline shot Ford a loaded glance, which Maple had no idea how to interpret. "What did my brother do to scare you off so quickly?"

Maple's fork paused halfway to her mouth. "You two are brother and sister?"

That made sense. No wonder they seemed so comfortable around each other.

"We are." Adaline pulled a face, as if being related to Ford was something to be ashamed of.

Maple decided right there and then that she liked Adaline Bishop. She liked her a lot. Too bad she'd never see her again—or eat any more of her delicious baked goods—after today.

Maple swallowed a forkful of pie, and it suddenly felt like a rock in the pit of her stomach.

"I didn't do anything to scare her off. This big-city wariness you're observing is Maple's natural state. I've been nothing but welcoming." Ford cut his eyes toward her. When he looked at her like that—as if his dreamy blue eyes could see straight into her soul—she sometimes forgot how to breathe. It was beyond annoying.

Maple focused intently on the rich red cherries on her plate. "Except for the part where you tricked me into examining a fake dog. And then dragged me to the hospital in the middle of the night. And then lied about being a doctor."

A bark of laughter burst out of Adaline. "Oh, this is getting good. She's got your number, Ford."

"She also has quite a flair for exaggeration," Ford countered. "Where's *my* pie, by the way? You just gave her a supersized slice, and I'm still sitting here empty-handed."

"Hold your horses. I was just getting to know my new bestie." Adaline shot Maple a wink as she cut a significantly smaller piece of pie for her brother. "Too bad you're not staying, Maple. I have a feeling we'd be great friends."

"Yeah," Maple said quietly. "I think we would, too."

A heaviness came over Maple that she wanted to attribute to lack of sleep, but it felt more like regret. Aside from her study group in vet school, she didn't have many friends in New York.

"Are you sure you have to go so soon?" Adaline picked up a mixing bowl and began measuring cups of flour to dump into it.

"I actually just missed my flight. I need to try and get another one later this afternoon. Everything right now is a little—" she swallowed and didn't dare venture a glance in Ford's direction "—complicated."

Adaline nodded as if she understood, but a flicker of confusion passed through her gaze. How could she possibly understand when Maple still hadn't managed to get a handle on her current circumstances herself?

"I need—" she began, ready to rattle off a list of perfectly rational reasons why she needed to get back to Manhattan, starting with her highly coveted position at the veterinary cardiology practice. But before she could utter another syllable, her cell phone rang, piercing the awkward silence that had descended at the mention of Maple's missed flight.

She dug the phone out of her purse and nearly dropped it when she spied her mother's name flashing across the top of the display screen. Lady Bird let out a long, drawn-out sigh.

Maple's gaze darted toward the dog, but the golden's sweet, melting expression only sharpened the dull ache of regret into something much more painful. What was going to happen to Lady Bird once she was gone?

Maple gripped her phone tight. "I should probably take this."

Lady Bird was practically the mayor of this town. The dog would have no trouble whatsoever finding a good home. Maple wouldn't be surprised if there ended up being a contest of some sort. She just needed to keep her eye on the prize long enough to get out of here.

The front door had barely closed behind Maple when Adaline abandoned her baking to give Ford a sisterly third degree.

"What do you think you're doing?" she said, pointing a wooden spoon at him for added emphasis.

Ford should've known this was coming. But truly, his sister was barking up the wrong tree.

"I'm eating my pie." He aimed his fork over his plate for another bite.

"Nice try." She slid the plate away from him, and his fork stabbed nothing but air. "You know what I'm talking about. What's going on between you two?"

Adaline cast a purposeful glance over his shoulder toward the town square, where Maple was now pacing back and forth as she talked on the phone. Lady Bird scrambled to her feet, trotted toward the door and proceeded to stare out the window at Maple while emitting a mournful whine.

"Nothing whatsoever is going on. Like I said, I'm just here for the pie. I'm perfectly content to mind my own business." Ford waved his fork between his sister and Lady Bird. "Unlike you two."

"Oh, please. From what Maple said, it sounds like you've spent an awful lot of time together in the past twenty-four hours." Adaline pointed her wooden spoon at him again.

Ford just wanted his pie back. Was that really too much to ask?

"For the record, Maple hasn't even been here twenty-four hours yet." He snagged his plate back while Adaline processed what he'd just said. "And she's already got one foot out the door, so I repeat—nothing whatsoever is going on."

His sister eyed him with thinly veiled skepticism. "You bought her a pie yesterday, and from the looks of things, you just spent the night together."

Ford loved his sister. He really did. He loved Bluebonnet too, with all his heart and soul…despite the fact that the general population of his hometown—Adaline, included—had never believed in the concept of privacy. Every place on earth had its downside.

"We spent the night at County General. *Working.* I had patients to attend to, and Maple brought Lady Bird for a therapy-dog visit. That's all. I promised to bring her here in exchange for coming to the hospital in the middle of the night."

Adaline's expression turned serious. "Was this for the little boy who has leukemia?"

Ford's teeth ground together. He'd already told his sister too much about Oliver. He'd never disclosed the child's name, but even talking about one of his patients in vague terms went against his ethics as a physician.

The similarities between Oliver's case and his memories of Bobby were too much, though. Same diagnosis, same age, same sickening feeling in Ford's gut. Every time he ran Oliver's blood count or checked the results of his most recent bone-marrow aspiration, Ford was plunged straight back to that awful summer when Bobby stopped showing up at the baseball diamond and his parents couldn't look him in the eye when they tried to explain what was wrong. In a moment of weakness, he'd shared only the bare basics of Oliver's story with Adaline. She'd known Bobby, too, and she'd been there when Ford's safe little world had been rocked straight off its axis. Telling her had felt right at the time, and for a moment, a bit of the weight had lifted off Ford's shoulders. He'd been able to breathe again.

It had been a mistake. He knew that much now. Things had been easier when Ford could compartmentalize his feelings and pretend everything was fine. He couldn't do that anymore now that Adaline knew the truth. It seemed Ford's sister had as much interest in his favorite patient as she did his romantic pursuits, and Ford had zero desire to discuss either.

"You know I can't talk about that," he said.

She held up her hands. "I know, I know. I just hope

he's doing okay. It's sweet that Maple came up there so late, whatever the reason. Staying all night is a pretty big deal. That's all I'm saying."

Ford shot her a sardonic look. "Is it really *all* you're saying?"

That would be a first.

Adaline crossed her arms and huffed. "Fine. You bought Maple an entire pie yesterday. That seems significant, wouldn't you agree?"

Granted, Ford wasn't generally in the business of feeding women baked goods. Until recently, apparently.

"The peach pie was Gram's doing, not mine. I was simply following orders." He gave his dessert an aggressive jab with this fork. Why did he feel the need to defend himself when he was telling the truth? Nothing had happened between him and Maple, and nothing ever would. Period. "I took Gram and Coco to the vet yesterday, and Maple works there. Or she did... Clearly, that's changed."

He was getting whiplash trying to keep up with Maple's plans. Not that where she lived or worked was any of his business. He just needed to know how to get ahold of Lady Bird, that's all.

Ford choked down the last bite of his pie and pushed away his plate. He'd lost his appetite all of a sudden.

Adaline took the plate and placed it in the sink behind the counter. Then she planted her hands on the smooth Formica and fixed her gaze with his, eyes wary. Obviously, she wasn't buying what he was selling. "Do I need to remind you what happened the last time you got involved with a woman who wasn't suited for small-town life?"

She absolutely did not. Ford couldn't have forgotten that particular disaster if he'd tried. And, oh, how he'd tried—many, many times. Certain heartbreaks had a way of burrowing deep, though.

"No need," Ford said.

"Are you sure? Because Maple seems really great. I was serious when I said I thought we'd be great friends. But she's obviously not cut out for Bluebonnet."

Ford knew better than to ask his sister to elaborate, because that would mean he was taking Adaline's warning seriously. Which he wasn't. He had no interest whatsoever in history repeating itself, and Maple had been trying to escape Bluebonnet since the moment they'd first met. How could he forget?

I'm from New York City. But I live here now...temporarily.

They'd practically been Maple's first words to him, and Ford had heard them loud and clear. It wasn't possible to place a bigger emphasis on *temporarily*.

"She'll be gone by tomorrow morning, and it can't come soon enough. You can stop worrying about me." Ford jerked his head toward Lady Bird, still pining at the door while she kept track of Maple's every move. Adaline's pristine, polished glass was rapidly becoming smudged with golden-retriever nose prints. "Lady Bird over there might be a different story."

"That dog loves everyone," Adaline said.

Ford shook his head. "This is different."

Adaline's forehead scrunched. "How can you tell?"

"I just can." Ford's heart went out to the poor dog.

He wondered if the golden could tell that Maple was related to Percy. A while back, he'd read an article in a medical journal that speculated dogs could identify blood relatives purely by smell. If that was the case, Maple was now the closest thing Lady Bird had to Percy, whom she'd adored with unfettered devotion.

"Mark my words. If you're worried about anyone, it should be Lady Bird," Ford said. For once, the dog didn't respond to the sound of her name. She kept her gaze trained out the window, laser-focused on Maple's every move.

"Are you sure you're not just projecting?" Adaline cleared her throat. "From where I'm standing, you and Lady Bird have matching puppy-dog expressions. That's all I'm saying."

"That's *all* you're saying? Again?" Ford arched an eyebrow. "Is that a promise this time?"

It was too early in the morning for a deep dive into his love life. Not that he had any love life to speak of, which was purely intentional.

"For now. As for the future, I make no guarantees." Adaline wadded up her dish towel and threw it at his face.

"Duly noted," Ford said dryly.

Ever the perfect therapy dog, Lady Bird abandoned her post to shuffle back to the counter and press the bulk of her warm form against Ford's leg. Then she rested her chin on his knee with an audible sigh, leaving Ford to wonder which one of them was supposed be on the receiving end of the comfort being offered.

Man, dog…or, quite possibly, both.

Chapter Seven

The best Maple could do was get on standby for a two o'clock flight out of Austin. She'd checked all the major airlines, and there wasn't an empty seat to be found, much to the dismay of her mother. *And* her father.

Once again, the Leightons had joined forces as soon as they'd found out that Maple had missed her morning flight. She'd done her best to assure her mother she still had every intention of returning to New York as soon as humanly possible. But no sooner had she admitted to missing her rideshare than her father had jumped on the line.

What was happening? Who knew the only way to get her parents back on speaking terms was for her to go rogue, flee to Texas, and accidentally discover she'd been adopted.

Surely, Maple could get a standby seat on one of the five flights scheduled to leave between afternoon and midnight. What were the odds she'd get stuck here… *again*?

"Not going to happen," she said out loud as she folded her cupcake pajamas and placed them in her suitcase.

Lady Bird lifted her head from her paws, where she was resting on the dog bed in the corner of Percy's bedroom. She tilted her gold head in the irresistible way that dogs had been doing since the dawn of time, and a fresh wave of guilt washed over Maple. How was she going to leave this sweet dog behind? Lady Bird was the only remaining tie she had to the father she'd never known. Was she seriously going to get on a plane and let someone else take care of her when Percy had specifically left the dog in her care?

You never knew him, she reminded herself. Things would be different if she'd known she'd been adopted before Percy passed away. It was too late to get to know her birth father, and it was definitely too late to build a life in a place like Bluebonnet. She'd spent a full year as an intern for her cardiology specialty. Small towns didn't need veterinary cardiologists. Even if she wanted to stay and follow in Percy's footsteps at his charming little pet clinic—which she didn't—doing so would mean wasting a large chunk of her education.

And then there was the matter of Dr. Grover Hayes. If she stayed, he would be her *partner*. Maple didn't know which one of them would find that prospect more horrifying. It would be a disaster, full stop.

"Why am I even thinking about any of this? I'm not staying." She slammed her suitcase closed and zipped it shut. Then her gaze fell to Percy's bedroom slippers sitting neatly beside the bed, where Maple had returned them to their proper place.

Her eyes immediately filled with unshed tears, and she squeezed them closed tight, determined not to get weepy about a total stranger who just so happened to share her DNA. What was wrong with her? She never let her emotions get the best of her like this. No wonder her parents were concerned.

Maple sniffed and squared her shoulders. Then she opened her eyes and found Lady Bird sitting at her feet, holding Percy's slippers in her mouth.

You've got to be kidding me, dog.

Maple stared as her throat squeezed closed.

"Fine." She gently snatched the shoes from the retriever's jaws. "I'm taking these with me. Happy now?"

Lady Bird's mouth stretched into a wide doggy grin as her tail swished back and forth on the bedroom's smooth wood floor.

"You're really something, you know that?" Maple whispered. She shook her head, unzipped her bag, and carefully placed the slippers inside.

The vintage rotary phone in the kitchen trilled, causing her to jump. It was a good thing she wasn't staying, because she'd never grow accustomed to that sound.

"We're not answering that," she said, but before the words left her mouth, Lady Bird was already trotting toward the source of the noise.

Maple followed, keenly aware of which party seemed to be in charge in this relationship. Spoiler alert: it wasn't Maple. But that was fine for now. So long as the dog was bossing Maple around, she didn't have much time to think about a certain pediatrician who seemed to possess a warm and wonderful center that was as soft and gooey and perfect as a cinnamon roll fresh out of the oven.

He healed sick children. He frequented his sister's pie shop. He pretended his grandmother's robot dog was real. Was Ford even a real human being?

She eyed Lady Bird while the phone continued to ring. "I already told you we're not answering that."

But what if it was County General again? What if something had happened to sweet little Oliver?

Maple plucked the receiver from its hook, all the while telling herself that answering the call had nothing whatsoever to do with Ford Bishop, even though a teeny tiny part of her heart did a backflip at the thought of seeing him one more time before she left Bluebonnet for good. "Hello?"

"Oh, good morning! So happy you picked up. Is this Maple Walker?"

Maple's entire body gave a jolt. *Walker.* Percy's last name, not hers.

Was there a single soul in all of Bluebonnet who hadn't heard that Maple was his long-lost daughter? Apparently not—yet another reason to get back to Manhattan, where the details of her birth certificate weren't front-page news.

Maple "Um. Yes, but—"

"Thank heavens," the caller said before Maple could point out that her last name was actually Leighton, despite whatever she might have heard via the town rumor mill. "Technically, I'm calling for Lady Bird, but she's yours now, right?"

Once again, Maple had no idea what to say. This time, she didn't even try to come up with a response. She just kept her mouth shut and frowned down at Lady Bird.

I told you we shouldn't answer the phone.

The dog's plumed tail wagged even harder.

"This is Virginia Roberts over at Bluebonnet Senior Living. We were expecting Lady Bird fifteen minutes ago for her regular weekly visit. Can you let me know when she might arrive?"

"Oh." Maple's stomach churned. She couldn't allow herself to get roped into another pet-therapy visit. No way, no how. "Well…"

"We have about a dozen residents gathered in the lobby, ready and waiting. I'd hate to have to disappoint them." Virginia cleared her throat.

Maple gritted her teeth and counted to ten, steadying herself to say no. Granted, she technically had time to squeeze in a pet visit since her ride wasn't coming for another three hours.

But still…

No.

Just say it, she told herself. *Sorry, but no*.

Then she made the mistake of glancing back down at Lady Bird. She blinked up at Maple with such trust and devotion in her soft brown eyes that Maple's resistance crumbled on the spot.

"We'll be there as soon as we can."

Luckily, the senior center was located just off the town square, a short two-block walk from Percy's house. Maple followed the walking directions on her iPhone's GPS, but she could've simply allowed Lady Bird to guide her there, because the golden clearly knew where they were headed. She tugged gently at the end of her leash, making the left at the town square, followed by an immediate right, without any guidance whatsoever from Maple. The closer they came, the harder Lady Bird's tail wagged. When the sign for Bluebonnet Senior Living came into view, Maple could barely keep up.

It was a blessing, really. Maple's social anxiety

didn't have time to kick in before Lady Bird dragged her through the door.

The young man who worked at the front desk lit up like a Christmas tree the instant they crossed the threshold. "Lady Bird! It's so good to see you! We've got a big crowd waiting for you, as usual."

The dog's tail swung back and forth, but her overall demeanor instantly changed. A steady calmness came over her, as if she knew she was here to work, just like it had at the hospital.

Maple couldn't help but swell with pride, even though she had nothing whatsoever to do with Lady Bird's training. That had been Percy's doing. Was it strange that she felt connected to them both, somehow?

"Hi, I'm Maple." She lifted a hand to wave at the young man stationed at the reception desk while he pulled a box of dog biscuits out of his bottom desk drawer. "Sorry we're late. I didn't realize Lady Bird had a visit scheduled for today."

"No worries," he said as Lady Bird rose up onto her hind legs and planted her front paws on the desk to politely take the treat he offered her. "We're just glad you were able to make it. Her visit is every Tuesday morning at eleven, just so you know. We always have it listed on the social calendar."

He tipped his head toward a wall calendar covered with colorful stickers and handwritten activities like bingo and movie night listed in bright magic marker. A paw print featured prominently on every Tuesday square beside Lady Bird's name.

Now would be the time to mention that Lady Bird's future visits were up in the air, but when Maple glanced beyond the reception desk and saw a large group of residents sitting in wheelchairs and peering toward her and Lady Bird in anticipation, she just couldn't do it.

She took a deep breath as the first tingle of nerves skittered down her spine. This wasn't like the calm, quiet visit with Oliver. This was an entire group of people who would all be focused on Maple and the dog.

More the dog, she reminded herself.

They could do this. *She* could do this, so long as Lady Bird was on the other end of the leash.

Finished with her biscuit, the dog licked her chops and hopped back down to all fours. She dropped into a perfect sit position and gazed up at Maple expectantly.

Maple stared back, unsure what the dog was waiting for.

"Go visit," a deep voice rumbled from just beyond the reception desk.

"Excuse me?" Maple leaned to the left, and that's when she spotted him. *Again.*

Maple's heart did a rebellious little flutter.

She swallowed hard. "You."

"You," Ford echoed, narrowing his gaze at Maple.

He hadn't expected to see her again, well…*ever.* Once she'd ended her call earlier at Cherry on Top and come back inside the bakery, she'd been all business. She'd been in such a hurry to get back to Percy's house so she could pack and make new travel arrangements that, much to Adaline's consternation, she hadn't even finished her pie.

Their goodbye had been strained and awkward, and all the while, Ford had told himself it was for the best. Life could go back to normal around here.

Never mind that the prospect of normal suddenly felt a little dull. A little predictable.

A little lonely.

Ford gritted his teeth and reminded himself he didn't have any romantic interest in this woman. She was going to leave skid marks in her wake when she finally left town.

"What are you doing here? I thought you had a plane to catch," he said bluntly.

"I did." She blinked her wide doe eyes, a deer caught in headlights. "I mean I do. It's not until later this afternoon."

Ford dropped his gaze to the dog sitting at her feet, wagging her little gold heart out. A pang of…something hit him dead in the center of his chest. As much as he wanted to believe it was pity for the poor animal, it felt more like empathy. "If Lady Bird and I didn't know better, we might think you didn't really want to go."

"Good thing you both know better, then," Maple said, but she suddenly couldn't seem to meet his gaze. She seemed to be staring intently at his forearms, visible below the rolled-up sleeves of his denim shirt. Then she gave her head a little shake and aimed those wary eyes of hers back on his face. "What are *you* doing here? You're a pediatrician. Shouldn't you be passing out lollipops somewhere?"

Ah, there she was—the mouthy outsider that seemed to love nothing more than getting under his skin.

The joke was on Maple, though. Ford could see right through the arrogant little act of hers. It was simply a way of keeping people at arm's length, like the armored shell on an armadillo.

"I'm off today. Once a week I do an overnight at County General, and my office is always closed the following day. I was here to play bingo with my gram." He gave the pocket of his denim shirt a pat. "But if you have a hankering for a lollipop, I might have one on me."

"Thanks, but I'm good." She held up her hand to stop him, which was just as well since he was only teasing. "What did you say a minute ago, though? I'm not sure I caught it."

"The part about you having a plane to catch?"

"No." Her forehead puckered. "It was something about a visit."

"Ah. 'Go visit.'" Ford cast a glance at the dog. "That's what Lady Bird is waiting for you to say. Percy always gave her that command at the start of a therapy-dog visit."

Maple's gaze flitted toward the golden. "Go visit, Lady Bird."

The dog immediately stood and started trotting toward her senior fan club, already assembled in the living room area of the lobby.

Maple flashed Ford a grin over her shoulder. "It worked! Thank you."

"You've got this, Maple," he said with a wink.

"Wait." She stumbled to a halt. "You're not leaving, are you?"

He'd planned on it. Visiting Gram had provided him with a welcome distraction from work, but Ford had other things to do on his day off. Bingo had ended a good twenty minutes ago, yet here he stood.

"Why? Do you want me to stay?" Ford shifted his weight from one booted foot to the other. The words had fallen out of his mouth before he could stop them. Of course, that's not what Maple wanted.

"Yes." She nodded vigorously, eyes pleading with him. "I mean, if you don't mind, that would be great. I really don't know what I'm doing, and you've clearly been around Lady Bird and Percy on their visits."

"There's really not much to it. That dog is a natural." He had no business staying and spending more time with her. Hadn't he just promised his sister earlier that he wasn't getting emotionally involved?

Good luck with that. A bitter taste rose up the back of his throat. Ford's emotions had been running roughshod over him for months now. What he needed to do now was lock the horse back in the barn.

"You're right. Sorry, it was just a thought." Maple cast a panicked glance toward the senior citizens, and Ford did his best to pretend he wasn't intrigued.

The woman was a study in contradictions. Why was she here when she so clearly wanted to be anyplace else?

"I'll stay," he said, telling himself he was simply doing her a favor, just like he would anyone else in town.

Her pretty mouth curved into a smile. "You will?" Ford ignored the telltale thump of his heart as relief flooded her features. Tried to, anyway.

He tipped his head toward the common area. "Yep, but you should probably go ahead and get started. Gram and her friends don't like to be kept waiting. They're going to eat you two alive."

Maple's face fell.

"I'm kidding, Doc." He leaned closer and gave her nose a playful tap. "Relax. Everyone's just happy you and Lady Bird are here. Trust me, you've got nothing to worry about."

"Except that I'm not certified to be doing this and everyone here has most likely been gossiping about me nonstop for the past twenty-four hours," she said with a wince.

She wasn't wrong, but dwelling on either of those things wasn't going to get her through the next half hour.

"Get through this visit, and I'll feed you more pie." Ford held up a finger. "Or better yet, barbecue. You can't leave Texas without a visit to Smokin' Joes."

Her nose wrinkled. "Why do I feel like now isn't the right time to admit that I don't like barbecue?"

That was downright blasphemous, but Ford had to cut her some slack. She'd obviously never had proper barbecue before. "That settles it. It would be a crime for you to leave Texas without giving our brisket a fair try. If you don't like it, fine. But you at least have to taste it."

She blew out a breath. "Okay, but only because you're saying."

"It's a d—" Ford swallowed the word *date* just in the nick of time "Deal."

"It's a deal," she repeated. Then she took a deep inhale and turned her attention toward Lady Bird. "Come on, Lady Bird. Let's go visit."

Chapter Eight

Maple really shouldn't have been so worried. Lady Bird knew exactly what to do, and as her handler, Maple was pretty much just along for the ride.

The dog moved deftly between wheelchairs, resting her head on the arm handles and allowing easy access for pats and scratches behind her ears. She didn't miss a beat, padding from one resident to the next, greeting everyone with happy tail wags and a wide doggy grin. Just a few minutes into the visit, Maple found herself relaxing into her role as Lady Bird's human sidekick.

Most of the seniors reminisced about dogs they'd known or shared stories about their childhood pets while Lady Bird worked her golden magic. A few residents even grew teary-eyed as they interacted with the dog, and Maple realized she shouldn't have worried so much about what to say. She didn't need to talk at all, really. Mostly, the retirees just wanted someone to listen.

Maple could do that. She liked hearing about the dogs that had meant so much to the seniors in years past, and it warmed her heart to see how simply petting Lady Bird for a few minutes could bring back such fond memories.

"Here you are again, you sweetheart," a woman with

short salt-and-pepper hair and dressed in a colorful muu-muu said as Maple and the dog approached her wheel-chair. "Oh, Lady Bird, I know I tell you this every week, but you remind me so much of my precious Toby."

The woman hugged Lady Bird's neck, closed her eyes and rocked back and forth for several long moments. Then she offered Maple a watery smile. "I had to give my dog up a few months ago. He lives with my granddaughter now."

"I'm so sorry to hear that." Maple pressed a hand to her heart.

"These visits help, you know. I never miss seeing Lady Bird. It's the highlight of my week." The woman cupped the dog's face with trembling hands. "Isn't that right, darling?"

Lady Bird made a snuffling sound and nodded her big gold head.

And so it went, from one bittersweet exchange to the next, until Maple's gaze landed on a familiar face.

"Hi, there," she said as they reached Ford's grand-mother, sitting at the end of a floral sofa with her walker parked in front of her. The infamous Coco sat propped in a basket attached to the front of the mobility device. "It's good to see you again."

Lady Bird touched noses with the stuffed animal as if they were old friends.

"I remember you." Gram's face split into a wide grin as she gazed up at Maple. "You're the pretty new vet-erinarian."

"That's right." Maple kneeled beside Lady Bird so she and the older woman were on eye level with one another. "How is your little dog feeling today?"

"Much better, thanks to you." Gram reached shaky fingertips toward Lady Bird and rested her palm on the dog's smooth head.

"I'm glad to hear it. Treating her was my pleasure," Maple said, and the tug in her heart told her that she meant it. She ran her hand along Coco's synthetic fur and the dog's mechanical head swiveled toward her. It blinked a few times, and then its mouth dropped open and the toy dog made a few panting sounds, followed by a sharp yip.

"Coco likes you," Gram said.

"I'm glad. I like her too." Maple smiled. She could feel Ford's gaze on her, and when she snuck a glance at him, he was watching her with unmistakable warmth in his eyes.

Maple's heart leaped straight to her throat, and she forced herself to look away.

"Next time, we're bringing Coco to you instead of Grover." Gram leaned closer, like she wanted to tell Maple a secret. "He won't like that, but he'll get over it."

Maple couldn't help but laugh, and for a second, she let herself believe that there really would be a next time. Would that seriously be so bad?

Lady Bird nudged her way between Gram and her walker, plopped her head on the older woman's lap and peered up at her with melting eyes. Gram placed her hands on either side of the dog's face and told her she was a good girl, just like Coco.

"It's so nice that you brought Lady Bird here today. Your daddy would be so proud of you, you know," Gram said, eyes twinkling.

For a disorienting second, Charles Leighton's face flashed in Maple's mind. Her dad had never been much of a dog person. Neither of her parents really understood her affinity for animals, but she liked the thought of making her family proud.

When Maple had been a little girl, before her parents' marriage had broken down for good, she'd often thought if she could just be good enough, she could make things better for her family. Looking back, that was certainly when her anxiety had started. She'd foolishly thought that if she could behave perfectly, she could fix whatever had gone wrong between her mom and dad. She'd tried her best in school, but no amount of straight A's on her report card or gushing reviews from her teachers about her polite classroom demeanor changed things. Her parents' relationship kept spiraling out of control, and the only other thing Maple could do was try and make herself smaller so she wouldn't get caught in the crossfire.

That was all a very long time ago, obviously. But old habits died hard. Maple loved her parents, as imperfect as they were. She still wanted them to be proud of her—maybe even more so than if she'd followed in their footsteps and gone to law school. All during veterinary school, she'd waited for one of them to realize how wrong they'd been. Surely, they'd noticed how passionate she felt about helping pets…how *right* it seemed. She'd found her purpose. Shouldn't that make any parent proud?

Her mom and dad still didn't fully understand, but that was okay. Maple was a fully grown adult. Now she chose to believe that somewhere deep down, they really were proud of her, even if they didn't share her love for animals. And even if they didn't show it. Still, she couldn't help thinking that even the Leightons might appreciate the power of a dog's unconditional love if they could see Lady Bird in action.

But then, as Maple was reminding herself that the golden would be the absolute last thing Charles and Meredith Leighton would care about here in Bluebonnet, the true meaning of Gram's words sank in.

Your daddy would be so proud of you, you know.

Maple's smile felt wooden all of a sudden. "Oh, you mean Percy."

"Of course, I do." Gram nodded. "You're so much like him it's uncanny."

"I—" Maple shook her head, all too ready to disagree.

She was nothing like her biological father. Clearly, Percy had been deeply devoted to his community. Lady Bird had a busier volunteer schedule than any human she'd ever met, but the dog couldn't spread joy and happiness without a handler. Their therapy-dog work had been Percy's doing. He'd lived in a quaint town in a tiny pink house with fanciful gingerbread trim. He'd paid for her entire education, despite the fact that she didn't have the first clue who he was.

Percy Walker had left behind some very large shoes to fill, and those shoes had nothing to do with the slippers Maple had so hastily shoved into her bag.

"I think Lady Bird's hour is up."

Maple blinked and dragged her attention back to the present. Ford must've picked up on her sudden feeling of unease, because there he was, swooping in to save her from the conversation. She wasn't prepared to talk about Percy. It hurt, and she wasn't altogether sure why.

This, she thought. *This is why I asked Ford to stay.*

Thank goodness she had. She'd choke down an entire plate full of barbecue in gratitude, if necessary.

"Gram, isn't it just about time for arts-and-crafts

hour?" he prompted with a glance toward the activities calendar.

"We're making crepe paper flowers today—dogwood blossoms, just like in the town square," Gram said.

"That sounds nice." Maple gave Lady Bird's leash a gentle tug to guide the dog out of the way while Ford helped his grandmother to a standing position behind her walker.

The woman in the muumuu who'd told her about Toby tugged on the sleeve of Maple's lemon-print Kate Spade dress. "You and Lady Bird are welcome to stay and make flowers with us."

"I'd love to, but I'm afraid Lady Bird and I already have plans this afternoon." Plans involving a food truck and a certain do-gooder who'd just rescued her right when she'd begun to feel out of her depth.

Oh, and catching a plane. She couldn't forget that crucial item on her agenda.

"Maybe another time," Gram said as she gripped the handles of her walker.

Maple didn't have the heart to admit that she and Lady Bird wouldn't be coming back. Instead, she simply smiled and said, "I'd like that very much."

Maple wasn't a thing like Percy Walker, but there was a certain type of magic about Lady Bird's therapy-dog sessions. Maple could feel it from the other end of the leash. She wasn't a patient, and these visits weren't about her, but accompanying the dog and seeing the effect she had on people filled her with hope. Joy. Peace…

And along with those precious feelings, the idea that perhaps it was okay that she wasn't just like her biological father. Maybe, just maybe, simply wanting to be like him was enough.

* * *

Ford cupped a hand around his ear and leaned closer to Maple, who sat opposite him at one of the picnic tables in Bluebonnet's town square. "I'm sorry, Doc. I'm going to need you to repeat what you just said. I'm not sure I heard correctly."

Maple's pupils flared. "You heard me the first time."

"Naw." Ford shook his head and offered Lady Bird a small bite of brisket, which she gobbled down with tail-wagging enthusiasm. "I don't think I did."

"Fine, you win." She pointed at the empty paper plate in front of her. "That was the most delicious meal I've ever eaten. Happy now?"

He winked. "Kinda."

"You're impossible." She reached to snag a Tater Tot from his plate.

He gave her hand a playful swat, but it didn't deter her in the slightest. "So I've heard."

After Lady Bird's visit to the senior center, Ford had made good on his promise to take her to Smokin' Joes. She'd hardly said a word during the short walk to the food truck, other than a quiet thank-you for intervening when Gram had brought up Percy. He'd swiftly changed the subject, poking fun of the fact that Maple continued to walk all over town in her fancy high heels, but she hadn't taken the bait. Not even when he promised her free medical services when she eventually twisted an ankle on the cobblestones in the town square.

It wasn't until she'd taken her first bite that she'd seemed to get out of her head. The second Joe's brisket passed her lips, she'd visibly relaxed. Within minutes, her eyes had drifted closed and the sigh she let out bordered on obscene. Ford had never been so jealous of a slab of beef, but there was a first time for everything, apparently.

"Seriously, where has real Texas barbecue been all my life?" Maple dabbed at the corners of her cherry-red mouth with her napkin.

"Right here in the Lone Star State, darlin'," Ford said.

Was he *flirting* with City Mouse?

It certainly appeared that way. Ford probably needed to reel that in. This wasn't a date, even though it sort of felt like one. It shouldn't, but it did. Or maybe Ford was just so rusty in the romance department that he'd forgotten what a real date felt like.

Probably that.

"Clearly, I should've made my way to Texas before now." Maple laughed, and then her forehead puckered like it always did when she was overthinking something. "Other than when I was a newborn, I guess."

She glanced around the town square, gaze softening ever so slightly as she took in the gazebo, the picnic tables surrounding Smokin' Joe's silver Airstream trailer and the dogwood blossoms swaying overhead. "I feel like I should remember this place. I know that's weird, but I can't help it. This could've been my home."

It still could.

He didn't dare say it. He shouldn't even be thinking it.

"There's so much I don't know about Bluebonnet… about my very own father." Maple swallowed, and then her voice went soft and breathy, as if she was telling him a deep, dark secret. "I wish I'd known him. Or, at the very least, that I knew a little bit more about him. Everyone in town seems to have known Percy, and I never got the chance to meet him."

"Maybe I can help. What do you want to know?" Ford didn't realize his fingertips had crept across the table toward Maple's until their hands were somehow fully intertwined. He told himself he was simply offering up moral support, pointedly ignoring the electricity that skittered over his skin at the softness of her touch.

"Everything." She shook her head and let out a laugh that was more than just a little bit sad around the edges. "Honestly, I don't even know where to start. He was a whole person with a whole life. It's easier to think of him as a stranger, but then someone will say something about him that resonates, and it catches me so off guard that I feel like the wind has just been knocked out of me."

Which is exactly what had happened at the senior center. He'd seen the pain wash over her face the second it happened, and in that fleeting moment, Maple's eyes had brimmed with a loneliness that had grabbed him by the throat.

He couldn't remember making a conscious decision to try and extricate her from the exchange with Gram. It had been pure instinct. He'd wanted to protect her, which was patently ridiculous. Maple was perfectly capable of taking care of herself. She'd made that much clear since day one.

But Ford knew there was more to Maple than the prickly image she seemed so hell-bent on showing to the world. She kept insisting she wasn't a people person, but last night when he'd seen her with her dainty feet swimming in Percy Walker's bedroom slippers, a hidden truth had shimmered between them. Maple wasn't a people person because she'd never had anyone in her life who she could fully trust with her innermost thoughts and feelings. She was hungry for connection, whether she wanted to admit it or not.

Against his better judgment, Ford wanted to help her find it. Adaline liked to say he was a fixer, and maybe she was right. He spent the better part of his time setting broken bones, mending scraped knees, and stitching childhood accidents back together. But bodies were like souls. No matter how tenderly they were cared for, they still bore the scars of yesteryear.

Just because he wanted to help her didn't mean he was in danger of developing feelings for her. And even if he was, he'd survive. Nothing would come of it. By this time tomorrow, she'd probably be busy examining a Park Avenue purse dog.

"What if we start small? That might feel less overwhelming. If you could ask me one thing about Percy, what would it be?" Ford gave Maple's hand an encouraging squeeze.

"Oh." Her bottom lip slipped between her teeth, and Ford was momentarily spellbound. "Just one thing. Let me think for a second…"

She glanced around as if searching for inspiration until her gaze landed on Lady Bird. The big golden panted with glee, and Maple instantly brightened.

"Oh, I know." She sat up straighter on the picnic bench, and Ford could feel her excitement like little sparks dancing along the soft skin of her hand. "He was so into pet therapy. I'd love to hear how that started… how he first got involved with that kind of volunteer work. You don't happen to know, do you?"

"As a matter of fact, I do," Ford said.

"So…" Maple leaned closer, until Ford could see tiny

flecks of gold in her warm brown irises. Hidden treasure. "Tell mè."

"Okay." Ford nodded.

This was going to be rough at first, but if she could stick with him until the end, he had a feeling it was a story she'd like. It would definitely give her a bit of insight into the type of man her biological father had been.

"About five years ago, Percy's mother was diagnosed with an aggressive form of breast cancer," he said, only mildly aware that he'd begun to move his thumb in soothing circles over the back of Maple's hand.

"His mother." Her breath caught. "That would be my grandmother."

Ford nodded. She'd found a family and lost it, all in one fell swoop. Percy Walker had died without a single living heir besides Maple. "She taught first grade at Bluebonnet Elementary when I was a kid. I wasn't in her class, but Adaline was. She could probably tell you stories about her sometime if you were ever interested. Miss Walker was a big dog lover. Never met a stray she didn't love, if word around town was to be believed."

"That must be why Percy loved animals so much." Maple grinned and shook off a bit of her melancholy. "Maybe even why he wanted to be a veterinarian."

"No doubt," Ford said. And that love—that passion— had found its way to Maple, too. Against all odds. The good Lord really did work in mysterious ways sometimes.

"Go on. Tell me more," Maple prompted.

"Miss Walker entered hospice care within just a few weeks of her diagnosis. Bluebonnet Senior Living has a skilled nursing unit, in addition to assisted-living and memory-care wings. They made space for Miss Walker in a private room once it became clear she was in her final days and needed around-the-clock care. From what I remember about that time, Percy would work in the clinic all day then head straight to the senior center and sit by her bedside for hours, long into the night. Like most late-stage-cancer patients, she slept a lot and drifted in and out of consciousness." Ford cleared his throat.

Maple was gripping his hand fiercely now, bracing herself for whatever came next. A bittersweet smile tipped her lips when Lady Bird moved to lean against her leg. That dog was more intuitive than any human being Ford had ever met.

"While Percy's mom was in hospice care at the senior center, one of his patients gave birth to a litter of puppies. There were some mild complications, so the mama dog stayed at the pet clinic for a few weeks so Percy and Grover could keep an eye on her. One day, Percy piled all the puppies into a big wicker basket and took them with him on his visit to see his mom." Ford shrugged. "That probably wasn't technically allowed, but everyone knew how much Miss Walker loved dogs."

"So the staff at the senior center looked the other way?" Maple asked.

"Pretty much. She was dying. I'm guessing everyone just wanted her to have one last puppy cuddle, even if she might not have been lucid enough to realize it was happening," Ford said.

Maple shook her head, her brown doe eyes huge in her porcelain face. "That is both the saddest and sweetest thing I've ever heard. Please tell me she woke up long enough to see the puppies."

"She did. In the eulogy he gave at his mom's funeral,

Percy said he placed the basket of puppies on her bed. Then he took her hand and ran her fingertips along one of the tiny dog's soft fur. He called what happened next a miracle." Ford had been at the funeral and heard Percy tell the story himself. When he spoke, the look on his face had been so full of wonder that there hadn't been a dry eye in the church.

"A miracle?" Maple tilted her head, and Lady Bird did the same in a perfect mirror image. Ford hadn't seen anything so cute in, well…ever.

Don't get attached to either of these two. Alarm bells clanged in the back of his head. *Ding, ding, ding.* Too late.

He swallowed. "Yeah. A bona fide miracle. Miss Walker opened her eyes, and as soon as her gaze landed on the basket, she broke into a glorious smile. Percy said for the first time in days, he had his mom back. She was herself again. She spent hours cradling those pups, cooing at them and laughing as tears ran down Percy's cheeks."

"Oh…" Maple's fingertips slipped out Ford's grasp and fluttered to her throat. "Wow."

"Yeah, wow." Ford's hands suddenly felt as if they had no purpose. He slid them into his lap. "Miss Walker passed away the following morning."

"Seeing her so happy with those puppies was Percy's last memory of his mom, and that's why he got involved with pet therapy. That's just…*incredible*." Maple's eyes went liquid.

"'There's no better medicine than a basketful of puppies,' your dad used to say. You want to hear something even more incredible?" Ford tipped his head toward Lady Bird. "This goofy dog who seems to have fallen head over heels in love with you was one of those puppies."

Maple gasped. "Lady Bird? Seriously?"

"Seriously." Ford's eyes flashed back to Maple, and he felt the corners of his mouth curl. He'd underestimated how good it would feel to help her put a piece of her family puzzle in place. He could've sat at that picnic table and kept talking and talking until he ran out of words.

If only she didn't have a plane to catch.

"Good girl, Lady Bird," Maple whispered against the soft gold fur of Lady Bird's ear.

The dog swiped Maple's cheek with her pink tongue, tail thumping happily against the square's emerald-green grass. Maple gave her a fierce hug, and for reasons Ford really didn't want to contemplate, an ache burrowed its way deep into his chest...all the way down to the place where he held his greatest hopes.

And his greatest hurts.

Ford shifted on the picnic bench. He needed space... just a little breathing room. But then Maple sat up and met his gaze, and he couldn't seem to move a muscle. She was looking at him in a way she'd never beheld him before—with eyes and heart open wide. Then her focus moved slowly, *purposefully*, toward his mouth.

Ford's breath grew shallow as Maple stood and leaned all the way across the picnic table. She came to a stop mere millimeters away from his face, lips curving into an uncharacteristically bashful grin.

"Yes?" she whispered.

"Yes," Ford said quietly. He couldn't get the word out fast enough.

Then she gave him what was undoubtedly the most

tender, reverent kiss of his life. Just a gentle brush of her perfect lips, and Ford was consumed with a kind of yearning he'd never known before.

More. The blood in his veins pumped hard and fast. *More. More. More.*

She pulled back just far enough to smile into his eyes. "Thank you."

"For?" he asked, incapable of forming more than a single, strangled syllable.

"For telling me that story about Percy and the puppies. It might be the best gift anyone has ever given me."

Ford really hoped that wasn't true. Maple deserved better than that. She deserved a lifetime of birthdays with cake piled high with pink frosting and blazing candles, Easters with baskets full of chocolate bunnies and painted eggs, a puppy with a red satin ribbon tied in a bow around its furry little neck on Christmas morning. She deserved the perfect kind of love she seemed so hungry for. Yesterday, today…always.

He reached and tucked a lock of dark hair behind her ear. "There are more stories where that one came from."

But to hear them all, you'd have to stay.

Maple's gaze bore into his, and neither of them said another word. Bluebonnet could've burned to the ground around them, and Ford would've scarcely noticed. Then she kissed him one last time, and her lips tasted of honey and barbecue. Of soft Texas sunshine. Of the slow, sweet dog days of summer.

And only just a little bit of goodbye.

Chapter Nine

"Good morning, Maple." June looked up from the receptionist desk as Maple walked into the pet clinic the following morning with Lady Bird prancing at her heels. "Good morning to you, too, Lady Bird."

Lady Bird's tail swung back and forth. Maple shifted the bakery box and coffee carrier she held in her arms and breathed a little easier. She thought she'd braced herself for anything. Not this, though. The last thing she'd expected was a friendly morning greeting delivered with a smile.

"Good morning, June." She handed the older woman a steaming cup of coffee in a paper cup with the Cherry on Top logo printed on its side. A peace offering, since Maple hadn't exactly been the easiest person to get along with the last time she'd breezed through the door.

"Oh, my. Thank you." June accepted the coffee and took a small sip. "Is this Cherry on Top's famous Texas pecan blend?"

"It sure is," Maple said. Points to Adaline for suggesting her house signature blend.

Maple had been nervous about showing up here again today, especially since everyone in town thought she'd gone back to New York yesterday, as planned. She'd walked to the bakery as soon as they'd opened and picked up treats for the office, figuring they couldn't try and turn her away again if she came bearing pie and coffee. Mission accomplished.

The funny thing was, Adaline hadn't been surprised to see her, either. She'd even invited Maple to a book-club meeting later tonight, and despite the fact that spending an evening with a new group of total strangers would ordinarily be an automatic no-go, Maple had found herself saying yes. If she was going to stay in town for a while, she might as well try and make some friends. Get a little involved.

It's what Percy would have done.

"You know we have one of those fancy K-Cup machines here, right?" June nodded toward the area behind the reception counter. "You don't have to walk all the way to the town square just for coffee."

"I figured. I just wanted to do something nice for you and Dr. Hayes." Maple felt her determined smile wobble a bit.

A fresh wave of dread washed over her at the thought of facing that man again, even though he was technically her partner. They were *equals*. There was no reason for her to be intimidated by him…

Except for his overall grumpy demeanor, along with the fact that this was his home turf and he clearly considered Maple an unwelcome interloper. Other than that, things between them should be just peachy.

June's face creased into a sympathetic smile. "Do you want to hear a little secret, sweetheart?"

"Um, okay."

"Grover's bark is a lot worse than his bite," June said

in a mock whisper. Then she winked and shifted her gaze over Maple's shoulder as the bells on the front door chimed. "Good morning, Grover. Maple is here for work, and she's brought us coffee and pie. Isn't that sweet?"

Great. He was already in the office. Any second now, he'd be standing right behind her.

Maple had hoped for a few minutes to get her bearings before her grump of a partner showed up. At the very least, she'd wanted to put her things down and slip a white lab coat over her flippy black-and-white polkadot dress. No such luck.

She straightened her shoulders, pasted a smile on her face and turned around to face her partner.

"Hi there, Grover." She shoved one of the coffees at him and pretended she belonged there. Because she *did* belong. This practice was half hers now, whether he liked it or not.

Maple really needed Grover to get on board, though. The ink on her veterinary school diploma was barely dry. Last night, she'd made the decision to stay in Bluebonnet and work at the clinic…at least for a while. She just couldn't go back yet, and she certainly couldn't leave Lady Bird. *Ever.* Now that she knew the dog's backstory, keeping her was one-hundred-percent nonnegotiable. Maple had informed her adoptive parents of her decision via text and then she'd turned off her mobile phone like a complete and total coward.

But at least she'd done it. She'd made her own decision about her own life, and she was sticking by it. So far, Maple's plan consisted of little more than staying in Bluebonnet for a bit and learning more about her birth father and the place he'd called home all his life...plus working alongside Grover Hayes.

All she needed now was his cooperation.

He plucked the coffee from her hand with a harrumph. "I hope this is decaf."

"Totally," she lied.

Note to self: no more caffeinated beverages for Grumpy McGrumperson. Maybe he needed to rethink that position. If anyone stood to benefit from a little caffeinated pick-me-up, it was Grover.

He took a gulp from his cup and glared at Maple for what felt like an eternity. Lady Bird started to drift off.

When Grover finally deigned to speak to her again, the dog's head jerked up with a start. "There's a kitten coming in at nine o'clock this morning for a routine checkup and her first round of shots. Do you think you can handle that, Dr. Leighton?"

Dr. Leighton.

He'd called her *Doctor*!

"Absolutely," she said, beaming.

Grover sighed mightily, but Maple couldn't have cared less. She'd take what she could get. At least he was willing to acknowledge her place at the clinic and give her a chance.

"Any questions or problems at all and you come find me. Understood?" He waved his coffee cup at her, and a drop sloshed out of the hole in the plastic lid. Lady Bird licked it up the second it hit the floor.

Grover sighed even harder.

Maple bit back a smile. "Understood."

After a cursory greeting aimed at June, Grover stalked past the reception area, headed for his office.

The instant the door slammed behind him, Maple shifted her gaze shifted toward the receptionist. "You're right. His bark really is worse than his bite, isn't it?"

"Told you," June said with a chuckle.

Maple glanced at the old-timey clock hanging beside the felt letter board that still listed Percy's name alongside Grover's in the reception area. Her feline patient was due in forty-five minutes—just enough time to locate the archaic file and familiarize herself with the kitty's history. How old was she? Where had the client gotten the cat? Was this their only pet?

But Maple lingered in the lobby, not quite ready to get to work.

"Can I do anything for you, Maple? Is everything okay?" June's forehead creased with concern. "Percy's office is yours now. Don't hesitate to get settled in there. If you need help clearing things out, I'd be happy to assist."

Maple shook her head. She wasn't ready to get rid of Percy's things yet. Not here, and not at home. She wanted to study them first. Who knew what sort of hidden treasures she might find?

"It's not that, but thank you for the offer." Maple cast a curious glance in Grover's wake. "He didn't seem all that surprised to see me here this morning. Come to think of it, neither did you."

At Cherry on Top, Adaline hadn't been fazed. She'd greeted Maple like an old friend, and now Maple had an entire novel to read before the book-club meeting tonight.

June peered at Maple over the top of her reading glasses. "Come on now. You've been in Bluebonnet long enough to know that nothing stays secret here for long."

"But I didn't tell anyone I'd decided to stay," Maple countered. Not even Ford.

Especially not Ford, lest he think that her decision had anything to do with him. Because it didn't.

Not much, anyway.

"You didn't have to, sweetheart. You kissed Ford Bishop right in the middle of the town square yesterday." June tutted, but her lips twitched with amusement. "Did you really think that would go unnoticed in a place like Bluebonnet?"

Maple hadn't been thinking at all. She'd acted with her heart, not her head, which was something that had always terrified her. She knew all too well what happened when people threw caution to the wind and let their feelings go straight to their heads. A year or three later, they ended up sitting in her mom or dad's law office, fighting tooth and nail over everything under the sun. There was an awfully thin line between love and hate. *Razor* thin, honestly. After everything Maple had seen and heard, particularly within the walls of her own childhood home, she preferred to stay as far away from that line as possible. Besides, she liked being in control of her emotions. Things were safer that way…more predictable.

But after Ford told her the story about Percy and Lady Bird, she'd hadn't been able to stop herself.

Who even was she anymore?

All her life she'd been Maple Maribelle Leighton— dog lover, introvert, perpetual good girl and overachiever extraordinaire. Now she was starting to think she might be another person entirely. The trouble was, she had no idea what Maple Maribelle Walker was really like. The more Maple got to know her alter ego, the more danger-ous she seemed. This new version of Maple had a pen-chant for straying far, *far* outside her comfort zone. She did things like purposefully miss flights, defy her fam-ily's expectations without thought to the consequences, and willingly throw away a shot at her dream job—not just once, but twice.

Oh, and she also kissed the local Hallmark hunk in the middle of the town square for all the world to see.

"That wasn't a regular kiss," Maple said primly. "That was a thank-you kiss. There's a difference."

"Oh, honey. Not from where I'm standing," June said with a knowing gleam in her eye. "I'm not sure how these things work up in New York, but here in Texas, a kiss is a kiss. Plain and simple."

There was nothing simple about it, though. Quite the opposite, in fact. Maple's feelings for Ford were grow-ing more complicated by the hour, especially consider-ing she shouldn't be having any feelings for him at all.

She blamed Bluebonnet for this entire mess. Every-one here seemed to think Maple was someone that she wasn't, and now she'd jumped right on the bandwagon and begun to believe it herself.

Even worse, she *liked* it.

Maple Maribelle Walker might be dangerous, but she was a heck of a lot of fun.

"Ford!" Oliver's hospital gown dipped off the child's bony shoulder as he struggled to sit up. "You're here! On a Wednesday!"

"I'm here. How's it going, bud?" Ford held up a hand for a high five.

Oliver gave it a weak slap. "Things are great now that you're here. Mom's at work again."

"I heard." Ford nodded.

He'd also heard that the child wasn't feeling well. Ordinarily, that wouldn't have been too much cause for concern. Chemotherapy treatment could be brutal, but according to the call Ford had gotten earlier in the day from Nurse Pam, Oliver had started running a fever after undergoing a bone-marrow biopsy early this morning.

Fever was always a concern for cancer patients. Chemo weakened the immune system, which sometimes led to infections. Oliver's fever had been running right around 100 degrees all day, and as long as it stayed low-grade, things would probably be just fine.

But a constant low-grade fever had also been one of Oliver's first symptoms when he'd been diagnosed with leukemia. His mom had brought him into Ford's office worried he might have an ear infection. Ford had assured her his ears were fine, but looking at the child's pale skin and the smattering of bruises on his extremities had sent a cold chill up and down his spine. He'd known something was wrong—something far worse than a simple childhood ear infection.

He'd been devastated to find out he'd been right.

"I also heard you weren't feeling so great." Ford glanced at the beeping monitor at the head of the bed. The body temperature reading flashed 99.3, and he breathed a little easier.

As soon as they got the bone-marrow biopsy results back, he could relax. Oliver was midway through treatment, and the test had been a routine check to monitor the effectiveness of the chemo. His oncologist expected good news, and Ford had taken the specialist at his word. Oliver was going to live a long and healthy life.

"I'm fine." Oliver's face spread into a hopeful grin. "Fine enough to play a board game."

"You got it." Ford nodded. An evening of board games with his favorite patient sounded great. Maybe it would help get his mind off the fact that Maple had kissed him silly yesterday afternoon.

He'd been busy all day today with back-to-back appointments and a quick lunch at the senior center with Gram. Adaline had called, but he'd ignored her voice mail. Knowing his sister, she'd heard about the kiss and wanted a thorough debrief…with a side of lecture about not letting himself fall for City Mouse.

Ford just wasn't in the mood. What difference did it make, now that Maple had gone back to New York? She'd kissed him, and then she'd fled.

Did she really, though?

He gritted his teeth. Nope, he wasn't going to let his thoughts go down that troublesome road. She'd missed one flight already. The odds weren't great that she'd willingly missed another. Besides, he had more important things to worry about.

Namely, keeping Oliver company.

"What's it going to be?" Ford scanned the collection of games, puzzles, and stuffed animals piled on the shelf below the window overlooking the rolling landscape of the Texas Hill Country. The sun was just beginning to dip below the horizon, spilling liquid amber over the hills and setting the wildflowers aflame. *"Apples to Apples? Candy Land?"*

Oliver groaned. *"Candy Land* is for kids."

"Noted." Ford swallowed a laugh. "My sincerest apologies. How about *Yahtzee*?"

"Yes!" Oliver punched the air.

See? The child is fine.

"*Yahtzee* it is, then." He grinned, feeling just a little bit lighter, a little bit more hopeful as he got the game set up on the bedside tray.

Then Ford noticed a small, greenish bruise on the child's forearm, and a weight settled on his chest.

He frowned at the tender spot on Oliver's arm and wondered where it had come from…how long it had been there. Why hadn't he noticed it before?

It's just a bruise. Kids get them all the time. A bruise doesn't have to mean anything.

Oliver spilled the dice onto the table, and the clatter pulled Ford back into the moment.

"Look, I got three fives already." The boy's eyes lit up as he pointed to the dice. "I'm so lucky. Right, Ford?"

Ford tensed at the choice of words, but he pushed down his worry and flashed Oliver a smile and a thumbs-up, even as his throat constricted, making a response almost impossible.

"You sure are, kiddo. The luckiest."

Chapter Ten

"Maple!" Adaline held her front door open wide and beckoned Maple inside. "I'm so glad you could make it. Come on in and meet the rest of the girls."

Maple hesitated for a beat. Here she was again, about to dive headlong into an uncomfortable social situation, and this time, Dr. Small Town Charm wasn't there for backup. But the smell of freshly baked pies wafted from the inside of Adaline's house, and Maple had spent every stolen moment today speed-reading her way through the book club's chosen novel. She'd never missed a homework assignment in her life, and she wasn't about to start now. Not even for a recreational reading club.

So in between administering kitten vaccines and removing porcupine quills from an understandably traumatized chocolate Labrador retriever—a task that veterinary school in New York City had in no way prepared her for—she'd snuck into Percy's old office for a few stolen moments and plopped into his chair with her nose in the book. She'd had to resort to speed-reading as the day wore on, but she was here.

And she was ready. Mostly, anyway.

"I hope it's okay that I brought Lady Bird with me,"

she said as she followed Adaline past the entryway toward the living room, where it sounded like a group of women were talking over one another with happy chatter.

Maple hadn't asked if the dog could tag along, but something told her that if Lady Bird was welcome at Adaline's bakery, her new friend wouldn't have a problem with the golden attending a book-club meeting. Also, the novel was part of a romance series that centered around an animal rescue called Furever Yours. Maple had a feeling she'd stumbled upon a group of pet lovers, which had only made her more excited about tonight. These were her kind of people. Maybe she'd make some genuine friends.

"Are you kidding?" Adaline cast an affectionate glance at the dog. "Lady Bird is practically a local celebrity. Everyone is going to love that you brought her."

Sure enough, the instant they crossed the threshold of the cozy living space, the animated conversation came to an abrupt halt as every head turned toward the dog.

"Lady Bird!" the other two women scattered about the room cried in unison.

A more timid dog probably would've turned tail and hid beneath the closest end table at the effusive greeting. Not Lady Bird. The dog thrived at being the center of attention. Tail swinging, she pranced toward the closest human and sat politely at her feet, waiting to be petted.

Adaline gave Maple a knowing grin. "Told you."

"You must be Maple." A woman with blond hair twisted into an artful bun stood and extended a graceful hand toward Maple. "Hi. I'm Jenna. I own the dance studio on Main Street, just around the corner from the town square."

"It's a pleasure to meet you," Maple said as she shook her hand.

A ballerina, she thought. That made perfect sense. Jenna definitely looked the part.

"We've all heard so much about you. I'm Belle," the woman sitting beside Jenna on the sofa said with a wave. "I'm the librarian at Bluebonnet Elementary School."

"Wait." Maple blinked. "You're a librarian, and your name is Belle?"

"I know, right? With a name like mine, I guess I didn't have much of a choice." The corners of Belle's mouth turned up. "It's a good thing I love books."

And so it went. The women chatted while Lady Bird shuffled from person to person and wagged her tail with such zeal that she nearly took out the wineglasses scattered atop the coffee table in the center of the room.

"Lady Bird, I would lay down my life for you, but if you knock over my cabernet, we're going to have a serious problem," Belle said with a mock glare in the dog's direction.

"I'm so sorry." Maple attempted to lure the dog back to her side, but she was too busy playing social butterfly to pay attention.

"Don't worry. There's more wine where this came from. I promise." Adaline handed her a glass.

"There's also pie. Adaline makes a new creation for every book-club meeting," Jenna said.

"I like to test out new recipes on our little group before I add them to the bakery menu. I hope you don't mind being a guinea pig." Adaline gave Maple a questioning glance.

"For pie? How is that even a question? Of course, I don't mind."

The conversation grew more boisterous over the next two hours, and the wine flowed while the women discussed the book. It didn't take long for Belle to ask Maple if Lady Bird might have time in her schedule to visit the school library and help struggling readers with their skills. She'd read an article online recently about therapy pets acting as reading education assistance dogs. Jenna piped up to see if Lady Bird could come to the first day of her toddler pre-ballet class in the fall and mentioned that a teacher friend of hers thought that having a therapy dog at Bluebonnet Elementary's back-to-school events would help ease nerves for new students.

Maple loved their enthusiasm, even as it quickly became apparent that she and Lady Bird would never be able to keep up with all the community requests for pet therapy. And so far, all the requests were the result of word of mouth. There was no telling what might happen if Maple put actual effort into building a comprehensive therapy-dog program. The possibilities were endless. Hospitals, nursing homes, schools, airports, courtrooms, crisis response…

During vet school, Maple had read extensively about therapy pets working in all these settings and more. She'd just never imagined she'd have one. There was no question that Lady Bird could help spread love and joy anywhere there were people who needed a little comfort, affection, and support.

But Lady Bird was just one dog. Not to mention the spectacular mess that was Maple's personal life. She didn't know how she was going to keep up with Lady Bird's commitments, as it was.

"Thank you so much for inviting me tonight," Maple said as she helped Adaline get the dessert ready in the kitchen once the book discussion was finished. "Your friends are really great."

"They're your friends now, too." Adaline waggled her eyebrows. "That's how things work around here."

Maple smiled to herself. She had a house, a job, and the best dog on the planet. Now, she even had friends here in Bluebonnet. Somehow, in a matter of days, she'd built more of a life here in this small town than she'd ever had back in New York. If she wasn't careful, she might end up staying for good.

"Don't let them pressure you and Lady Bird, though." Adaline snuck a nibble of piecrust to the dog, who'd been staring intently at the kitchen counter, nose twitching. "You're just getting your footing here, and they know that. But you've also got an amazing dog."

Maple's heart swelled. "I do, don't I?"

"Should I thank her for convincing you to stay, or did that decision have to do with something else?" Adaline's smile faltered ever so slightly as she slid a slice of pie onto a china plate with a pretty rose pattern and handed it to Maple. "Some*one* else, maybe?"

"Oh, you mean Percy?"

"No, not quite." Adaline gave her a sideways glance as she plated another slice of pie. "Here's another fun fact about small towns—there's only one way to stop people from talking about the latest hot gossip. Do you know what it is?"

I wish. Maple shook her head, riveted. As one of the

most recent subjects of the Bluebonnet grapevine, this seemed like valuable information. "I don't, but really I'm hoping you're about to tell me."

"You wait it out, because sooner or later something else scandalous will happen, and everyone will start talking about that instead. People have notoriously short attention spans."

"So you're saying eventually everyone will lose interest in my family situation." Maple couldn't wait. Whatever the new scandal might be, she was ready for it.

Adaline's forehead creased. "Oh, honey. Didn't you know? They already have."

"What's the new scandal?" Maple couldn't believe she'd missed it.

Adaline pointed the pie slicer at her. "You kissing my brother in the middle of the town square, obviously."

Oh.

Oh.

Maple's cheeks burned with the heat of a true Texas summer. "That wasn't what it looked like."

Adaline's eyebrows shot clear to her hairline. "So you didn't lock lips with Ford at a picnic table by Smokin' Joes?"

"It was a thank-you kiss," Maple countered.

"That's not a thing," Adaline said flatly.

Why did people keep saying that?

Because it's not, and you know it.

Maple longed for the floor of Adaline's kitchen to open up and swallow her whole. This wasn't a conversation she wanted to have with Ford's sister, of all people.

Of course, Maple found Ford attractive. Very, *very* attractive. And, yes, she might even have feelings for him.

But how was she supposed to make sense of those feelings when her entire life had so recently been turned upside down?

"Look, I like you, Maple. A lot. I hope you stay in Bluebonnet forever. Not just because I worry about my brother, but because I want us to be friends. Real friends." Adaline put down the pie cutter and took both of Maple's hands in hers. Lady Bird's furry eyebrows lifted as her gaze darted back and forth between them. "When you live in a town as small as Bluebonnet, new friends aren't very easy to come by. I'm so glad you're here."

"I am, too," Maple said, breathing a little easier. "But can I ask why you're worried about Ford?"

"That was probably an exaggeration. Ford is a grown man, and he can obviously take care of himself. Goodness knows, he takes care of practically everyone else in this town."

"So I've noticed," Maple said. It was one of his most endearing qualities.

Adaline paused, as if weighing her next words carefully. "Did he tell you he left once…just a few years ago?"

"Ford left Bluebonnet?" Maple couldn't wrap her head around it. She couldn't imagine him living anyplace else. He seemed as deeply ingrained in this community as Lady Bird was.

Adaline nodded. "He took a job up in Dallas at a state-of-the-art children's hospital there. I could tell straight away he didn't love it like he loves Bluebonnet, but Ford is very serious about his work. He was excited about the many opportunities to help kids up there. Then he met someone—another doctor, whose father happened to be chief of staff at the hospital. After dating for about six months, Ford asked her to marry him."

Maple's stomach instantly hardened. Spots floated in her vision as a wave of jealousy washed over her so hard and fast that she swayed on her feet.

Ford had been *engaged*?

It shouldn't have come as a surprise. Ford Bishop was clearly the marrying type. He doted on his grandmother, frequented his sister's bakery and devoted his life's work to caring for sick children. If that wasn't the very definition of *family man*, Maple didn't know what was.

Still, the revelation came as a shock. Maple didn't want to think about Ford slipping a diamond on another woman's finger or, heaven forbid, watching someone else walk toward him down the aisle of some cute country church. Someone vastly unlike Maple, obviously. Someone who belonged by his side. Someone gentler, sweeter…kinder. Someone who'd fit right in someplace like Bluebonnet, Texas.

Then again, maybe not, because Adaline's expression turned decidedly sour as she prepared to finish recounting the story. She took a deep breath and seemed to make an effort to neutralize her expression, but the smile on her face didn't come close to reaching her eyes.

"I was so happy for him. I missed seeing him nearly every day, obviously. Our parents retired and moved to Florida right about the time Ford and I graduated from college, so other than Gram, my brother was all the family I had in Bluebonnet." Adaline blew out a breath. "Then one day Gram had a bad fall. She'd been having some mild memory issues up until then, but the fall changed things. Gram just didn't bounce back. Ford rushed home as soon as it happened. He was only supposed to be here for a few days, but then…"

Adaline's voice drifted off, and Maple could guess what came next.

"He decided to stay, didn't he?" She knew it, because that's the kind of person Ford was. He valued things like family and community and responsibility. He would want to be here with his grandmother when she was at her most vulnerable, no matter how capable Adaline and Gram's caregivers at the senior living center might be.

"He did." Adaline nodded, and her smile turned bittersweet. "I can't say I was disappointed. It was so nice to have him back, and I could tell straightaway that Ford was happy to be home, despite the circumstances. His voice had taken on a certain edge whenever I spoke to him on the phone. Once he came back, he was like his old self again. Even when Charlotte postponed her plans to join him, he seemed unfazed. I don't think it ever crossed his mind that she'd never come here."

Maple swallowed. *Charlotte.* Putting a name to Ford's ex made the woman all the more real, and a fresh stab of envy jabbed Maple right in the heart. Ridiculous, considering they'd very clearly broken up. Somehow, that didn't make her feel any better.

"Never?" Maple asked. "You mean she didn't even give Bluebonnet a chance?"

She wasn't sure why she felt so indignant on behalf of a town she'd first set foot in only a few days ago. It wasn't as if Maple had been thrilled at the prospect of spending one measly year in Bluebonnet.

But here you are, even after getting handed a get-out-of-jail-free card.

"Charlotte kept putting it off, over and over again. Her parents put a lot of pressure on her, especially her dad. Since he was head of the hospital up there, he thought moving to a place like Bluebonnet was akin to career suicide," Adaline said.

Maple shifted her gaze to the countertop as shame settled in the pit of her stomach. She'd had the exact same thought…more than once. How could she not, when there was a prestigious cardiac practice in New York ready and willing to give her a job?

"There's more to life than work, you know?" Adaline said, as if she could see straight inside Maple's head. "Even when your work is something vitally important, like looking after children's physical and emotional health."

That's right. They were talking about Ford's work, not Maple's. Still, she couldn't shake the feeling that this conversation had more to do with her than she wanted to admit.

"Anyway, like I said, I want us to be friends. I really like you, Maple." Adaline handed her the last slice of pie, neatly plated and topped with whipped cream. "But until you're sure that you want to stay in Bluebonnet for good, I hope you'll think twice about giving Ford any more 'thank-you kisses.'"

And there it was.

Adaline was calling her bluff on the entire concept of a thank-you kiss, and Maple didn't blame her one bit. Who was she kidding? She hadn't kissed Ford simply because she'd been grateful. She'd kissed him because the longer she stayed in Bluebonnet, the more she wanted to know what it felt like to press her lips against his…

To feel his strong hands cradle her face with a gentleness that made her forget how to breathe… To open her heart just a crack to the possibility of not spending the rest of her life alone…

"You can see why it might get confusing, don't you?" Adaline said with a kindness in her tone that Maple didn't deserve.

"I do." Maple nodded. Boy, did she ever. She'd never been so confused about things in her life.

What happened to the carefully orchestrated plan she'd made for herself? In less than a week, all her dreams had completely fallen by the wayside. Just because she'd discovered she'd been adopted didn't mean she had to change her entire life.

But what if you want to change, a voice whispered in the back of her head. *And what if your dreams change, too? A new life is possible, and so are new dreams.*

Maple blinked hard. She felt like crying all of a sudden, and she absolutely refused to get weepy in Adaline's kitchen over the prospect of something silly like not kissing Ford Bishop again.

It didn't feel silly, though. It felt like another heartbreak, another loss—the loss of yet a different life she'd never experience.

"Don't worry." The effort it took to smile was monumental. "You have my word. It won't happen again."

She wanted to reel the words back in the very second they left her mouth. Maple knew better than to make promises when she was in the midst of an existential crisis. It seemed like she'd completely lost control over rational thought, particularly when she was anywhere in the vicinity of Ford. What made her think she could exert any sort of sensible decision-making where he was concerned?

Because you care about him, and the last thing you want to do is hurt him.

And she wouldn't. *Couldn't.* The next time Maple saw Ford, she'd just turn off her feelings like a light switch. She'd simply have to learn to ignore the way his eyes crinkled in the corners, as if kindness and laughter came naturally to him… The irresistible pull she felt toward him every time he was near… The breathtaking habit he had of seeing past her frosty exterior, all the way down to her tender, aching heart.

That shouldn't be a problem, right? Maple had all sorts of practice at erecting a nice, strong wall around her innermost thoughts and emotions. She'd been doing it her whole life.

But then the back door of Adaline's quaint little kitchen swung open, and there he was—Ford, in the flesh, looking casually heroic in a pair of hospital scrubs that made his eyes sparkle bluer than ever. And the second those eyes homed in on her, they widened in surprise. Maple practically melted into a puddle as he drank in the sight of her, and the corners of his lips curved into a slow and easy grin.

"Well, look who missed her flight." He arched a single, all-too-satisfied eyebrow. "Again."

Chapter Eleven

*S*he's still here. The tension in Ford's body began to ease the instant he spotted Maple. *Not just here in Bluebonnet, but right here in Adaline's kitchen.*

Never had there been such a sight for sore eyes.

Since he hadn't heard a word from her since their kiss the day before, he'd assumed she'd really left this time, as planned. Once he'd checked on Oliver and realized some of his initial symptoms had returned, Ford's singular focus had been on his patient. The fact that he'd missed such an important piece of local gossip was a testament to how distracted he'd been.

"I decided to stay a bit longer." Maple swallowed, clearly caught off guard by the sight of him. She crossed her arms, then uncrossed them, and recrossed then again, as fluttery and nervous as the day they'd met.

Ford tilted his head. "You okay there, Doc?"

"Fine," she said. A lie, if he'd ever heard one before.

What exactly was going on here?

Alas, Ford didn't have a chance to ask because Lady Bird had finally torn her attention away from the pie plate on the kitchen counter and registered his arrival. The dog's paws scrambled for purchase on the slick floor in her haste to get to him. Ford braced for impact as she crashed into his legs and threw herself, belly-up, at his feet.

"Hey there, sweet girl." He crouched down to give her a belly rub. "At least someone's happy to see me."

Maple let out a cough, and Ford winked at her.

"Maple is here for book club. We're finishing up soon." Adaline frowned down at her brother. "What are you doing here? And why are you in scrubs? You already did your shift at the hospital this week."

Ford straightened. "I did, but I wanted to stop by and check on a patient who wasn't feeling well. I ended up staying for a while."

After spending the evening playing *Yahtzee* with Oliver, he hadn't felt like going home to an empty house. Plus he knew that his sister always made fresh pie on book-club nights, so he'd swung by, hoping Adaline would take pity on him and let him crash the festivities. The last person he'd expected to find here was Maple.

Not that he was complaining.

"I hope everything is okay." Concern glowed in Maple's big brown eyes.

A look passed between them. She'd met Oliver and likely had a good idea how special that kid was to Ford.

He wished he could say more, but he couldn't discuss his patients. Ford's face likely said it all, though, as Maple's look of concern only deepened after their eyes met.

He gave his head a small shake, indicating they all needed to move on to a different, safer topic of conversation.

"We have pie." Adaline offered him a plate.

He took it and reached for a fork. "Thanks. I was hoping you might."

Adaline's gaze flitted toward Maple. "Come on in. You can join the rest of the book chat."

"But I haven't read the book."

Adaline shrugged. "It doesn't matter. Right now, everyone is pretty much just gushing over Lady Bird, anyway. If Maple isn't careful, that dog is going to be booked twenty-four-seven with therapy dog visits."

"Grover would love that. I'm not even joking. I think he'd actually prefer it if I was out of his hair and he could handle the pet clinic all on his own," Maple said.

"I doubt that," Ford countered as they headed toward the living room, even though he was fully aware the elder veterinarian could be a little rough around the edges.

Maple knew her stuff, though. Surely, Grover could see that, or maybe Ford just needed her to believe she was welcome at the pet clinic...welcome enough to make her stay in Bluebonnet permanent.

Maple aimed a sideways glance at Ford. "Have you met Grover Hayes?"

"Point taken." Ford laughed, but before he could offer a word of encouragement, Adaline swept between them and steered them toward chairs on opposite ends of the room from each other.

Lady Bird immediately left him in the dust to follow Maple. No big surprise there, but Ford felt lonely all the way on the other side of the living room, despite being surrounded by Adaline's friends. As the evening wore on, his gaze kept straying toward Maple. And once the pie had disappeared and the women had decided on their next book-club read, the night came to its inevitable close.

"Maple, where's your car?" Adaline peered toward the driveway from the front porch, where everyone was saying their goodbyes. "I figured you'd be driving Percy's truck."

Maple shook her head. "We walked."

Adaline's gaze dropped to Maple's feet, once again clad in a pair of strappy high-heeled numbers that looked more appropriate for a beauty pageant than walking a dog. "In *those*?"

"My wardrobe options are limited," Maple said, and Ford could see her blushing even in the silvery moonlight.

"I need to take you shopping," Adaline said.

"Here? I didn't realize Bluebonnet had much in the way of fashion."

Adaline grinned. "Oh, you just wait."

"Meanwhile, I'm happy to give you and Lady Bird a ride home," Ford interjected before someone else could offer.

"Oh." A look of a panic flitted across Maple's face. "That's really not necessary. Lady Bird and I have been walking all over town together. We like it, don't we?"

Lady Bird wagged her tail, which meant nothing whatsoever. The dog would've agreed to anything Maple asked her in that soothing, singsong voice of hers.

"It's late." Without warning, Ford reached for Lady Bird's leash and slipped it out of Maple's hand. "And dark."

And Ford wanted to spend more time with her. Mostly, he wanted to know why she suddenly seemed keen to avoid him. He'd thought those days were over. The last time he'd seen her, she'd leaned over a picnic table in the middle of the town square and given him the most perfect kiss of his life.

"Ford, you know better than anyone that Bluebonnet is perfectly safe. If Maple wants to walk, you should let her," Adaline said with a slight edge to her voice. "She doesn't need your permission."

All at once, Ford knew exactly what was going on.

He turned toward his sister. "Adaline."

"Ford," she said with a tiny quiver in her chin.

Jenna and Belle fled toward their cars, no doubt eager to avoid a sibling squabble. Maple stayed put, and Ford knew good and well it was only because he still had Lady Bird's leash wrapped around his hand.

He knew he shouldn't be angry with Adaline. His sister loved him and didn't want to see him hurt again. She'd already said so at the bakery, but she also needed to mind her own business. He was a grown man, and if he wanted to give Maple a ride or walk her home, there wasn't a pie in the world that could stop him…

Provided Maple let him, of course.

"Maple, may I walk you home?" he asked quietly. He suddenly liked the idea of a nice quiet stroll. It would give them time to talk, which suddenly seemed quite necessary.

Lady Bird's head swiveled toward him, and she let out a booming bark at the word *walk*.

"Your dog seems to love the idea," Ford said. He owed Lady Bird a dog biscuit now…possibly three.

Maple's eyes sparked with amusement. "You truly are impossible, you know that?"

"So you've said." Ford shrugged. "Several times, in fact."

"For the record, I concur. You *are* impossible." Adaline glared at him and then turned toward Maple with an apologetic smile. "Don't let me stop you. I should probably start letting my brother live his own life."

"You really, *really* should," Ford muttered.

"Good night, Maple. I'm really glad you came tonight. I hope to see you at our next book club." Adaline gave Maple a quick hug and, with a wave at Ford, she disappeared inside the house, leaving the two of them alone on the porch.

Ford offered Maple his arm. "Well, what do you say? It's a nice night for a walk, and we wouldn't want to disappoint Lady Bird."

"She might never forgive me, so I should probably say yes." Maple wrapped gentle fingertips around the crook of his elbow. "For Lady Bird."

"For Lady Bird," Ford echoed and smiled into the velvety darkness as the golden retriever guided them toward home.

"So tell me the truth." Ford gave Maple a sidelong glance that somehow felt as real as a caress, despite the darkness that surrounded them.

A nighttime Texas sky was nothing like the neon lights of New York City. Out here, the darkness was so thick that the stars glittered like diamonds overhead. For the first time ever, she could see the constellations. It made her feel tiny and larger than life, both at the same time.

"The truth about what?" she asked in a whisper. That was another thing about Bluebonnet after hours—the silence. There were no sirens, no honking cabs, no city noises to keep her up at night. Just a casual walk home felt intimate in a way that made goose bumps dance across her skin.

"What's the real reason you're not driving Percy's truck around town?" Ford said with a smile in his voice. "You don't have a driver's license, do you?"

She gasped in mock horror. "I beg your pardon, I certainly do. Just because I'm from Manhattan doesn't mean I don't know to drive."

"And when exactly was the last time you were behind the wheel of an automobile?"

Touché. He had her there.

"The day I got my license." She cleared her throat as Ford chuckled with self-satisfaction. "But I *do* possess one. I know how to drive—at least according to the State of New York."

"I guess I'll have to take your word for it." He gave her shoulder a little bump with his. "Yours and the State of New York's."

"Do you have any idea how much parking costs in Manhattan? Garage fees are outrageous. Plus, we've got the subway and cabs and Uber. It's just easier to take public transportation."

Ford laughed under his breath again. "Yeah, we don't have much of that here."

"So I've noticed," Maple said. And soon, she'd have the blisters on her feet to prove it.

More than that, she was beginning to worry about the heat. The temperatures were already hovering around ninety degrees at high noon, and it was only the beginning of summer. In a matter of weeks, the pavement would be too hot for Lady Bird's sensitive paws.

At least the evenings were still pleasant. Soft and fragrant with the perfume of wildflowers, almost like walking through a dream.

"I could help you practice," Ford said.

Maple narrowed her gaze at him beside her. "You seriously want to give me *driving lessons*?"

"Not lessons. You already know how to drive, Doc." His grin turned far too sardonic for Maple's liking. "I just thought you might feel more comfortable if you had a little practice. Also, if you started using Percy's truck, you could bring Lady Bird to the hospital more often."

Right. This was about Lady Bird, her therapy-dog work and, by extension, Oliver. No wonder Ford wanted to volunteer as tribute.

Even so, it was a kind offer and one that Maple would probably be wise to accept. It wasn't like she could accidentally let herself kiss him again while she was operating a moving vehicle.

Stop thinking about kissing.

She bit down hard on her bottom lip as punishment, but, of course, her gaze flitted straight toward his mouth.

"I'd like that a lot. Thanks—" she managed to squeak out the last word "—friend."

How awkward could she possibly be?

Ford looked downright puzzled. This was beyond her usual social anxiety. The way she couldn't seem to think straight around him felt like something else entirely.

Something almost like...

Don't you dare think it, Maple! Not even for a second. Love?

She released her hold on his arm, because *whoa*. Being attracted to Ford was one thing, but thinking about the *L* word was more than she could handle. More than she'd *ever* be able to handle. In keeping with the automotive topic at hand, she needed to seriously pump the breaks.

"Maple, I'm not sure what exactly Adaline said to you tonight, but—" Ford began.

"Your sister was nothing but welcoming. Truly. I really like her," Maple said in an effort to cut him off.

She really meant it, too. She liked Adaline, and she'd had a great time meeting her friends. But even though Adaline had backed off somewhat and encouraged Maple to let Ford walk her home when he'd obviously figured out she'd been interfering in his personal life, the warning she'd given Maple still rang true.

Ford had already been hurt once by someone who'd turned her back on Bluebonnet. Maple cared too much about him to risk doing it again.

It would be different if she knew she was staying for good, but Maple couldn't make a promise like that right now…not even to herself. She'd only just recently given herself permission to take things one day at a time. Even that had been a massive leap of faith for someone who'd had an entirely different life mapped out for herself just a few short days ago.

"She told you about Charlotte," Ford said, cutting straight to the chase.

"Yes, but I don't want you to think I was trying to pry. For the record, I don't think that was Adaline's intention, either." This discussion was getting more uncomfortable by the second. How was that even possible?

"I know better than to think you'd try and interject yourself into my business, Maple. Quite the opposite, in fact. For a while there, I wondered if you were actively trying to avoid me." Ford's footsteps slowed. Maple had been so consumed by their conversation and the thoughts spinning in her head that she hadn't realized they'd reached her house until Lady Bird's tail stopped waving in front of them. The dog plopped into a down position at their feet. "Until you kissed me yesterday, that is."

"I shouldn't have done that. It's practically turned into front-page news around here. I keep telling people it was just a thank you kiss, and no one seems to think that's a real thing. Maybe it's not. I don't know. It was kind of a new experience for me. Believe it or not, that was rather out of character."

Maple was babbling. She couldn't seem to stop the stream of nonsense coming out of her mouth, and the more she said, the more tenderly Ford seemed to look at her—so tenderly that she wanted to lose herself in those kind eyes of his. Forget-me-not blue.

As if I could ever forget Ford Bishop, she thought. *Never in a million years.*

"I'm sorry," she blurted, apologizing once and for all for the kiss heard—and more importantly, *seen*—around the world. Or at least Texas, which had begun to feel like the only place on earth.

"I'm not," Ford said in a voice so low and deep that it scraped her insides. Then he took a step closer and gazed into her eyes with such intensity that every sliver of space between them cracked with electricity. "In fact, I want you to do it again."

"You do?" Maple heard herself say. She wasn't sure how, because her heart had never pounded so hard and fast in all her life.

Ford nodded, and tipped her chin upward with a gentle touch of his fingertips until her mouth was positioned just below his. "I do. Right now, in fact."

"Right now," she repeated, as weak and small as a kitten. If she didn't give in, the longing just might kill her. So much for flipping her feelings off like a light.

He wasn't like any man she'd ever known before. He was passionate about his career, just like she was. But when he was with her, he was fully present. He made her feel like there was nowhere he'd rather be than with her. She'd shown him exactly who she was—the messy side of her that she never let anyone else see. And somehow, it only seemed to make him like her more.

How was she supposed to resist that?

She rose up on tiptoe, and just as the yearning became unbearable, her lips met his. And this time, there was no hesitation…no restraint. The warmth of his mouth on hers sent a hum through her body that made her wrap her arms around his neck and pull him closer.

Yes. It was the only semi-coherent thought in her head as his hands slid into her hair. *Oh, my, my, my. Yes, please.*

She felt her soul unfold like the petals on a flower, inviting him in. She needed him even closer—so close that she could feel every beat of his heart crashing against her rib cage. No one had ever kissed her like this before. Like she was special, like she was cherished. Maybe even adored.

Then, without warning, it was over almost as soon as it had begun.

Ford pulled back, and when Maple dragged her eyes open, she found him looking down at her with the strangest expression on his face. He was as still as stone, but his eyes were wild and dark with desire. Maple wished she could press Rewind and live the last two minutes of her life over and over again on constant repeat.

She wanted that so much it scared her a little. "What is it?"

Ford pressed a fingertip to his lips, signaling for her to be quiet.

"I think I just heard something," he whispered.

Maple blinked. *You certainly did. It was every last shred of my resistance crumbling down around me.* "Wh-what did it sound like?"

"A whimper. Or a cry, maybe. Like someone in pain." His head jerked toward the right and he peered over her shoulder. "There. I just heard it again. Did you?"

"Maybe?" She couldn't be sure. Her head was all fuzzy after that kiss, brief as it had been.

But then she glanced down at Lady Bird and snapped back to awareness.

"Ford." Maple's fingers curled around the fabric of his shirt and she balled it into a fist as a shiver coursed through her—and not the good, yummy kind of shiver she'd been experiencing just seconds before. "Look at Lady Bird."

The gentle dog's ears were pricked forward, and her hackles were raised. She'd obviously heard something, too, and whatever it was had her spooked.

"It's okay, girl." Ford rested a hand on Lady Bird's back.

The golden panted and relaxed a bit at his touch, but then a mournful cry pierced the air.

Maple's gaze immediately collided with Ford's.

"That sounds like a hurt animal," she said.

Lady Bird barked and sprang into action. She darted past Ford, dragging her leash behind her before either of them could stop her.

"Lady Bird!" Ford shouted, chasing after the dog.

Maple followed with her heart in her throat. Lady Bird was just a streak of gold in the darkness, dashing sideways across Percy's lawn toward the pet clinic next door.

Now, Maple *really* wished she'd given up on her fashionable stilettos. She could barely keep up. She finally kicked them off and ran barefoot toward the front porch of the pet clinic, where she could scarcely make out the silhouette of Ford's profile in the moonlight.

"It's a dog," he called out, and the tone of his voice alone told her it was bad. *Really* bad. "She needs help!"

Chapter Twelve

Bile rose to the back of Ford's throat as he crouched down next to the small copper-and-white dog. "It's okay, little one. Maple will get you all taken care of."

It didn't take a genius or a medical professional to see that the dog was pregnant and in active labor. Her belly was hard and swollen, but the pup was as a limp as a dish-rag, stretched out on the welcome mat to the pet clinic with her eyes closed. She didn't have a collar, tags or any other type of identification. Something wasn't right, and if Ford had to guess, whoever had dumped her here knew it.

How could someone do this? He felt sick just think-ing about it.

Lady Bird seemed equally upset as she gently dropped to her belly and curled her body in a protective barrier around the distressed dog. The small pup gave a weak wag of her tail at the contact.

"What is it? What's wrong?" Maple caught up with them, stumbling onto the porch barefoot. She kneeled beside Ford, and her face crumpled as she assessed the situation. "Oh, no. You poor, poor thing."

"The puppies are coming, right?" Ford asked.

"They're trying. We need to get the little mama inside so I can see what's going on, but I'm guessing it's dystocia. She can't push them out." Her hands trembled as she rooted around her purse for her keys.

"Here, let me. I'll get the door." Ford took Maple's bag, found her key ring and unlocked the clinic while she gently scooped the dog into her arms and carried her inside.

The little thing couldn't have weighed more than twenty pounds, even heavily pregnant. Ford thought it best to let Maple handle her, since she was the veterinary professional. He did what he could, turning on lights and making sure Lady Bird didn't get in the way while she carried the dog directly to a table in the clinic's operating room.

Ford winced at the streak of blood on Maple's arm as she set down the pup and slipped into a white coat. Things weren't looking good. The dog could barely keep her eyes open, and she'd started shivering. Maple spoke to her in soothing tones as she did a quick exam, checking the dog's eyes, gums, body temperature and pulse. She scanned the dog for a microchip but couldn't find one.

Then she glanced up at Ford while she gently palpitated the pup's abdomen. "She's a little Cavalier King Charles spaniel. From the looks of it, not even a year old. Dogs really shouldn't have puppies that young. Their bodies aren't mature enough to handle the strain. Plus, Cavaliers have a high incidence of mitral valve disease. No responsible breeder would breed a dog like this until at least two and half years of age, and only then if she's been health-tested and found to be heart-clear, preferably by a veterinary cardiologist."

Ford gritted his teeth. "The very fact that we found her dumped on the welcome mat is a pretty good indication that whoever owns her isn't all that concerned with ethics."

"Owned." Maple's eyes flashed. "No collar, no microchip… Whoever had her before made sure we wouldn't be able to locate them. She belongs here now, and we're going to do everything we can to save her and her puppies. She likely came from a puppy mill, and when they realized it wasn't going to be an easy delivery, they got rid of her. At least they had the decency to drop her off at a vet clinic."

"I can't believe we found her," Ford said. If they hadn't, she wouldn't have made it until morning. That much was obvious. "What should we do now?"

Maple bit her bottom lip as she studied the dog. "Ordinarily, we'd start with a dose of oxytocin. It enhances uterine contractions. Lots of things can cause dystocia—low calcium, uterine inertia. This dog's small size doesn't help. I doubt she and her puppies have gotten proper nutrition during the pregnancy. She's probably also dehydrated."

"So you don't think the oxytocin would work?"

"It might, but we don't know how long she's been like this. The longer the labor goes on, the more dangerous this situation gets. She needs a C-section." Maple swallowed. "As soon as possible."

"Okay." Ford nodded. They were two medical professionals. They could handle this, couldn't they? "Let's do it. Tell me how I can help."

She glanced up from the dog long enough to flash him a smile. "You seriously want to assist while I do an emergency canine Cesarean section?"

"Of course, I do, but you might need to give me some instructions. We didn't cover this in med school," Ford said as Lady Bird shuffled closer to lean against his leg.

"You know what us veterinarians say, right?" Maple twisted her hair into a bun on the top of her head and miraculously secured it in place with nothing but a pencil from the pocket of her lab coat. "Real doctors treat more than one species."

It was such a Maple thing to say that he couldn't help but laugh, despite the seriousness of their circumstances.

He folded his arms. "Go on, then. Let's make a real doctor out of me."

"I take back what I said." Affection sparkled in her eyes. "You might not be so impossible, after all."

With Ford's help, Maple had the dog—whom she'd christened Ginger, because the sweet thing deserved to be called by a name—prepped for surgery within minutes. Once she'd gotten an IV catheter in place and administered the anesthesia, she got to work shaving Ginger's abdomen while Ford prepared a whelping box for the puppies. He placed a heating pad at the bottom and lined it with blankets for warmth.

With any luck, they'd be able to save Ginger's litter and actually get to use it.

"Ready?" she asked as she positioned the scalpel over the dog's abdomen for a midline incision.

"Ready, Doc." Ford nodded, eyes shining bright over his surgical mask. "You've got this."

She soaked up the much-needed encouragement. Maple had performed C-sections in vet school, but never in an emergency like this. She desperately wanted to save this dog...*and* her puppies. It might seem crazy, but finding a Cavalier in distress like this almost felt like a sign. Like Maple was in the right place at the right time. Like ending up here in Bluebonnet was meant to be, beyond the names that were printed on her birth certificate. A new Cavalier mom and her babies would certainly benefit from having a certified canine cardiologist in town.

But Maple was getting way ahead of herself. She still needed to perform the surgery. Plus, there was the matter of Grover. He was going to flip his lid when he found out about this. He'd demand to know why she hadn't called him before taking matters into her own hands, which was probably a valid question.

Except they didn't have that kind of time. Ginger's pulse was already thready. She couldn't let the dog down.

Maple pushed aside all doubts and got down to business. She held her breath as she made the incision, and then her eyes filled with tears as she caught her first glance at Ginger's moving uterus.

"We've got two puppies, and they're both alive." She pointed toward the squirming pups for Ford to see.

"Well, would you look at that?" he said in an awe-struck voice.

"Get ready. I'm going to incise the uterus, and as soon as I remove the first puppy, I'm going to hand it over so you can clear its airway and stimulate breathing."

Ford stood poised with a towel in one hand and a suction bulb in the other.

Everything that happened next seemed to move in fast motion. Maple got the puppies out as quickly as she could. One of them was tiny and delicate, and the other was a downright chunk. The big pup, a boy, had likely been too large for the young mama's birth canal, contributing to her distress. The smaller puppy was a girl, and Maple had a feeling she'd end up looking just like

Ginger someday. Mom and her babies all had the chestnut and pearly white markings that the Blenheim variety of Cavalier King Charles spaniels were famous for.

So whoever had unloaded Ginger on the doorstep had definitely been an unscrupulous breeder, angling to crank out a litter of purebred puppies for profit without regard to the health of the mother or her litter. Later, Maple would allow herself to feel properly enraged about that, but right now, all she felt was pure gratitude.

This was why she'd become a veterinarian. Maybe she'd lost sight of some of the reasons she'd gone to vet school in the first place after she'd become bogged down with exams and all-nighters and the extra effort it took to get a specialty certification. After her disastrous attempt at dating one of her study-group partners, she'd closed herself to other students. She'd always been a driven pupil, but she'd doubled down after Justin had taken advantage of her academic prowess.

She'd once heard her mother tell a client that the best revenge was massive success, and Maple had internalized that message without even realizing it. The one time she'd put her heart on the line, she'd gotten hurt. So somewhere deep down, she'd decided to believe all the things her bitterly unhappy parents had told her—and *shown* her—about love. She'd closed ranks around her heart even stronger than before and decided the only path forward was to be the best. Untouchable in every possible way. In the long run, she could love herself better than anyone else could.

Except for dogs.

Maple had always known they knew how to love better than humans did, which was why she'd chosen this life to begin with. It's why she'd dug her heels in and taken the grant when her mom and dad refused to fund her education. But she didn't need to work in a sleek high-rise building or cater to wealthy Upper West Siders to help animals. She could make a difference right here in Bluebonnet. Maybe that's what Percy's grant and his requirement to work for a year at the clinic had really been about.

It was a humbling thought, and it made Maple's throat close up tight as she clipped the second puppy's umbilical cord. She handed the tiny girl to Ford, and the way he looked at her nearly did her in.

He still didn't get it. They weren't alike at all. She wasn't special. She really wasn't…

But this moment certainly was. And Maple wouldn't have traded it for anything.

"Hey there, welcome to the world," Ford cooed as he massaged the puppy with a soft towel to get her breathing.

Maple couldn't wait to join in and check the new babies out from head to toe, but first she needed to get Ginger stitched up. She wouldn't be able to relax until she knew for a fact that the new mom was out of the woods.

But once Ginger was resting comfortably, Maple finally allowed herself to breathe, take a look around and bask in a happiness so bone-deep that it took her breath away.

Ford was bottle-feeding the girl puppy while the boy slept in the whelping box. Lady Bird couldn't seem to decide whether she should stand guard over the puppies or Ginger, so she alternated between all three, keeping a watchful eye over the whole furry family as best she could. And as crazy as it seemed, Maple could almost sense Percy's presence there, too…or maybe that was just wishful thinking.

One thing she knew for certain: he would've been proud, just like Ford's Gram had tried to tell her the other day at the retirement home.

"You okay, Doc?" Ford looked up from the puppy in his hands, sucking greedily at the bottle. Once Ginger was awake, they'd introduce the puppies to their mama. She'd been through a lot, but it was important for her to try and nurse so she could bond with her babies. Even so, the pups would likely need supplemental bottle-feeding for the next few weeks. "That was a lot."

"It was a lot." Maple laughed and plucked the boy puppy from the whelping box so she could feed him. "But I'm good. I'm more than good, actually. I loved every minute of it. Tonight was…"

She shook her head and held the puppy close to her heart. "I don't think I have words for what tonight meant to me."

Ford stood, and without missing a beat of bottle-feeding duty, he walked over to Maple and kissed her cheek. "You did it, Doc."

"No." She shook her head and grinned up at him, half-delirious. Maple had no idea what time it was. The past few hours had passed in a blur, but she didn't want to close her eyes. She didn't want to miss a single, solitary second of this magical night. "*We* did it."

The magic ended early the following morning when Maple jerked awake to the sound of Grover's gravelly voice echoing throughout the pet clinic's operating room.

"What in tarnation is going on in here?"

Her eyes snapped open, and for a second, she forgot where she was. What was she doing, sleeping on the floor of the clinic, of all places? And what was *Ford* doing here, too? Other than providing her with a nice, strong shoulder to use as a pillow...

Maple sat up, blinking against the assault of the clinic's fluorescent lighting, convinced this was all a stress-induced nightmare. She'd been feeling so out of sorts lately, not to mention the calls and voice mails from her parents, which she'd been ignoring for days. A nightmare seemed par for the course at this point.

But then her gaze snagged on the whelping box beside Ford, who was just beginning to stir, and the events from the night before came rushing back to her. The abandoned dog... The surgery... Two perfect puppies.

And Ford had been there for all of it.

Magic.

"Good morning, Grover," Maple said. Even Grumpy McGrumperson couldn't spoil her mood today. Although it would be really great if he stopped looking at her like she was a teenager who'd just been caught making out with her boyfriend in a parked car. "I can explain."

Grover glanced around the room, frown deepening as he noticed Ginger resting on a soft dog bed in a kennel piled with blankets. "Please do, because for the life of me, I can't figure out if this is a slumber party or a veterinary emergency."

"Both, actually." Maple laughed. Grover, pointedly, did not.

"Hi, Grover." Ford stood and held out his hand for a shake. He had an adorable case of bed head, which probably would've look ridiculous on anyone else but somehow only made him more attractive. "You should've seen Maple last night. She saved that dog's life."

Grover accepted Ford's handshake, and eyed Maple dubiously.

"I would've called you, but there was no time. Someone abandoned Ginger on the steps of the clinic. She was in the latter stages of labor with obvious dystocia and needed an immediate C-section." She glanced at Ford. "We're lucky we even found her."

Grover regarded Ford, still dressed in the scrubs he'd worn to the hospital yesterday. "You assist with veterinary surgery now, Dr. Bishop?"

"Apparently so." Ford chuckled, and something about the deep timbre of his voice sent Maple straight back to last night and the lump that had lodged in her throat at the sight of him cradling a newborn puppy in his strong grasp. "It was fun. Maybe I can do it again someday."

He snuck a glance at Maple, and a million butterflies took flight in her belly.

I'm really in trouble now, aren't I?

Last night had changed things between them, and now there was no turning back. She knew he felt it, too. Ford held her fragile heart in his hands as surely as he'd held those puppies, and it terrified Maple to her core.

What was she going to do?

"Perhaps we shouldn't make a habit of it." Grover's eyes cut back toward Maple. "You do realize the pups will probably need supplemental bottle-feeding for the first few days, don't you?"

Maple nodded. "Yes, sir. We've already given Peaches and Fuzz two feedings, three hours apart."

"Peaches and Fuzz?" Grover's eyebrows rose. "You named them already?"

"Yes, and the mother, too. I'm calling her Ginger."

Grover's mouth twitched, as if he was trying not to smile. No way. Impossible. "So all these dogs are yours now?"

Overnight, she'd gone from owning one large dog to owning two adult dogs and two newborn puppies. It was going to take a full-size moving van to get her to New York when she finally moved back.

If she moved back.

"It's just temporary," she said, doing her best to avoid Ford's gaze. "For now, they're completely my responsibility."

"Have you introduced the pups to the mother yet?" Grover asked.

"Yes, and it went really well. But she was still drowsy from the anesthesia, and I didn't want her to accidentally roll over the puppies, so I didn't think it was best to leave them all together unsupervised."

"And you're keeping them warm?"

"Yes."

"And you offered Ginger a small amount of food and water a few hours after the birth?"

"Yes." Again, Maple nodded.

The interrogation continued, with Grover barking out question after question about the surgery, Ginger's post-op treatment, and the care and feeding of her puppies.

Finally, when he'd exhausted his long list of concerns, he waved toward Ginger's kennel, the whelping box and the pile of old blankets Maple had found in the clinic's donation closet and used for a pallet for her and

Ford to get some shut-eye in between puppy feedings. "Now clean all of this up, would you? I've got a poodle coming in for a spay this morning."

He stalked out of the operating room before Maple could respond.

She sighed and glanced at Ford. "Well, that went pretty much exactly like I thought it would. That man really needs to reconsider his stance on caffeinated coffee."

Ford grinned and raked a hand through his hair. "Speaking of caffeine, why don't I run over to Cherry on Top and get us a couple of large coffees real quick? I know I could use it before my practice opens in—" he glanced at his watch and winced "—just under an hour."

"I'd *love* one of their hazelnut cream lattes, if you have time. I think Adaline calls that drink Texas Gold. I'll get all of this cleaned up. For today, I think I'll see if June can keep an eye on Ginger and her babies up front in the reception area. I'll take everyone home with me tonight," Maple said.

She started folding one of the blankets and tried not to think about what Ford's sister would say when she found out they'd spent the night together...*again*. Not that medical emergencies should count. But still...

The purely innocent sleepovers seemed to be occurring with alarming frequency.

"Sounds like a plan," Ford said, and just as he swept a lock of hair from her face and Maple thought he might be about to kiss her goodbye, Grover stormed back into the room.

"One more thing," he bellowed.

Maple's heart hammered against her rib cage as she sprang backward away from Ford. "Y-yes?"

Grover jerked his head toward Ginger and the puppies, and his expression morphed into something approximating an actual look of approval. "You did a good job here last night."

She couldn't believe her ears. Grover wasn't Percy, but he'd been his business partner for a long, long time. She'd never get the chance to hear her father utter those words, but having Grover say them was the next best thing.

"Thank you, Grover. That means a lot," she said before he could stomp off again. "Especially coming from you."

"Right. Well." He shifted his weight from one foot to the other, clearly unaccustomed to issuing such effusive praise. "Keep up the good work."

Happiness sparkled inside her, and just this once, she didn't worry about tomorrow. Or the days or weeks that followed. All that mattered was this day. This place.

This *life*.

"I will."

The text came just after Ford dropped off Maple's hazelnut cream latte with June at the front desk of the pet clinic.

He'd gotten a coffee for June as well, and the older woman had gushed about what a fine man he was to help Maple deliver the puppies. Peaches, Fuzz, and Ginger were all snuggled together in a cozy playpen-like contraption behind the reception desk. Maple had already jumped right into an appointment when a walk-in client had shown up with a lethargic hedgehog.

Ford assured June that was just fine. He needed to get going, anyway. But he'd still paused to watch Ginger and her pups for a moment. The mama Cavalier's tail wagged as soon as she caught sight of him, and Ford couldn't help but marvel at the dog's sweet and trusting disposition, after all she'd been through. Joy warmed him from within just looking at the furry little family.

Something had shifted inside Ford the night before. He'd been drawn to Maple since he'd first set eyes on her—that much was undeniable. But even when she'd kissed him—even when he'd challenged her to do it a second time—he'd thought he'd had his emotions under control. He and Maple were nothing alike. She'd been clear about that right up front. She'd never once tried to hide who she was, unlike his former fiancée, who'd never once told him she had reservations about moving to Bluebonnet. In retrospect, he should've known she was lying. The signs were all there. That relationship had always felt too much like work, unlike the time he spent with Maple. With Maple, he could be himself. He could relax. He could breathe easy, because there was no danger of losing his heart. Maple been perfectly honest about the fact that she couldn't wait to put Texas and all it contained in her rearview mirror, Ford included.

But then she'd stayed.

She'd had chance after chance to make good on her word and leave, but she'd never actually gone. And still, somehow it wasn't until Ford helped her save that dog and her puppies that he'd realized he was falling.

In truth, it had been happening all along. He knew that now. How could he not, when he'd watched her spread joy and light on her pet visits with Lady Bird, even when she insisted it didn't come naturally to her at all? Maybe that's why her commitment to it meant more.

Or maybe she was more tenderhearted than she wanted to believe. Either way, it had been a sight to behold. Ford couldn't have looked away if he'd tried.

Then it had felt so nice last night when she'd fallen asleep with her head on his shoulder. So *right*. Ford had stroked her hair and stubbornly refused to move, even when his arm fell asleep. He'd told himself he was simply savoring the moment. Holding on to something—some*one*—whom he'd known from the outset was never meant to be his.

Ford had been doing the right thing his entire life. He'd come back to Bluebonnet to care for Gram. He put his family and his town and his patients first. Always. He'd never once regretted any of it. Just this once, though, he'd wanted to give in to what he really and truly wanted. And he'd never wanted anyone as badly as he wanted Maple.

So he'd let himself believe it was okay to let his guard down…to brush the hair back from her face and caress her cheek and let his fingertips linger on her soft skin while he held her and let himself fall. It might be his only chance to feel this close and connected with the enigmatic woman who'd found her way into his heart when he least expected it.

When morning came, everything had still been okay. Sure, Ford felt like he was walking around with his heart on the outside of his body, but he was good. *They* were good. Even Grover was being decent for a change.

Then Ford's phone chimed with an incoming text.

"See you later, June. Thank you for keeping an eye on the little ones for Maple," he said as he reached inside his pocket for his cell.

He was already outside on the sidewalk soaking up the first rays of the Hill Country sunshine when the message popped up on his screen. He'd half expected it to be from Maple, but instead, the name that popped up above the text bubble was Pam Hudson's from County General Hospital.

Oliver Taylor's bone-marrow biopsy results are in. It's not good news. Thought you'd want to know. I'm sorry.

Chapter Thirteen

Maple had now been in Bluebonnet long enough to expect that word about Ginger and her puppies would spread through town like wildfire. She'd actually been looking forward to it since, according to Adaline's small-town-gossip theory, the next newsworthy event would make everyone forget about the kiss in the town square. If that was the case, bring on the collective amnesia!

What she hadn't expected was the cake. Or the casseroles. Or the pair of giant wooden storks that appeared in her front yard—one pink and the other blue, holding tiny bundles in their beaks labelled Peaches and Fuzz.

Maple peered out her kitchen window at the wooden birds as she handed Adaline a bottle filled with puppy formula. "I don't get it. Can you shed any light on this?"

"You're way overthinking it. They're just yard signs, like the ones people put on their lawns when a new baby is born." Adaline nudged the tip of the bottle into Fuzz's tiny mouth, like Maple had shown her on the first day she'd brought the dogs home to Percy's charming house next door to the clinic.

The puppies had just turned five days old. Ginger was recuperating nicely from her surgery and nursing the babies every day, but because she'd been neglected during her pregnancy, Maple was concerned about her nutrition. She didn't want to exhaust the little mama, so she'd kept the puppies on a supplemental feeding schedule.

Luckily, there was no shortage of volunteers to help out. Like today, when Maple had found Adaline, Belle and Jenna waiting on her front step after work, ready for dog duty. The book-club girls had been taking shifts since she'd brought the dogs home and were still eager to help.

"We don't have yard signs in Manhattan." Maple laughed. "We don't even have *yards*. I have no idea who put those out there. They just appeared out of nowhere the other day."

Belle held Peaches close while she offered her a bottle. "You did an amazing thing. The town just wants to celebrate you."

And they certainly were. The cake had been from Adaline, naturally—a triple-layer, funfetti-flavored wonder, dotted generously throughout with rainbow sprinkles and *Bluebonnet Thinks You're Pawesome* piped in decadent frosting. Then the casseroles had started appearing, wrapped snugly in tin foil. Thankfully, most of them came with heating instructions since Maple had never cooked a casserole in her life. Yesterday, a teacher from Bluebonnet Elementary School had even stopped by the clinic with a stack of drawings of the puppies her first graders had made for Maple.

It was all so...*kind*.

And nothing at all like her job would've been like at the cardiology practice in New York. Maple knew it wasn't fair to compare, but she couldn't help it. She'd always done her best to keep to herself and fly under the radar. That was impossible in a place like Bluebonnet, and to her surprise, she didn't mind so much anymore. It felt nice.

"Maple, are you doing therapy-dog visits with Lady Bird, or are you too busy with Ginger and the puppies?" Jenna asked.

Ginger sat in her lap while Jenna ran her hand in long, gentle strokes over the dog's back. Maple had noticed a pattern: while everyone else fawned over the puppies, Jenna seemed more drawn to the mama dog. She was glad. That poor dog needed as much love and affection as she could get.

"Are you kidding? The phone is still ringing off the hook, and it's never for me." Maple glanced at Lady Bird, glued to her legs as usual. "Is it, girl?"

Lady Bird woofed right on cue.

"I'm this dog's glorified assistant. The town might riot if I stopped taking her on visits. Why?" Maple asked.

"I have ballet camp starting at the dance studio in a few days, and I was hoping you could bring Lady Bird in for our first morning? Just to put the littlest ones at ease?" Jenna grinned. "I have a tutu Lady Bird can borrow."

"Then how could I possibly say no? Sure, we'll be there."

The answer flew out of Maple's mouth before she had a chance to feel a twinge of anxiety. Oddly, even after she'd spontaneously agreed, the twinge never came.

She buried her fingertips in the soft fur on Lady Bird's broad chest and gave the golden a good scratch. *You did this, sweet girl.* Social anxiety didn't go away overnight. Maple knew she'd probably have a lifelong struggle feeling confident in social settings. But she had the dog to thank for getting her acclimated to the pet-therapy visits and interacting with strangers—strangers who were becoming friends.

Day by day. Visit by visit.

Maple wasn't the same person she'd been two weeks ago. She'd breezed into town intent on changing things, and instead, the town had changed her.

But it wasn't all Lady Bird's doing. Someone else had been there alongside her every step of the way. And much to Maple's confusion, she hadn't set eyes on him for five straight days.

Ford had returned to the pet clinic and delivered her latte, as promised, on the morning after the pups were born. Since then...nothing.

At first, Maple had chalked up his absence to the fact that they'd both been exhausted. He had a medical practice to run, just like she did it. She figured he was simply getting caught up on things. But then one day had turned into two, two turned into three, and so on. With each passing day, Maple had started to feel more and more like a lost puppy herself.

It's for the best. You were scared to death of your feelings for him, and now you don't have to worry about that anymore.

Maple clung to that thought, just like she'd been clinging to it for the past five days. But the more she repeated the mantra, the less she believed it. Because now that he was gone, she was more terrified than ever.

She'd texted a few times and gotten nothing but short, generic responses. Even when she'd sent photos or videos of the puppies, she'd gotten nothing but a heart emoji in return. If it hadn't been for those brief missives, she would've been worried that he'd had an accident or something. But no. He was simply pulling away, just like Justin had done in college, only this was a gradual withdrawal instead of a clean break. She was beginning to realize that the latter would've been far less agonizing. This felt like death by a thousand paper cuts.

"Adaline, can I talk to you for a second?" Maple tipped her head toward the hallway.

She'd sworn to herself she wouldn't do this. Adaline had never been thrilled about Maple and Ford spending time together. She was probably the last person who'd want to shed light on why he was semi-ghosting her.

But she also knew Ford better than anyone else in Bluebonnet. They were close. So Maple had finally decided to swallow her pride and ask.

"This is about Ford, isn't it?" Adaline said as soon as they were out of earshot of the rest of the group. She didn't even give Maple time to answer before her shoulders sagged with relief. "Thank goodness. I was beginning to worry that you weren't ever going to say anything."

The ache that had taken up residence where Maple's heart used to be burrowed deeper, and deeper still. So she hadn't been imagining things. Ford wasn't just busy. Something had happened to make him stay away.

She wrapped her arms around her middle, bracing herself for whatever was to come. "I know you don't think I'm good for him, and I understand why. I happen to agree with you, but—"

"What? No, Maple." Adaline grabbed onto Maple's arm and gave it a tender squeeze. "I don't think that at all."

"But that night at book club, you told me you didn't think we should be together."

"That's not what I said. I remember distinctly telling you that I didn't think it was a good idea for you to kiss him anymore until you knew for certain you were going to stay in Bluebonnet." Adaline's eyes welled up. "I never thought you weren't good for him. You two are so alike. I think you'd make a great couple."

Maple shook her head. "No, we're really not—"

"Stop. You may seem like total opposites on the surface, but you're alike in the ways that matter most. *That's* why I was worried. My brother is head over heels for you, whether he realizes it or not. I knew if you left, he'd be heartbroken. Because you belong together, not the opposite."

Sorrow closed up Maple's throat. She'd spent the past five days trying to convince herself that she and Ford had never stood a chance, and now his sister was trying to tell her they were soul mates or something.

She wished it was true. She'd never wished for anything so hard in all her life.

"That's not what it's like between us," Maple protested.

But Adaline wasn't listening. "I promised to stay out of his business. I swore. So when I realized he'd been spending all his time at the hospital, I didn't say anything. I thought for sure you knew, and then when I realized you didn't, I knew it wasn't my place to bring it up. I figured he'd come to his senses sooner or later, but clearly he's not."

She was talking in circles, and the more she said, the more Maple realized she should've pushed harder. She should've trusted that Ford wasn't the sort of person who'd vanish from her life without good reason. He'd never given her any reason to believe that.

Maple's past had, though. All her life, she'd been taught that feelings couldn't be trusted and love never stood the test of time. Her own limited experiences with dating had confirmed everything her parents had impressed upon her, either by their words or actions. So she'd kept her heart under lock and key. The less she shared herself with other people—people who would only end up hurting her in the long run—the better. Then Ford had come along and stolen her heart when she wasn't looking. And instead of telling him how she felt, she'd held her breath and waited for the other shoe to drop.

Was it any wonder it had?

"Adaline," Maple snapped. "You're scaring me. What's going on? Why is Ford spending all his time at the hospital?"

She didn't need to ask, though. She knew, even before Adaline said it.

Oliver.

The child had been on Maple's mind ever since the teacher from the elementary school had given her the colored drawings of Peaches, Fuzz, and Ginger. She'd brought the pictures home and tacked her favorites to Percy's refrigerator with magnets, and every time her gaze landed on the strokes of bold crayon, she thought about Lady Bird's visit with Oliver.

My mom says when I'm better, I can get a dog of my own. When I do, I want one just like Lady Bird.

She could still hear the little boy's voice, so upbeat

and happy, despite his circumstances, just like she could still see his tiny form, dwarfed by the hospital bed…the tired shadows beneath his eyes.

He wasn't getting better, was he? And Maple had been so wrapped up in her own messed-up life that she hadn't for a moment considered that Ford might've been experiencing a crisis of his own.

"He's got this patient." Tears shone in Adaline's eyes, and she let out a ragged breath. "Ford is very attached, and let's just say things aren't looking good. He can't tell me much, but I'm worried. My brother is a mess, and I'm not sure there's anything any of us can do to make things better."

Maple just stood there, shell-shocked, until Lady Bird pawed at her foot, pulling her out of her trance. She dragged her gaze toward the dog, eyes blurry with tears. She blinked hard, and her vision cleared a bit…

Just enough for hope to stir as she realized that maybe there was one small thing she could do to help.

It took longer than Maple would've liked to get ready to go to the hospital. She made an excuse for the book-club girls to leave and then packed things up as quickly as she could, heart pounding all the while.

Lady Bird followed her around the house with her tail hanging low between her legs. Empathy was the dog's strong suit, after all, and she could tell Maple was a jittery jumble of nerves—as evidenced by the way she nearly jumped out of her skin when there was a knock on the front door just as she was almost ready to leave.

Lady Bird, mirroring Maple's disquiet, released a sharp bark. In turn, Ginger let out a low growl in the kitchen. The sweet dog probably thought whoever was at the door must be a threat to her puppies.

"Everyone, let's just calm down," Maple said, as much to herself as to the dogs. "I'm sure that's just Adaline, Jenna, or Belle. One of them probably forgot something."

She swung the front door open without even checking the peephole. Big mistake…

Huge.

"Mom." She gaped at Meredith Leighton, unable to process what she was seeing. Then her gaze shifted to the man standing beside her mother. "And Dad?"

They'd flown clear across the country to Texas and taken a car to Bluebonnet, all the way from Austin? *Together?*

Maybe she was hallucinating. That seemed far more likely.

"Well?" Maple's mother peered past her toward Lady Bird, who'd chosen this most awkward of moments to lose her sense of decorum and bark like she'd never set eyes on a stranger before. Perhaps she'd picked up on the fact that her parents weren't dog people. Either way, it was mortifying. "Can we come in, or will that dog attack us?"

"Lady Bird wouldn't hurt a fly. She just knows I…" Maple shook her head. She couldn't tell her parents she was about to run after a man. They'd probably kidnap her and forcibly drag her out of Texas like she'd joined a cult and needed to be deprogrammed. "Never mind. We were on our way out, that's all."

"Come on in." She waved them inside, then cut her gaze toward Lady Bird. "You're fine. It's all good."

Her mother tiptoed over the threshold, sidestepping

Lady Bird as if she was the star of that Stephen King story, *Cujo*.

Dad rolled his eyes at his ex-wife, but once he was inside, he scrunched his nose. "It smells like dog in here."

They still had so much in common, even after decades of trying to tear each other apart. How they couldn't see it was a mystery.

"That's because I rescued a lovely Cavalier King Charles spaniel a few days ago. She was in the late stages of labor when I found her, and I had to perform an emergency C-section. We ended up saving her and her two darling puppies." Maple gestured toward the kitchen. "Would you like to see them?"

Meredith Leighton looked at her like she'd just sprung an extra head and it was wearing a ten-gallon cowboy hat. "No, Maple. We're not here to look at puppies. We're here to take you home."

"What?" Maple shook her head, but somewhere deep inside, she felt like a naughty child who'd done something terribly, terribly wrong. The urge to smooth things over and obey was almost crushing. "If all you wanted was to try and talk me into leaving, you could've just called."

"We've been calling. You never pick up," her father said.

Yes, she'd dodged a few calls. And maybe she'd also deleted a couple voice mails without listening to them. But she knew they'd never understand why she liked it here.

For a second, when she'd first seen them standing there on Percy's doorstep, a sense of profound relief had coursed through her. She'd actually thought that now that they were here, she could show them what made Bluebonnet so special.

The Leightons weren't interested in that, though. Just like they'd never been interested in why she wanted to be a veterinarian instead of going to law school. She knew they loved her, but that love came with strings attached. Too bad they had such an aversion to dogs. Her mom and dad could've learned a thing or two about unconditional love from Lady Bird.

"I'm not going back." Maple took a deep breath and finally let herself say the words out loud that had been on her heart for days. "*Ever.* I'm staying here in Bluebonnet."

Her father's face turned an alarming shade of red.

"You've got to be kidding." Meredith threw her hands up in the air. Lady Bird's head swiveled to and fro, as if she'd just tossed an invisible ball. "You're just going to throw your entire life away for a birth father you never even met? He gave you away, Maple. Maybe let that sink in before you dig in your heels."

Maple reared back as if she'd been slapped.

No wonder she had such a hard time trusting people. She'd been told over and over again she couldn't count on anyone. She might still believe it, if not for Ford.

Ford!

Maple turned away to grab her purse, Lady Bird's leash, and the other items she'd set aside for her trip to County General.

"What are you doing? Where are you going?" Her mother's voice was growing shriller by the second. *"We just got here."*

"I know you did, and I'm sorry. But like I told you, we were just on our way out," Maple said. She'd never spoken to her parents like this before, and she marveled at how calm she sounded.

"Let's all just settle down." Charles Leighton huffed out a sigh. "Maple, sit."

He pointed at the sofa, and even Lady Bird refused to obey.

"No," Maple said as evenly as possible. "I'm leaving now. The two of you can either stay here and wait until I get back, or you can go back to New York. Either way, I won't be going with you. I want to stay here and learn more about my birth father, but that's not the only reason. This town is special. So are its people. They've inspired me in ways that would amaze you."

Her parents exchanged a glance, and Maple could see the fight draining out of them. They were scared, that's all. They were afraid of losing their only daughter.

"I love you both. That hasn't changed, and it never will." Maple beckoned to Lady Bird and the dog sprang to her feet. "Now, like I said, we have to go. We have someplace very important to be, and it really can't wait another second."

Chapter Fourteen

Oliver grinned as he moved a red checker in a zigzag pattern of jumps, ending in the king's row on Ford's side of the playing board. "King me."

Ford then watched as the little boy plucked two more of his black checkers out of play and added them to the sizable stack of Ford's castoffs piled on the hospital bedside tray. This game was going to end just like the others had, and if things kept going at the current pace, he was about to get trounced in record time.

He placed a red checker on top of the one that had just annihilated half of his remaining pieces. "There you go, bud."

"Are you even trying to win?" Oliver cast him an accusatory glance. "You're not letting me beat you just because I'm sick, are you?"

"Absolutely not. I'm genuinely this bad at checkers." Ford made a cross-your-heart motion over the left pocket of his scrubs.

Granted, the fact that that he was preoccupied with keeping an eye on Oliver's vital signs as they flashed on the monitor beside the bed didn't help matters. He was doing his best under the circumstances, though. He could never beat Gram at board games, either—probably because she was a notorious cheat.

"You're even worse at Go Fish." Oliver snickered.

"Careful, there. Or I'll tell your mom you know where she hides the chocolate bars." Ford winked.

He'd never tell. The kid had him wrapped around his little finger. Never in his career had Ford spent every waking moment of his free time at the bedside of one of his young patients. Then again, no other child had touched his heart in the way that Oliver had.

If only he wasn't fighting the same exact disease that had claimed the life of Ford's childhood friend… If only Oliver's most recent bone-marrow test hadn't indicated that this latest round of treatment wasn't working… If only there was something more Ford could do to help…

If only.

"It's your turn again," Oliver prompted.

Ford slid one of his few remaining checkers from one square to another, and Oliver immediately jumped over it with a double-stacked red playing piece. That's right, kings could move in any direction. Ford had forgotten.

He needed sleep. He was so exhausted from trying to keep up with his regular appointments while also monitoring Oliver's progress as closely as possible that he could barely think straight. Was playing games and coloring with the child in the evenings while his mom worked the night shift doing anything to beat Oliver's cancer?

Doubtful. But Ford wasn't about to let that little boy spend his evenings alone when the odds of him beating the disease were suddenly in doubt. He hadn't been there to spend time with Bobby all those years ago. When his friend passed away, the rug had been pulled out from underneath Ford's entire life. He'd never doubted for a minute that Bobby would recover. Kids like them didn't *die*.

That's how naive he'd been back then. That's how idyllic growing up in Bluebonnet had been. Ford knew better now, and he wasn't going to let the rug get yanked out from under him again without a fight.

He hadn't been around when Oliver had his last bone-marrow test. There hadn't been a reason for him to be there since he was only the child's primary care doctor, but that was beside the point. The kid had very little in the way of a support system, hence his deep attachment to Lady Bird, even though pet-therapy visits typically only took place once a week.

The boy needed a friend, especially now, and Ford could be that friend. *That*, he could do. That much he could control.

He'd dropped the ball for a bit, that's all. Rationally speaking, he knew his feelings for Maple had nothing at all to do with Oliver's illness. But the night the puppies had been born had marked a turning point—Ford had finally let loose and given up control. He'd let himself want. He'd let himself yearn. He'd let himself love. And then, when he'd been the happiest he could remember in a long, long time, he'd gotten the text from Oliver's nurse.

It was a gut punch Ford had never seen coming.

The chemo wasn't working. *No change*, the oncologist had said. Ford didn't understand how that was possible. Oliver was handling the treatments like a champ. His spirits were up. His color looked good. Even the nausea was getting better.

The cancer, on the other hand, wasn't.

"Can we play again?" Oliver asked as he leaped over Ford's last checker. "Please?"

"I don't know, bud. It's getting late, and you have another bone-marrow test in the morning." This one would be different. It had to.

Ford scrubbed his face.

When was the last time he'd slept? He wasn't even sure. Every night when he got home from the hospital, he fell into bed, closed his eyes, and dreamed of Maple. She didn't deserve to be treated like an afterthought. Ford didn't know how to let her in anymore, though. He couldn't wrap his mind—or his heart—around allowing himself to be vulnerable and strong all at once. It was easier—*safer*—to not let himself feel anything at all.

When did you turn into such a caveman?

He wasn't. That was the problem. He couldn't turn it off. No matter how much Ford tried, he couldn't stop thinking about Maple. He had this fantasy that she'd walk through the door of Oliver's hospital room one evening and suddenly, everything would go back to feeling right and good. Ford knew it would never happen. Even if she came, she'd never look at him the same way again. How could she? His actions over the past week had been shameful. Ford knew Maple had trouble trusting people, and in the end, he'd shown her that he was the least trustworthy of them all.

"Lady Bird!" Oliver shouted, fully ignoring Ford's reminder that tomorrow was an important day and he needed to get some rest.

Ford paused from pressing his fingertips against his eyelids to slide his gaze toward the child. He'd known this was going to happen, eventually. Maybe he could get Pam to call Maple and request a visit from the therapy dog, and Ford could make himself scarce before she got there.

No, that would never work. She'd need a ride to the hospital. He'd volunteered the last time, and Pam wouldn't hesitate to ask him again.

"How about one more game of checkers?" Ford offered. "You really need to rest up. Lady Bird can visit another time."

Oliver's face scrunched. "But she's already here."

He pointed toward the door, and Ford's chest grew so tight that he couldn't breathe as he slowly turned to look.

And there she was. Maple, just like in his fantasy—smiling, with Lady Bird wagging happily at her feet. The only difference between his dreams and the impossible reality taking place was the addition of a large wicker basket in Maple arms.

"Hi, there," she said, nodding toward the basket as she lingered in the doorway. "Lady Bird and I brought you a little surprise, Oliver. Is it okay if we come in?"

Her gaze flitted toward Ford, and his dread coiled in his gut as he waited to absorb the full blow of the inevitable hurt in her gaze—hurt that he'd put there. But when their eyes met, the only things he saw in her beautiful expression were affection and understanding and a tenderness so deep that he very nearly wept with relief.

"Yes! Come in!" Oliver demanded, then clamped a hand over his mouth as he remembered his manners. "Please?"

"Come on, Lady Bird." Maple's eyes glittered. "Let's go visit."

* * *

Maple's legs wobbled as she entered the hospital room.

She wasn't sure why she was nervous. The look on Ford's face when he'd first spotted her standing in Oliver's doorway had said more than any words of apology ever could. He'd blinked—hard—as if trying to convince himself he wasn't dreaming. And his eyes, the exact shade of blue as Texas twilight, flickered with regret.

Everything is going to be okay, she wanted to tell him. But she couldn't make that kind of promise. Maple wasn't sure exactly what was going on with Oliver, but whatever it was had sent Ford reeling. That was okay… that was *human*. They could figure out the rest later, but the important thing was she wanted to be here for him now, the same way he'd shown up for her—again and again—since the day she'd come home.

Home to Bluebonnet.

"Hi," she said as he rose from the chair beside Oliver's bed and walked toward her.

He looked exhausted to his core—much more so than the morning after they'd stayed up bottle-feeding puppies. That had been a happy sort of exhaustion. This… This was something else. This was a bone-deep weariness that made Maple worry he might break.

"Hi." Ford cleared his throat, and the smile he offered her was the saddest she'd ever seen. "Thank you. I don't how you got here or how you knew how badly Oliver needed this, but thank you. From the bottom of my heart."

"I'm not just here for Oliver," she said as Lady Bird licked Ford's hand in greeting before trotting toward the hospital bed.

Ford looked at her for a long, silent moment until, at last, the smile on his face turned more genuine.

"You could've told me, you know," Maple whispered. "You don't always have to be the strong one—the one holding up the world for everyone else. It's okay to need people. We all do from time to time. That's a lesson I only learned just recently, by the way."

His tired eyes twinkled. "Oh, yeah?"

"Yeah. From someone I've grown quite fond of." *Someone I just might love.* She took a tremulous inhale. Now wasn't the proper time or place to tell him she was in love with him, but she would…soon. "As for how I got here, let's just say there's a pickup truck taking up two spaces in the parking garage downstairs. For the life of me, I couldn't get that thing to squeeze in between the two yellow lines."

Even if she'd heard from him in the past few days, there would've been no time for driving practice. Caring for Ginger and the puppies was practically a full-time job, and Maple was busier than ever at the clinic since Grover had decided she was, in fact, competent. Just this morning, he'd surprised her by adding her name to the felt letter board in the reception area. It was listed right alongside his, where Percy's used to be. *Dr. Percy Walker* was spelled out directly beneath, along with the years of his birth and death.

"You finally drove Percy's truck?" Ford arched a disbelieving eyebrow.

"I had to do it sooner or later." A smile danced on Maple's lips. "I can't live here permanently if I don't drive, can I?"

He gave her a tentative smile that built as the news sank in that she was staying. For good.

Maple had made up her mind even before she'd told the Leightons she wasn't going back to New York with them. She'd decided a few days ago, and she'd been weaving new dreams for her future ever since. There were still a lot of things to figure out, but she was resolute.

"I just told my parents. They're here, if you can believe it." She blew out a breath. "Or they were. I left in a hurry, so I wouldn't be surprised if they're already headed for the airport in Austin."

The look in his eyes turned gentle, as if he knew how hard it was for her to tell the Leightons she wanted to start a new life here in Texas. He probably did. Ford had always seemed to understand her like no one else could.

"I don't know. From what I've seen, your family doesn't have the greatest record when it comes to travel plans. Maybe they'll surprise you and stick around for a while," he said.

"Maybe." She took a deep breath. She might like that, actually. Bluebonnet would probably do them some good.

She'd meant it when she'd told them she loved them, just like she'd meant it when she'd said she wanted to learn more about her birth family and this town that had embraced her and made her feel like she belonged. Those two things could be true at the same time. The Leightons had loved her as best as they could. It was the only way they knew how.

"I would've been here sooner if they hadn't turned up out the blue. The only other person who knows so far is

Grover." Maple shifted the basket in her arms to hide its contents from view until the big reveal. "I didn't want to tell anyone else until we had a chance to talk. I wanted you to hear it from me, not someone else."

"You're just full of surprises tonight, Doc. I haven't slept much in the past few days. If this is a dream, please don't wake me up."

"This isn't a dream." As crazy as it seemed, it was real life. And Maple was finally ready to grab on to it with all her might.

Ford shook his head and grinned like he still couldn't believe it. "So you're really standing here with a basket full of—" He mouthed the next word so Oliver wouldn't hear, although that was doubtful since the child was chattering away to Lady Bird, who'd traveled all the way to the end of her leash to plant her front paws on the edge of the bed. The boy and the dog were in their own little world. "Puppies?"

"Yes and no." At last, she thrust the basket toward him for a closer look. "Peaches and Fuzz are far too young to leave their mom for any length of time, plus they shouldn't get out and about until they're vaccinated. So I brought the next best thing."

Ford's mouth dropped open as he got a good look at the three battery-operated golden-retriever puppies nestled together inside the basket. They were robotic companion animals, just like the one his Gram had. Except these were miniature versions of Lady Bird, Bluebonnet's unofficial town mascot. As soon as Maple had discovered them on the internet, she'd known they were perfect for her new venture. She'd ordered a dozen of them on the spot.

"You're *certain* I'm not dreaming? Because for the life of me, I can't figure out why you'd have these." He shook his head in disbelief.

"I bought them for Comfort Paws." Maple bit her lip. This was the part she couldn't wait to share with him. She hadn't told a soul—the idea had begun as a passing thought at book club, and the more she saw all the good that Lady Bird did in the community, the more it had taken root.

Ford angled closer, lips curving into a slow smile, almost like he already knew. "What's Comfort Paws?"

"It's what I've decided to name the new pet-therapy organization I'm starting. I have a lot to learn, obviously, but Lady Bird has been a pretty great teacher so far. Ginger's puppies will be perfect for this type of work. Cavaliers love people and make great therapy dogs, just like goldens do. Something tells me I know a few dog lovers who'd want to help get a new group up and running." She grinned, thinking of the book-club girls.

"Oh, there's no doubt you're right about that." He looked at her with a combination of wonder and affection that left her breathless.

She could get used to Ford Bishop looking at her like that, and now she had all the time in the world to do just that.

"So you think this is all a good idea?" Maple nodded at the litter of robot companion animals. "Until we get things off the ground, I've bought some of these guys to share with patients like Oliver and your gram."

Ford pressed a hand to his heart, and she wondered if he, too, was thinking about the day they'd met and tussled over Coco and her dead batteries. She'd been so sure she had him figured out, and she'd never been so wrong in her life. She'd never seen love coming, but it had found her, anyway.

That's the way love worked sometimes—it bowled you over when you least expected it. Love could sneak up on you in the form of well-worn bedroom slippers that felt just right, in the steady presence of a dog with a heart of gold…

In the arms of a man who made you believe in yourself again, even when you hadn't fully realized how lost you were to begin with.

"It's a great idea, sweetheart. It's also rather poetic." The warmth in his gaze seemed to reach down into her soul.

"I like it when you call me *sweetheart*. It's a much better nickname than Doc."

"This might be the best dream I've ever had." His eyes crinkled in the corners. "Shall we introduce these guys to Oliver?"

"I thought you'd never ask."

"Hey, bud." Ford turned his smile on his patient. "Wait until you see what Maple and Lady Bird brought for you."

Maple followed him as he walked closer to the bed, and then she set the basket on the edge of the mattress, right next to Lady Bird's front paws. Oliver's mouth formed a perfect *O* as he peered inside. All three puppies wagged their mechanical tails, and when Lady Bird gave one of the puppies a nudge with her nose, it blinked its eyes and yipped.

Oliver gasped and let loose with a stream of giggles.

"They're real! I thought they were stuffed animals, but they're *real*."

And just like that, Maple's heart lodged in her throat. It was such a small thing, but to a boy confined to a hospital bed, this trio of tail-wagging, battery-powered companions meant the world. The light in his eyes was unparalleled.

Maple prayed with all her might that he would be okay.

"Not all the way real, but as real we can get for now," Ford said.

The distinction didn't matter to Oliver. He couldn't have been happier.

"They look just like you, Lady Bird." Oliver scooped a puppy out of the basket as gently as if it was a living, breathing animal, and he held it up to Lady Bird's nose for a sniff.

"Good girl, Lady Bird." Maple massaged the golden behind her ears, praising her for playing along.

"I can feel the puppy's heartbeat!" Oliver held the stuffed animal close to his chest. "Can I keep him?"

"Of course, you can. You can keep all these pups, for as long as you want. They're all yours. Lady Bird and I wanted to make sure you had some doggy company when we're not around."

"I love them," the boy said with a yawn. "And they love me, too. I'm going to sleep with all of them in my bed tonight."

"There's no better medicine than a basketful of puppies." Maple tilted her chin up and swallowed the lump in her throat. "At least that's what my dad always used to say."

Ford caught her gaze as he took her hand in his and squeezed it tight. "Your dad was a good man."

"He sure was." Maple smiled.

And hopefully, in time, I'll learn to love the way that he did. I'll keep growing, keep dreaming, keep believing. I'll hold people dear instead of hiding my heart away.

And through it all, I'll become my father's daughter.

Epilogue

The true dog days of summer came in late August, weeks after Oliver Taylor had been found to be in full remission. On the morning the child had been declared cancer-free, Ford called Maple to tell her the good news, and later that night, after they'd celebrated with champagne and cupcakes from Cherry on Top, she'd found him with his arms around Lady Bird's thick neck, weeping quietly into the dog's soft fur.

They'd been happy tears, but they'd also been much more. Ford had told Maple about his childhood friend Bobby shortly after she'd surprised him at the hospital with the basket of puppies for Oliver, and she knew that in so many ways, their friendship had made Ford into the man he was today. Driven, responsible, fiercely protective of the people he loved. But once Oliver was released from the hospital—an occasion marked with a goodbye party, complete with cake and a real, live golden-retriever puppy that Maple had helped his mom adopt from a local rescue group—Ford seemed less wistful when he talked about his old friend. He shared good memories of their years together. Bobby's grandfather sometimes gave them sugar cubes to feed the ponies at the family ranch, and Ford smiled when he told Maple about the feel of the horses' velvety muzzles against his sticky palm. He drove her down a dusty country road to show her the ranch where Bobby's family used to live and whooped with joy when he realized the treehouse where they'd played together still stood among a cluster of live oak trees. The grief was still there and always would be, but it was less sharp than it had been before. Ford could finally let his dear friend rest in peace.

Between the pet clinic and trying to get Comfort Paws off the ground, Maple was as busy as ever—but not too busy to slow-dance in the kitchen whenever Ford's favorite country song came on. Adaline had made good on her promise to take Maple shopping for more practical footwear, but she'd instantly fallen in love with a pair of western booties so bedazzled with rhinestones that they could've doubled for a pair of disco balls. She wore them almost daily, and they glittered like crazy every time Ford spun Maple in a twirl and sang to her with his warm lips pressed against her ear.

Ginger grew healthier by the day and, with Lady Bird as their self-appointed canine Mary Poppins, the puppies had hit all their biggest milestones on the holidays that dotted the summer calendar. On Memorial Day, their bright little eyes opened. By the time Bluebonnet's annual Fourth of July parade marched through the town square, they were eight weeks old and ready to explore the big wide world outside the Sunday house. Peaches and Fuzz loved everyone they encountered, greeting strangers with an adorable wiggle that always transitioned smoothly into a sit position without any prior training. Maple knew without a doubt they'd both make perfect therapy dogs. Both pups displayed the true Cavalier King Charles spaniel temperament—gentle, affectionate and eager to please.

And now, on the Saturday of Labor Day weekend, the time had come for them to go to their new homes. Adaline was adopting Fuzz, whom she'd taken to calling Fuzzy. Belle had staked her claim on Peaches, and both women were fully invested in completing therapy-dog training. So was Jenna, who couldn't wait to bring Ginger home and give her all the love and spoiling she deserved. Comfort Paws was really happening! On Maple's birthday, her parents had surprised her with a large donation—enough to fund dog training, buy T-shirts with the new Comfort Paws logo, and purchase therapy-dog-in-training vests for the pups scheduled to start class in the fall. Charles and Meredith Leighton hadn't been back to Bluebonnet since their surprise trip a few months ago, and when she'd come home from County General that night, they'd already gone. But slowly and surely, they were coming to accept the fact that Maple had decided how she wanted to live her life and she wouldn't be swayed.

"Ford, what's going on in there? The girls are going to be here any minute," Maple called from the living room, where he'd ordered her to stay put while he got the puppies ready for one last picture with her before they left for their new homes. He'd been holed up with the dogs in the kitchen for several long minutes. She had no idea what they could possibly be doing in there.

"We're just about ready. This is a big day. Peaches and Fuzz are the foundation puppies of Comfort Paws. It seemed like they should dress up for the occasion," Ford yelled from the kitchen.

Dress up? Where had that idea come from? Maple had never once mentioned putting costumes on any of the dogs before. However, Lady Bird was going to make an awfully cute pumpkin when Halloween rolled around.

"Here they come!" Ford announced. Then, in a whisper just loud enough for Maple to overhear, he said, "Wait, Peaches. Come back here. Fuzzy was supposed to go first."

Too late. Peaches came bounding around the corner, scampering toward the living room in a Tiffany Blue sweater with white lettering that Maple couldn't quite make out.

"He dressed you in a sweater?" Maple squatted and called Peaches toward her. "Does he realize how hot it is outside?"

The little dog's tail wagged so quick and fast that it was nothing but a blur. Her paws skidded on the hard wood floor as she flung herself at Maple before landing in a clumsy sit.

She scooped up the puppy and inspected the sweater. An *M* and an *E* were positioned over the dog's back.

ME? Maple was more confused than ever. "Ford, this is super cute, but I'm not sure I get it."

Fuzz came stumbling into the room next, ears flying as he tripped over his own paws. The sweater stretched over his pudgy little body was identical to the one Peaches had on, with one notable exception.

"What does yours say, Fuzzy?" Maple set Peaches back down on the ground and tucked her hair behind her ears for a closer look.

MARRY.

She glanced back and forth between the two dogs. "Me marry?"

Ford strolled into the room behind the dogs with a sheepish grin on his face, the likes of which she'd never seen before. "Fuzz was supposed to go first."

He reached down to rearrange the puppies. "See?"

MARRY ME.

Maple's heart flew to her throat. She was so stunned that she hadn't realized Ford had dropped to one knee when he'd bent to rearrange the dogs and pulled a small velvet ring box from the pocket of his denim shirt—the same one he'd been wearing on the day they'd met, with the sleeves rolled up to reveal his forearms, just the way she liked.

"Is this a puppy proposal?" she blurted through giddy tears.

"It seemed only appropriate. How else would I propose to a woman like the love of my life? I'm not sure you realize this, but you have a thing for dogs." He flipped open the box to reveal a sparkling emerald-cut solitaire surrounded by a frame of slender baguette diamonds. Maple had never seen another ring like it before.

"I love you, sweetheart. I want to keep building this crazy, unpredictable life with you," he said as the puppies climbed all over him in their delight at having one of their favorite humans down on their level. "Me marry?"

It was the most ridiculous proposal Maple could've imagined—as ridiculous as a man bringing a robot dog into the vet's office with a dead battery and a green bean stuck in its mouth.

And that's precisely what's made it perfect.

"Yes, a thousand times *yes*."

* * * * *

SIT STAY HEAL

Chapter One

Jenna Walsh really should've seen it coming. The signs were all there—from the banner strung over Main Street, to the new chill in the air the past few mornings when she walked her rescue dog Ginger, to the crimson blush on the leaves of the dogwood trees that stood near the crisp white gazebo in the quaint town square of Bluebonnet, Texas. Because autumn in Texas was about one thing and one thing only: football. And as the aforementioned banner screamed in the Bluebonnet Bulldogs team colors of royal blue and yellow, the arrival of football season meant the town's favorite occasion was right around the corner...

Homecoming, y'all!

That's literally what the banner said. The wording, like everything else even remotely having to do with homecoming, was a Bluebonnet tradition. Jenna had been looking at that same banner every fall, year after year, for the entirety of her twenty-eight years on earth. She'd only aggressively despised it for the past decade.

Still, when Jenna first pulled up to Bluebonnet Physical Therapy & Rehab on that crisp October morning, she remained blissfully unaware that Homecoming was a mere seven days away. She'd been so wrapped up in her new status as a dog mom to the sweet and adorable Ginger that football season had barely registered in her consciousness. That alone made the small fortune she'd spend on girly, plush dog toys over the past two weeks more than worth it. Thus far, the little copper-and-white Cavalier King Charles spaniel was the proud owner of a whole slew of stuffed toys from mock doggy luxury brands like Chewnel, Sniffany & Co., and Chewy Vuitton. Jenna probably needed to stop shopping for the dog, but after what Ginger had been through, the little Cavalier deserved to be spoiled. At least that's what Jenna told herself yesterday when she'd plunked down a near-obscene amount of money on a set of polka dot Kate Spade dog bowls.

This morning, however, there was no ignoring the signs of impending homecoming season doom. As soon as Jenna entered the rehab facility lobby with Ginger prancing alongside her in her Comfort Paws therapy-dog-in-training vest, her gaze snagged on a massive vase of chrysanthemums decorated with a profusion of blue and yellow ribbons sitting smack in the middle of the front desk. The floral arrangement was so large that the receptionist had to bob her head sideways to see around it. Even then, she was forced to bat away one of the miniature plastic footballs that protruded from the vase on a bouncy spring, like sports-themed antennae.

"Jenna!" Denise beamed at her as she flew to her feet. "We're all so excited about Ginger's pet therapy visit today."

"Great," Jenna said, stomach turning as she took in the royal blue bunting decorated with shiny sequin footballs that hung over Denise's desk.

The staff at Bluebonnet Physical Therapy & Rehab was always happy to see Ginger, but the dog's presence had never prompted a spontaneous standing ovation before. Still, Jenna didn't think too much of it. She was too busy wondering how she could've forgotten about her least favorite week of the year.

"You're not going to believe who's here." Denise's eyes glittered as she spoke in a loud whisper. Then she mimed zipping her lips. "I'm not supposed to talk about it. But you'll see soon enough."

Jenna's gaze dropped to the silver and black 57 splashed across the front of the football jersey Denise was wearing. *No*, she thought. *Surely not.*

Bile rose to the back of her throat.

Impossible.

Nearly everyone in town had a jersey just like it. As far as fashion statements went during Homecoming Week, a Houston Rattlers jersey was second only to Bluebonnet Bulldogs gear in terms of popularity. Jenna wouldn't have been caught dead in one, but to each his own.

This isn't about you. Or football. It's about your dog.

Jenna took a deep breath and refocused her thoughts. At dog training class, she'd learned that emotions traveled straight down the leash, from handler to pup. The last thing she wanted was to make Ginger nervous.

"We're happy to be here." Jenna swallowed. "As always."

Everything was going to be fine. Ginger's therapy dog certification test was in seven short days. Practice like this—at an actual medical office—was invaluable to their training. Like most Cavaliers, love and affection came naturally to Ginger, despite her background. Since she was a rescue, no one could be sure what her life had been like before she'd turned up on the front steps of Bluebonnet Pet Clinic late one summer night a few months ago. But the poor thing had been malnourished, pregnant, and in distress, so wherever she'd come from hadn't been a good place.

Despite it all, Ginger was now happy, well-adjusted, and eager to please. She *adored* socializing and was friendly to everyone she met. Jenna just knew she'd make a perfect therapy dog, but the pup's confidence was still a bit shaky. She needed this.

They needed this.

"Dr. Nick is expecting you." Denise darted from her desk to the door separating the lobby from the rest of the rehab office. "He's in the gym with a client. I'll walk you guys back there."

Weird. Jenna knew how to find the gym. This was her fourth practice visit at the office with Ginger. Plus, Jenna herself had been a patient here, once upon a time. But before she could say so, Denise was walking alongside Jenna and the dog, buzzing with excitement.

Something was definitely up. Jenna tried to tell herself that even in the highly unlikely event there was a famous athlete getting physical therapy right here in Bluebonnet—even if, horror of horrors, said athlete was a football player—it didn't mean her worst nightmare was about to come true. Why would *he* come home, after all this time?

Maybe because that's the very definition of homecoming.

As if Cam Colden cared a lick about what, or who, he'd left behind. Jenna would've bet the deed to the dance studio she owned just off town square *and* her entire handbag collection that he hadn't given Bluebonnet a second thought in years. He probably wouldn't be able to find the town on a map anymore without using the GPS in one of his fleet of sports cars.

Not that Jenna in any way kept track of the man. But when ESPN had done a special on his car collection and his River Oaks mansion, the show had been the talk of the town. Plus, it was just kind of hard to avoid seeing his face every year during football season when it was plastered all over the television. And the front page of the *Bluebonnet Gazette*. And the cereal boxes at Luke's Grocery.

Good grief, Jenna really, *really*, hated football season.

She'd get through it, though. She always did. This year, with Ginger by her side, it would be easier than ever.

Jenna glanced down at the pup. Her huge, melting eyes were trained on Jenna, just like they always were. Ginger always looked at her like she was the dog's everything. The stars, the moon, the sun. It never failed to put a lump in her throat.

Her focus was still on the dog as they entered the physical therapy gym and Dr. Nick greeted her with a smile in his voice.

"Jenna and Ginger, hi! We have an extra special guest today, and I'm sure he could use a dose of canine medicine."

"That's exactly why we're here," Jenna said, feeling more like herself after the brief eye contact with her dog. In her Comfort Paws training class, she'd learned that merely looking at a cute animal could lower anxiety, relieve stress and enhance a person's mood.

Mission accomplished, she thought as she swept her gaze away from Ginger, toward Dr. Nick and his mystery patient.

And just like that, the delicious boost in oxytocin and serotonin she'd gotten from a tiny bit of eye contact with the sweetest dog in the world vanished before it even fully hit her bloodstream.

There he was: Cam Colden in the flesh, looking just as yummy as he did on a box of breakfast cereal. Jenna had always assumed those glossy photos must be photoshopped. Apparently not.

He was big—six-foot-five at least, with a chiseled build that could've only come from years of being one of the country's highest-paid professional athletes. Jenna's face went warm when she realized he was shirtless. Worse yet, she was *staring*, and she'd only vaguely taken notice of the physical therapy tape wrapped in a complicated pattern around his right shoulder. But goodness gracious, no wonder that man's body was insured for millions of dollars. *If* the tabloid cover stories were to be trusted, that is. At such close range, Jenna was inclined to believe it.

But once she managed to drag her gaze away from his touchdown-throwing biceps and forced herself to look him in the eyes, she caught a glimpse of a deeper, more unsettling truth.

It was all still there—the same crooked smile, the same dimples beneath the layer of scruff on his face, the same sparkle in his sea-green eyes. The same boy who'd stood alongside her on that grassy field when the crown had been placed on her head and the sash strung over her shoulder.

They'd been the golden couple of Bluebonnet High— the ballerina and the quarterback. Homecoming queen and king. He'd been her first kiss, her first love, her first everything.

And then it had ended just as it started, with Jenna's feet on that same green turf, blinded by the stadium lights and her own sweet naïveté while the entire population of Bluebonnet looked on.

"Jenna." He smiled, as if all that pain, all that heartache was water under the bridge.

Maybe it should be…maybe it could be. The man had left Bluebonnet behind without a backward glance. He'd moved on, and so had she. She wasn't that trusting, starry-eyed girl anymore. She was a grown woman now. A hashtag #girlboss who ran her own business.

So why did she feel so small all of a sudden?

"You're back," she finally managed to say as Ginger moved to sit her bottom squarely on the toe of Jenna's ballerina flat.

He nodded. "I'm back."

At least he had the decency to stop smiling like the Bluebonnet Chamber of Commerce was about to throw him a homecoming parade.

Oh, no. Jenna tightened her grip on Ginger's leash. *There's going to be a parade, isn't there?*

Of course there would be. This changed everything. When word got around, the entire town would roll out the proverbial blue-and-gold carpet. People were going to lose their football-loving minds.

Cam Colden, America's favorite quarterback and Bluebonnet's golden boy, had finally come home.

Chapter Two

For a split second, Cam forgot about the pain in his shoulder as his eyes met Jenna's.

He'd known he'd see her eventually. Bluebonnet was a small town, and even if it hadn't been, Jenna had always been deeply involved in her community. It was one of the things Cam had always loved best about her. She genuinely cared about people, hence her very presence at his rehab appointment with a cute dog in tow. They'd have crossed paths eventually, even in a town that boasted more than a single stoplight.

Still, when the physical therapy doc had mentioned that the clinic had been working with a volunteer therapy dog team, Cam hadn't for a second guessed that the dog handler might be Jenna. She hadn't even had a pet back in high school. Not even a hamster.

Cam waved at the dog with his left hand. He didn't dare move his throwing arm while Dr. Nick was busy taping his injured shoulder. The pup responded with an enthusiastic full-body wiggle that made him laugh. Cam hadn't laughed much recently. This might've been the first time he'd cracked a smile since separating his shoulder in the game yesterday, but when he lifted his gaze to Jenna's again, he felt the easy grin die on his lips.

"Hello, Cam," she said coolly.

Never in his life had he set eyes on a woman who was so clearly unhappy to make his acquaintance. Ordinarily, it was the opposite. He had a substantial female fan base. Just this morning, a giddy mom in the frozen food aisle of Luke's Grocery had asked him to sign her baby's diaper.

"Oh, do you two know each other already?" The receptionist's eyes danced as she bounced on her toes and glanced back and forth between them.

"We do," Jenna said flatly before Cam could respond.

"Oh, that's right. I'd completely forgotten that you two…" Dr. Nick's voice trailed off, and the temperature in the gym seemed to drop ten degrees or so in the wake of Jenna's icy stare.

Cam reached for his shirt, wincing as he pulled it over his head.

"Are you okay, Cam? Do you need some help?" the receptionist gushed, ready and willing to lend a helping hand.

Jenna's gaze flicked toward his and she rolled her eyes so hard that Cam half expected them to roll straight out of her head and tumble down Main Street.

"Thanks, Denise. I'm fine."

Cam was not fine. Not even close, frankly.

Just after halftime at the Mile High stadium in Denver yesterday, he'd taken a hit at the thirty-yard line. He'd been off his form all day, and his team, the Houston Rattlers, were leading by a mere three points in what should've been a blow-out game. The instant he'd landed face down on the turf, he'd known something was wrong.

Still, he'd never expected to be placed on the injured reserve list. IR meant the coach expected him to be out for several weeks, not days. The team needed him out on the field. More important, Cam needed to get back out there. He couldn't remember the last time he'd had time on his hands during football season, and frankly, the idea didn't sit well. Now here he was, back in his hometown for the first time in years, being hailed as a hero by everyone except the one person whose opinion truly mattered.

"Denise, we've got everything under control here. You can go back to your desk." Dr. Nick nodded toward the lobby, and the receptionist retreated with a pout.

"Okay, well." Nick scrubbed the back of his neck as he shifted his attention awkwardly between them. "Jenna, the trainer for the Rattlers has diagnosed Cam with a separated shoulder. He's come home to Bluebonnet for the duration of his treatment and, based on my initial assessment, I agree with the diagnosis. What I haven't mentioned to Cam yet is that I purposely scheduled his appointment today to coincide with your regularly scheduled visit because I think you could be a real asset to his recovery."

"Um." Jenna's forehead scrunched like it always had back when she'd been trying to work out an algebra problem in Mrs. Matthew's class during senior year. The memory was as visceral as if it happened yesterday.

Cam's chest gave a pang nearly as painful as his shoulder.

"Right. Okay." She nodded, obviously stalling for time. "How can we help? Ginger loves to play fetch. Last week, we worked with a patient who was rehabbing a shoulder and the physical therapist had him toss a ball for Ginger for twenty minutes. Would something like that work?"

"Is that what therapy dogs do?" Cam asked, genuinely curious as he nodded toward the words *therapy-dog-in-training* on Ginger's working-dog vest. A heart-shaped patch with a logo for an organization called Comfort Paws was placed just above the embroidered text. "They help with a patient's exercise regimen?"

"Sometimes." Jenna nodded, and for the first time since she'd set eyes on him, her lips curved into a genuine smile. "Therapy dogs provide comfort, support and unconditional love to people in health care settings, schools and other kinds of facilities. Sometimes their role is as simple as curling up in a patient's lap and being petted, and other times, the dog is a more active participant in treatment. Ginger isn't an official therapy dog yet. Her certification exam is coming up soon."

The little dog wagged her tail as if she knew good and well that she was the topic of the conversation.

"She seems like a great dog," he said.

"She is. The best, really. Sweet as pie. Playful. Loving..." Jenna's eyes flashed. "Loyal."

Oof. That last adjective hit with a blunt force that rivaled the tackle that had put Cam on the injured reserve list. He just wasn't sure why...

He'd never knowingly done anything to hurt Jenna, and he hadn't so much as looked at another girl when they were together during their school days. They'd been so young, though. Kids, basically. The likelihood that he'd accidentally done or said something stupid was high.

"Jenna," he started as the pang in his chest blossomed into a full-blown ache.

Dr. Nick cut him off. "Some ball tossing would be great, and we should definitely include that in Cam's sessions here at the rehab center, but I actually had something else in mind—some additional therapy that would take place outside the gym."

Jenna shook her head. "I don't understand."

Neither did Cam, but the mere thought of working together outside the gym had every last drop of color draining from Jenna's face.

"You're still teaching your *Ballet is for Everyone* class, yes?" Dr. Nick pressed on.

Jenna nodded. "Of course, but—"

The doctor turned toward Cam. "My grandmother benefited a lot from Jenna's class after her rotator cuff surgery last spring."

His *grandmother*? Was this a joke?

"Ballet?" Cam coughed. "You can't be serious."

"This isn't regular ballet. It's a special class designed to enhance upper body movement. If memory serves, Jenna offers a group class once a week, but I was hoping she'd agree to daily private lessons while you're here in town." Dr. Nick shot Jenna a questioning glance. "What do you say, Jenna? You know how much Bluebonnet loves our hometown hero here."

Cam sensed another eye roll coming on.

"I highly doubt Cam wants to take ballet lessons, even something like *Ballet is for Everyone*." Her eyes narrowed as she cut her gaze toward him. "You heard him just now."

Cam held up his hands. The simple movement sent a shot of pain from his shoulder all the way down to his elbow. "I didn't mean to offend anyone. The suggestion caught me off guard, that's all. If Nick thinks it might help, I'm all for it."

That's how desperate he was to get back on the field, not that he'd ever have a chance to put his money where his mouth was. Jenna would never go for it. That much was clear.

"I think it would be very beneficial to your recovery." The doctor's eyebrows rose. "Jenna? The entire town would owe you a debt of gratitude. We all want to see Cam back in action. I'm sure you do too."

"I'd love nothing more, actually. The sooner he's back in action, the better," she said stiffly. Translation: the sooner he was *gone*, the better. "But I have a lot on my plate right now. I only have a week to get Ginger ready for her certification test."

Cam knew an excuse when he heard one, and he wasn't going to pretend otherwise. "Your dog seems perfectly well-behaved to me already."

Ginger wagged her feathery tail, accepting Cam's compliment with grace. Her ballerina mistress, on the other hand, glared at him as if he'd just kicked a whole litter of puppies.

"There's more to a therapy dog certification exam than simply being well-behaved."

"Such as?" Cam prompted. He wasn't going to let her off the hook that easily. If she didn't want to teach him how to flutter around like a swan, so be it. He'd find another, more conventional way to heal. But not until he found out why Jenna seemed to despise him so much.

They'd been so close back in high school. There'd even been a moment when he'd considered turning down his football scholarship to the University of Texas to stay here in Bluebonnet.

For *her*.

His father never would've let that happen, though. And that was a good thing, because as soon as he'd moved away, everything had changed. If anyone had a right to be angry about the past, it was Cam. But all of that was ancient history. And even back then, when Jenna had moved on with someone else, all Cam wanted was for her to be happy.

Even when it had hurt like hell.

"A therapy dog needs to know basic obedience, as well as show an interest in interacting with strangers," Jenna said just as Ginger left her side to scurry toward Cam, wiggling with excitement.

He couldn't have scripted the moment better if he'd tried.

"Well, aren't you just a sweetheart?" Cam bent to pet the dog and she sat politely at his feet, leaning into his touch while she closed her eyes, clearly basking in the attention. "I think she's got the 'willingness to interact with strangers' part down pat."

He arched a single eyebrow at Jenna. "Unless it's just me that she likes?"

The color came rushing back to her face in the form of a furious blush. "Hardly."

Cam got the definite feeling that if Nick hadn't been present and watching their interaction with obvious interest, she would've said more. Probably something along the lines of *don't flatter yourself.*

Instead, she took a tense breath and squared her shoulders. "Ginger's biggest challenge is working on her confidence. During the exam, she'll have to perform a sit-and-stay exercise while I leave the room for a full minute. So far, she hasn't been able to hold a sit-stay for longer than three seconds."

"I suppose I could help you practice," Cam said.

"It's not just her stay that we're working on. She also needs to work on her confidence around medical equipment. Ginger is a rescue dog and hasn't been exposed to the world in the same way other dogs have. That's the entire reason we've been coming here to the rehab clinic."

"Jenna was a patient here years ago. When we heard she needed a place for Ginger to practice interacting with patients and staff, we were eager to help." Nick turned a knowing smile on her. "I'm sure she's happy to return the favor, pay it forward, and work with you on your rehabilitation."

Cam wouldn't bet on it.

Except Jenna wasn't the sort of person to say no…to anybody. During senior year, she'd been dubbed Miss Bluebonnet in the yearbook because of her unwavering love for their town. She'd racked up more volunteer hours than all the other students in their civics class combined. The very fact that she was training to volunteer as a therapy dog handler told him she was still the same generous girl she'd always been, albeit with a frostier exterior.

Besides, the frostiness was solely for his benefit. That much went without saying.

"Cam, didn't you mention you're going to County General Hospital later today to visit the children's ward?"

Cam nodded before he had a chance to fully realize what the doctor had in mind.

"Do you think they'd be amenable to bringing Jenna and Ginger along with you?" Nick slipped a cell phone from the pocket of his white coat. "I have some contacts there. I could give someone a call if you two would like."

"Wait." Jenna's eyes went wide. "So now you're suggesting that Cam and I do ballet training *and* go on hospital visits together?"

"You just said that Ginger could use more practice in medical environments before her therapy dog test. Doesn't the certification exam include role-playing with pretend patients? At County General she'd get plenty of real-life experience." Nick bent to give Ginger a gentle scratch under her chin. The Cavalier's mouth spread into a doggy grin. "And like I said, your *Ballet is for Everyone* curriculum would be a significant help with Cam's recovery."

The doctor was proposing a trade. Whether Jenna was willing to admit it or not, it was a good one. Even Cam could see it.

"Take a minute to think about it, if necessary." Nick stood. He raised his brows, held up his phone and aimed a meaningful glance at both of them. "I'm happy to make the call to County General. This seems like a uniquely workable solution. All things considered, it sounds like you two need each other."

He was right, and Cam knew it. Still, when his eyes shifted toward Jenna, she seemed anything but convinced.

He crossed his arms. "I'm in if you are."

It came out sounding more like a challenge than he'd intended. But for better or worse, it was out there.

All she had to do was say yes.

Chapter Three

Why on earth did I say yes to this?

Jenna held Ginger close to her chest while she watched Cam and a little girl with plaster casts on both of her legs play catch with a foam football. The scene was about as heartwarming as a greeting card commercial—the kind that made you cry ugly tears and reevaluate all your life choices. Except Jenna was perfectly fine with her life choices, thank you very much. This wasn't the real Cam Colden, anyway. At least Jenna didn't think it was…

It was awfully convincing, though.

Ginger let out a soft sigh in Jenna's arms, as if Cam had charmed the dog the same way he'd charmed every man, woman, and child they'd come across since they'd arrived at the hospital. By all appearances, Jenna was the only holdout. And her resistance was wavering, ever so slightly.

She was only human, after all. Who wouldn't go all gooey inside at the sight of a big, strong, world-famous athlete interacting with sick children like it came as naturally to him as breathing?

"He's so great with the kids, isn't he?" Nurse Pam, the hospital employee who was accompanying them as they moved from room to room, said in a whisper. "I mean, I'd heard he was pretty amazing, but I didn't expect all this."

She waved at a wheeled cart loaded down with signed jerseys, foam footballs, blankets, and heaps of other items emblazoned with Cam's number and the Rattler's team logo. There were even bandanas for the kids undergoing chemo to use as headscarves. Cam's first order of business when he'd unloaded the boxes of goodies from the trunk of his car had been to tie one of the bandanas around Ginger's neck.

The Cavalier, traitor that she was, had squirmed with delight—so much so that Jenna was seriously rethinking her grand speech about dogs being loyal.

"I think your dog is a fan," Cam had said with a wink.

Jenna had wanted to die right there on the spot.

"Does Cam do this sort of thing often?" Jenna asked the nurse. He must, seeing as he traveled with a trunk full of Rattlers gear and news of his empathy and compassion for children had reached Nurse Pam even before he'd rolled back into town.

"Oh, yes. Haven't you heard of his foundation?" Nurse Pam gave her a little shoulder bump. "He visits children's hospitals and hospice centers in Houston and also organizes events during the holidays and brings other teammates along."

Jenna's heart gave a rebellious tug. "That's really something."

"Beneath the football pads and the Rattlers jersey, he's a really special person," Nurse Pam said.

Jenna wanted to disagree, but how could she?

"I caught it!" The little girl with the casts on her legs

beamed as she clutched the football, head resting against the pillows of her hospital bed.

Like every other child they'd visited, she hadn't missed a single catch. The way Cam could aim the ball straight into the hands of each patient was uncanny and more than a little adorable. Jenna tried to tell herself that throwing a football with pinpoint accuracy was his literal job. He was a professional quarterback. There was no reason to get emotional about it. Somehow, though, seeing him toss a ball to a kid in a hospital gown was a lot more swoonworthy than watching him in action on television.

"Touchdown!" Cam threw his arms up when the young patient caught the ball again.

She let loose with a stream of giggles and Ginger whimpered. If Jenna didn't get out of there, she was in danger of whimpering herself.

"Would you like to meet my friend, Ginger?" Cam pointed the toy football toward Jenna as she stood off to the side holding the Cavalier.

The child's smile dimmed slightly as she regarded the two of them. "Does she bite?"

Cam answered without hesitation. "Not at all. That dog is a total marshmallow. She's as squishy as this football."

He threw the ball again, and Ginger's ears perked up as she tracked it while it sailed through the air.

"Why don't you try throwing it for her? I'll bet she'll bring it back to you." Cam waggled his eyebrows at the little girl.

Her eyes went wide. "Really?"

"Really," Jenna said as she placed Ginger on the floor. "Go ahead and give it a toss."

"If she brings it back, it means she really likes you." Cam grinned at the child.

Her cheeks went pink. "Go get it, doggy."

She gave the ball a wobbly toss, and it bounced across the slick tile floor.

Ginger scrambled after it, chasing the ball into the corner of the room. As soon as she snatched it in her jaws, she trotted toward the bed, tail wagging. Then she dropped the toy beneath the bedrails and gazed up the child with an expectant gleam in her eyes.

"She fetched it! She likes me!" The little girl's eyes danced. "Can I pet her now?"

"Of course you can. Ginger loves to be petted." Jenna scooped the dog up and held her while the girl ran her fingertips gently over Ginger's soft fur. Her movements were unsure at first, but the last of her hesitation seemed to melt away when Ginger licked her hand. "Look at that, she gave you a puppy kiss. Would you like me to put her beside you on the edge of the bed? She really likes to snuggle."

The girl nodded. "Yes, please. I like to snuggle too."

Ginger settled into a contented ball next to the young patient and stayed that way for several long minutes while the girl lavished attention on her, and Jenna's heart swelled. This was perfect—just the type of practice that she and Ginger needed.

Cam's gaze met hers from where he stood on the opposite side of the bed, and for a minute, it hurt so hard to look at him that Jenna forgot how to breathe. So much shared history glittered in those lovely green eyes of his. Jenna had put great effort into forgetting the good times they'd shared, but there they were, staring right back at her, daring her to remember. Weekends at the town animal shelter volunteering as puppy bathers. The way he'd always come to her dance recitals bearing a huge bouquet of blush-pink roses sprinkled with baby's breath. The day he'd earned his team letter jacket and slipped it over her shoulders later that night at the homecoming bonfire.

She'd sat beside him in the bleachers with a cup of hot cocoa warming her hands, thinking she was the luckiest girl in the whole state of Texas.

Now here we are again, building more good memories together, without even trying.

Jenna purposefully aimed her attention back toward the patient, but she could still feel his tender gaze on her long after she'd looked away.

Chapter Four

Later that night at book club, Jenna picked at a slice of warm, homemade pie with her fork and then put the utensil down without taking a bite. "I think I'm in trouble."

Her friends Adaline, Maple, and Belle all looked up, mouths full.

They usually met at Adaline's house for book club, but since early summer when Ginger's puppies had been born, they'd begun gathering at Maple's charming pink house near the center of town. Her kitchen was already equipped with a puppy pen, so Belle and Adaline, who'd each adopted one of the pups, had brought Peaches and Fuzz along so they could play. Lady Bird and Ginger watched from the sidelines, curled together on a fluffy plaid dog bed.

Maple's house was also the temporary new headquarters of Comfort Paws, their fledgling new therapy dog organization. But they were all on the hunt for somewhere bigger and better to hold training classes for new therapy dog prospects. They all had big plans for Comfort Paws, but since the puppies weren't quite old enough to train as therapy pets, Ginger was next in line to get certified.

Jenna could've waited until the group was ready to

host its own training program and evaluation process, but she wanted to get started with pet therapy work sooner, if she could. The therapy dog certification exam Ginger was scheduled to take was put on by a national therapy dog group. She'd have to drive all the way to Austin for the exam. It had seemed like a great idea at first, but the closer Jenna got to the big date, the more intimidating the prospect seemed. She wouldn't know a soul at that exam. She really didn't want to let her friends down, but at the moment, dog training was the last thing on her mind.

"Is there something wrong with the bluebonnet cream pie?" Adaline, who owned the Cherry on Top bakery on Main Street and always experimented with new recipes on book club nights, frowned down at her plate. "You know it's not really made from bluebonnets, right? Bluebonnets aren't edible. This is mostly creamed custard with a dash of crushed blueberries for color. The crystallized petals on top are from violet blossoms. Totally safe to eat. I'm just calling it bluebonnet cream pie because I'm experimenting with recipes for the Bluebonnet Festival next spring."

"There's a Bluebonnet Festival?" Maple, who'd only recently moved to town after inheriting her birth father's veterinary practice—along with his golden retriever Lady Bird, Bluebonnet's first therapy dog and the inspiration for Comfort Paws—tilted her head and scanned the group with her gaze.

"It's a whole thing." Belle, Bluebonnet Elementary School's librarian and proud new dog-mom to one of Ginger's puppies, shrugged. "Prepare yourself for bluebonnet soap, bluebonnet candles, bluebonnet tea…"

"Bluebonnet nail art," Adaline added with a flutter of her fingertips.

"Bluebonnet bubble bath." Belle ticked off another item. "The list goes on."

"But none of those things are actually made with real bluebonnets?" Maple's forehead creased. "Because they're toxic."

Adaline nodded. "Correct."

"Everything is simply bluebonnet-*inspired*," Belle clarified.

"Because it's also illegal to pick bluebonnets in Texas, since they're the state flower." Adaline took a sip of coffee from a mug that boasted the Cherry on Top logo.

Belle rolled her eyes. "*Not* true. How many times do I have to tell you that's just an urban legend?"

Adaline snorted. "Tell that to Cam Colden. Didn't he spend a night in our silly excuse for a town jail after he picked Jenna a whole bouquet of them during sophomore year?"

"I will never understand this town. Or this state, for that matter." Maple laughed and shook her head.

"Oh, please. You love it here. You're one of us now." Jenna sat back and crossed her arms. "And for the record, it was junior year. Not sophomore."

Then, without any warning whatsoever, she burst into tears.

The three other women froze. Lady Bird abandoned her spot by the exercise pen where Peaches and Fuzz, Ginger's puppies, were engaged in a boisterous round of puppy-tumbling and trotted over to plant her head in Jenna's lap. Ginger pranced on the golden retriever's heels and pawed at Jenna's shins when she reached the table.

Great, she'd even alarmed the dogs with her outburst.

"Hon, are you okay?" Adaline reached to give Jenna's hand a squeeze. "What am I saying? Of course you aren't. Something has upset you, and it's obviously more serious than pie."

"Whatever it is, it's going to be okay. We're here for you." Maple offered Jenna a paper napkin. "This isn't about Ginger's certification exam, is it? It's okay if she's still having trouble with her sit-stay. If she doesn't pass the first time, you can always test again."

That seemed likely, given that her new training partner was Cam Colden, of all people. The man didn't know the meaning of the word *stay*.

Jenna took the napkin Maple offered her and pressed it against her closed eyes. *Get a grip on yourself. You've cried enough tears over Cam for one lifetime.*

"I said I might be in trouble, but scratch that. I'm definitely in trouble." She sniffed and scooped Ginger up to sit in her lap, then pushed her plate away, out of reach of the dog's twitching nose. "He's back."

"Oh, no." Belle's eyes went wide.

Maple frowned. "Who's back?"

Adaline shook her head. "Not the bluebonnet thief himself. Not after all this time. No way."

"Yes way. Cam Colden is right here in Bluebonnet. Ginger and I just spent the entire afternoon with him, visiting sick children at County General Hospital." Jenna stroked Ginger's soft ears, a move that usually brought her endless comfort when she'd had a tough day. Still, her stomach roiled.

Had today actually happened? It felt so surreal now, almost like a fever dream.

"Why does that name sound so familiar?" Maple set her fork down on the table. No one was in the mood for pie or book talk anymore, apparently.

Jenna blamed Cam. Did the man have to ruin *everything*?

"Because he's the star quarterback for the Houston Rattlers. You've probably seen his commercials for Calvin Klein underwear. They're kind of hard to miss," Belle said with a raise of her eyebrows.

"Oh, *that* guy." Maple toyed with the engagement ring on her left hand. No doubt she could appreciate an advertisement for designer boxers featuring a manly, chiseled professional football player, but everyone knew she only had eyes for her fiancé, Adaline's brother, Ford. "He's from right here in Bluebonnet?"

"Mm-hmm." Belle nodded. "He and Jenna were high school sweethearts, until…"

Her voice drifted off as her gaze sifted toward Jenna.

Maple waved her hands. "Never mind. We don't have to talk about it, Jenna. You're obviously upset."

"No, it's okay. Really." Jenna swallowed. She never spoke about what happened the fall after they'd graduated. She tried her best to never even think about it. But she wanted to tell the story now…*needed* to tell it. If only to remind herself why she didn't have any business falling for his Mr. Nice Guy act again.

"We started dating sophomore year after we got assigned lockers right next to each other. I was the shy ballerina, and he was the big man on campus, even in tenth grade. He'd been the starting quarterback right off the bat as a freshman. A phenom, they called him."

"His dad certainly called him that," Adaline said. "God rest his soul."

"True. His father was one of those really obnoxious sports parents, but he was right. There was just something special about Cam. He wasn't just talented. He was kind and smart and thoughtful. The teachers all loved him. And from the second he turned all that star power on me, I was a goner." Jenna's throat went thick. She'd been so open back then, so trusting. It was hard to believe she was still that same person.

"He was equally as besotted with you as you were with him, though. Once, at one of your ballet performances, I looked over at him and he had tears in his eyes while he watched you dance." Adaline shook her head. "I just couldn't believe it when things went sideways."

"How did it end?" Maple asked quietly. Lady Bird shifted to lean against her legs and the big gold dog sighed.

"When we were seniors, we were crowned homecoming queen and king. That whole year was a whirlwind. College recruiters came to all of Cam's games, and I was busy auditioning for apprentice positions at various ballet companies. After graduation, Cam left to go to school in Austin, and I signed on to dance in the *corps de ballet* with a dance company in Fort Worth. We promised each other we'd come back to Bluebonnet for homecoming. It's school tradition for the prior year's king and queen to come back and pass down the honor to the new homecoming court. There's a big ceremony during halftime, right on the fifty-yard line."

"It's always a huge deal, but that year was like no other. The whole town couldn't wait to see Jenna and

Cam together again. They were like the king and queen of Bluebonnet, not just the high school," Belle said.

"I didn't care about all the pageantry, really. I just…" Jenna swallowed around the lump in her throat. "…*missed* him. I was so busy with dance that I hadn't been able to go to any of his college games. He had a lot going on too, obviously, so he'd missed seeing me dance *Swan Lake* for the first time. We barely had time to talk on the phone. None of that mattered, though. We both had homecoming weekend off, and we'd promised each other we'd be there. It was never any question, really."

She'd been living for that weekend. Ballet hadn't been going well. Her left ankle had been giving her trouble, and she'd been too afraid of losing her coveted position at a professional dance company to say anything about it or seek treatment from the company trainer. She just danced through the pain, again and again, pinning all her hopes on a weekend away from it all. Homecoming would fix everything. All she needed was to go home— home to Bluebonnet, home to the boy she loved with her whole heart.

"He didn't show, did he?" Maple winced.

Jenna shook her head. "No. He had practice in Austin the day of the game, so I knew I wouldn't see him until later that night. When he wasn't at the high school stadium for kickoff, I figured he was simply running late. As halftime crept closer, I got distracted helping the dance team get ready for their halftime performance. Cam had never broken his word before. *Ever.* I knew he had to be around that stadium somewhere. I even started to think it would be romantic for us to wait and see each other again for the first time out on the field, wearing those stupid homecoming crowns."

She took a deep breath. Revisiting this story wasn't as humiliating as she'd expected. Now, more than anything, it just made her sad.

She'd spent a good long time heartbroken over the crushing end of her first love, but she'd never really grieved the loss of the old Jenna. That autumn had been one aching loss piled right on top of another, and she'd never quite been the same.

"When the announcer called our names, I walked out onto the field, convinced he'd be there. I don't know what I was thinking. That he'd materialize out of thin air? Come rushing into the stadium at the last second?" Jenna shook her head. "I never gave up hope until I found myself standing under the glare of those Friday night lights with a crown on my head and all eyes on me and me alone. You could've heard a pin drop. I think everyone else in Bluebonnet was just as surprised as I was."

But they'd moved on. So had Cam. Which begged the question…

Why couldn't she?

"And you never heard from him again? He never called or came back to town?" Maple asked, incredulous.

"Not until today." Jenna forced a smile. Maybe if she pretended not to be in any way affected by his presence, it would eventually be the truth.

There was no fooling her best friends, however. Especially after she'd just sobbed at the mere mention of the bluebonnets he'd picked for her way back when.

She spent the next few minutes telling Adaline, Belle and Maple all about Dr. Nick's plan for Cam's recovery and their visit to County General. The only thing she left out was the part where her heart had just about beat right out of her chest while she'd watched him interact with the children. No one needed to know about that.

"Are you sure you're really up for all of this? Cam broke your heart. You are under no obligation whatsoever to teach him ballet or go on hospital visits with him." Adaline scowled. "I'm honestly kind of furious that Dr. Nick even asked."

"Of course he did. Cam is the best thing to ever come out of Bluebonnet. There's not a person in town who wouldn't bend over backward to help him get healthy again," Jenna said.

If she refused, everyone within a one-hundred-mile radius would know about it before the sun came up the next morning. That's how things worked in small towns. And once the greater population of the Texas Hill Country heard she didn't want a thing to do with Bluebonnet's homecoming hero, they'd all think she'd never gotten over him.

Jenna couldn't let happen. Not in a million years...

Even if it was the truth.

Chapter Five

The house where Cam had grown up near downtown Bluebonnet somehow felt exactly the same and completely different, both at the same time.

"You can sleep in your old bedroom for as long as you like. I got it all ready for you today, and there are fresh sheets on the bed." His sister Kelsey hitched a thumb toward the hallway off the living room. "The boys can share the bunk beds in Hunter's room while you're here."

Cam shook his head. His sister and her twin six-year-olds had moved into their childhood home last year after their father passed away and their mother subsequently left Bluebonnet to go live with their aunt in Florida. The house might look the same, but it belonged to Kelsey now, and he didn't want to get in the way. He certainly didn't want to force one of his nephews out of his own bed. "Not necessary. The couch is fine."

Cam dropped onto the sofa and stared at his dad's old recliner, pointed straight at the television in the same spot where it had sat for as long as he could remember. It was a wonder the paneled walls of the living room didn't echo with the sound of Martin Colden screaming at the flat screen the way he always had whenever a football game was on television.

"No." Kelsey shook her head. "Absolutely not. You can't sleep on the couch with a separated shoulder. You need rest. That's the entire reason you're here. I'm still surprised you wanted to stay at the house with us instead of staying someplace nicer. I love having you here, but are you sure you wouldn't be more comfortable at the B and B in town square? I'm almost positive the mattress in Hayden's room dates back to our elementary school years."

Cam was pretty certain it dated farther back than that, but he also wholeheartedly doubted the Bluebonnet B and B had the kind of Tempur-Pedic mattress his team doc recommended. Even if they did, Cam wouldn't have cared. He didn't want to stay in town square and have the staff fawn all over him twenty-four hours a day. He wanted to feel normal while he was in Bluebonnet. This was supposed to be his home.

Which was something dear old Dad never seemed to understand.

Cam's gut churned. He hadn't wanted to stay away, but every time he mentioned coming for a visit, his father urged him to stay in Houston.

It would be better for your conditioning to stay and work with the team trainers during the off-season, don't you think, son?

I hear that new gym at the Rattlers stadium is state-of-the-art. You owe it to your team and your fans to make use of it every single day.

Do you know how many people wish they were in your position? Make the most of it while you can. Life is short.

Year after year, it was always the same until Cam finally stopped trying. It was easier not to bring it up…easier to let his family come see him instead of the other way around. Those visits always involved football, though— box seats for home games or fancy hotel suites when the Rattlers were on the road. Martin Colden's favorite Christmas of all time didn't involve any heartfelt or cozy family memories. Instead, it was the holiday when Cam had played in the Armadillo bowl as a college sophomore on Christmas Day in freezing drizzle and sleet.

"I'd much rather stay here with you guys," he said. "But only if you and the boys don't mind."

"Are you kidding? They'll be bragging about it like crazy at school. You're staying in Hayden's room, case closed. Don't be surprised when you see the Rattlers bedspread and the posters of you all over the walls. Try not to let it go to your head." Kelsey threw a pillow at his face, but Cam caught it one-handed before it made contact. "The twins are in the bathroom right now, getting dressed for bed and brushing their teeth, but I'm pretty sure I heard the thud of a football hitting the wall just now. They've never been so excited in their lives."

"I could've come home sooner, you know." Cam's gaze flitted toward the recliner again.

His sister's smile went sad around the edges. "Come on, Cam. You know Dad loved you. He wasn't an easy man, but he loved you the best way he knew how. He wanted you to keep looking forward, not backward."

Cam took a ragged inhale. She was right, but at times, their father's particular brand of affection had felt more like hero worship than love.

No one had been more invested in Cam's sports career than his dad. He'd *lived* for football season for as far back as Cam could remember. Even when he'd played peewee football, his tiny shoulders sagging beneath the weight of his first set of pads, his father had attended every single game. Every single practice, even. And he always had a few choice words for the coach when he felt like Cam wasn't getting the right plays called to show off his talents.

Sometimes Cam marveled at the fact that his dad's overbearing involvement hadn't ruined his love for the game. Despite it all, he still loved what he did…still wanted to get his shoulder healed as quickly as possible so he could get his life back. But it had been such a long time since he'd been home.

Too long.

"I could've at least come home for the funeral," he said as evenly as he could. "I still regret that I didn't."

His sister gaped at him. "Are you crazy? That was playoff season. If you'd missed a single day of practice or, heaven forbid, an actual game for Dad's service, he would've turned straight over in his grave."

"Or come back to haunt me." Cam laughed a little under his breath.

"He would've haunted us both." Kelsey nodded toward the recliner. "As it is, I'm almost scared to get rid of that hideous thing. The minute I do, it will probably reappear out of nowhere on the next game day."

"He was a strong-willed man." Cam's jaw clenched. "To a fault."

His dad had been right about one thing, though—life was short. Cam couldn't go back and do things differently now that his father had passed and his mother had moved away. All those hometown holidays and missed birthdays in Bluebonnet were gone forever, and there was no getting them back. But he could change things going forward, and that's what this visit to Bluebonnet while he was on the injured reserve list was really about. Still, it was hard not to think about how different things could've been.

It had been all too easy to listen to his father once he'd lost Jenna. There'd been nothing left for him in Bluebonnet after that first semester of college...after she'd given up on them.

His chest ached every time he thought about the way she looked at him now—as if they'd never meant the world to each other when they were kids. As if he was a complete and total stranger. Or worse, her enemy.

There'd been a moment this afternoon at the hospital, though. A moment when their eyes had met, and she'd let her guard down. The tenderness in her gaze had been almost too much to bear. It had catapulted Cam straight back to the past, when everything had been simpler.

Happier...

His jaw clenched. What would his father think if he could hear his thoughts right now?

"I saw Jenna Walsh today," he said before he could stop himself.

"Oh." Kelsey's face went as white as a sheet. "Wow. That must have been..."

She looked away and her voice trailed off without finishing her thought.

It was just as well. What he and Jenna once had was water under the bridge. He didn't want to talk about the past with his sister. He didn't much want to *think* about it, but he couldn't stop.

He'd wanted to kiss Jenna this afternoon. The urge

had been almost overwhelming, and they'd been at a sick child's bedside. It didn't even make sense. What was *wrong* with him?

It was this injury, that's all. He just needed to get himself healed and he could go back to life as normal. Maybe he should've stayed and rehabbed his shoulder in Houston like the team doc suggested.

No, he'd needed to come home. He wanted to see his sister…wanted to build a real relationship with his twin six-year-old nephews. Kelsey was a single mom, and he wanted to be here for her and the boys. Now that Dad was gone, she'd finally been open to the idea.

"I thought you'd forgotten all about Jenna. Do you think you'll see her again while you're here?" Kelsey tucked a lock of dark hair behind her ear and nibbled on her bottom lip.

"Yes. Tomorrow morning, in fact. Dr. Nick seems to think ballet might help my injury."

"Ballet?" Kelsey's lips tipped into a smile. "That… unexpected."

You're telling me.

"I've got to try," he said. "For the team."

"You sure that's the only reason?" His sister arched a brow.

No, not at all.

Cam dropped his gaze to his interlocked hands. He hadn't been sure of anything since he'd seen the devastated expression on Jenna's face when she first saw him.

Something wasn't right. Cam had no idea what, but he could feel it.

"Listen," Kelsey said, casting a sidelong glance at their father's empty recliner. "I should probably tell you—"

But before she could finish her thought, Hunter and Hayden burst into the living room from the hall, running toward Cam at full speed.

"Uncle Cam! Mom said we could have a bedtime story. Will you read it to us?" Hayden took a flying leap at his lap.

Cam braced for impact as his other nephew tugged at his good arm. "Pleeeeeease, Uncle Cam!"

"Boys," Kelsey said, sounding eerily like their dearly departed father. "Be careful of Uncle Cam's arm. He's not a plaything. He's a world-class athlete."

"It's fine." Cam scooped one twin onto his good shoulder while the other one tried to climb his leg like a tree. "Of course I'll read you guys a bedtime story. Let's do it."

Kelsey crossed her arms. "Please don't hurt yourself any worse than you already are."

"Relax, sis." He flashed her a grin.

Some things never changed, even while others were so easily lost to time and distance. Things like first loves and whispered promises. Things that Cam had once held so dear that he still ached at the memory of letting them go. Things he still wanted even to this day, despite the impossibilities of it all.

You can never go home again.

That old adage had been around forever, and maybe there was some truth to it. Cam's father had certainly thought so.

But this was autumn in Bluebonnet, and if Texas believed in anything this time of year, it was homecoming. Despite it all, a flicker of hope stirred deep inside Cam's chest and he wondered if he just might believe in it too.

Chapter Six

Jenna glanced around her dance studio the next morning, wondering what it might look like through Cam's eyes.

Her pre-ballet class for toddlers had just ended, and he was due to meet her here in just under half an hour. She'd been jittery all morning, anticipating their first lesson.

Why does he have to come here, of all places? She tightened the bow on her chiffon wrap-around ballet skirt, a nervous habit since her early days of dance training, way before she'd slipped on her first pair of pink satin pointe shoes.

She should've insisted on doing Cam's ballet exercises at the physical therapy office. The high school gym, maybe. Anywhere but here.

Bluebonnet Ballet School had been Jenna's safe space since she'd first opened its doors to students eight years ago. On the heels of the horrible homecoming episode, she'd returned to the dance company in Fort Worth, but her heart hadn't been in it. She wasn't able to dance through the pain in her ankle anymore. Trying to fake having her life together when she was falling apart at the seams both physically and emotionally was just too much. Days after returning to rehearsals, she tumbled on the landing of a triple pirouette.

Again, Miss Walsh, the ballet master had said.

So Jenna had hopped back up and launched herself into another turn on the tip of her pointe shoe while her ankle seemed to ache and throb in time with her broken heart. When she fell out of her pirouette a second time, the stumble was accompanied by the unmistakable sound of bone against bone as the undiagnosed stress fracture in her ankle gave up the fight.

She returned to Bluebonnet the following day with an orthopedic boot on her foot, broken in both body and spirit. In a way, it had been a relief. She'd been free to start her entire life over from scratch, and after she'd finished long months of treatment at Bluebonnet Physical Therapy & Rehab, Jenna rebuilt herself anew.

Stronger than before, just like a bone after it mended.

Except that oft-repeated saying wasn't actually true. Bones weren't any stronger after they healed from a break, especially for a dancer. Jenna's career as a professional ballerina had ended as abruptly as her reign as homecoming queen.

But that was okay. She'd wanted to brush off everything about her past. She'd wanted to do whatever it took to make herself invincible. Opening her own dance school meant long-term security. She could *teach* dance forever. And if she opened a school in Bluebonnet, she could carve out a place for herself in the town she loved that would always be untouched by Cam Colden. It would be the one place in Bluebonnet where they'd never shared a single memory. Not a hug, not a kiss. Not even so much as a tender glance.

The studio would be hers and hers alone. That had been the plan, anyway. And it had worked…

Until today.

"Hey, there." Cam strode inside the dance school dressed for exercise in a pair of slim fit track pants and a shirt that seemed to hug every muscle of his lean physique. Despite the duffel bag in his left hand that could've easily doubled as a dance bag, he looked woefully out of place.

He was just so *big. Did the room just shrink by three sizes, or is it only my imagination?*

Jenna took a shaky inhale and reminded herself that he was only a man and this was simply a private lesson, like any other.

Still, the effect of his image being reflected back at her in the floor-to-ceiling mirrors was more than a little overwhelming. He was everywhere. There wasn't a single safe place to look.

"You're early," she said, picking an invisible speck of lint from her black leotard while she took a deep breath and tried to calm the frantic boom of her pulse.

Stage fright. That's what this sickening sensation felt like. She had all the classic symptoms. Sweaty palms, racing heart…the way her mouth had just gone so dry that she couldn't seem to swallow.

Get a grip on yourself. You're about to show a football player how to do some simple arm movements, not dance the lead in The Nutcracker *at Lincoln Center.*

"Are you okay?" Cam lowered his aviator sunglasses and regarded her through narrowed eyes.

Why did people keep asking her that question? "I'm perfectly fine. You're just…"

The first boy I ever loved. The only *boy.*

She cleared her throat, still as dry as sandpaper. "…early."

"So you said." He slid his sunglasses off, folded them with care and zipped them into the side pocket of his duffel bag. "I like to be prompt when I have an appointment, particularly when someone is going out of their way to try and help me."

Jenna was dying to remind him about the time he'd failed to show up altogether, but she refrained. Doing so would only make him think she still wasn't over him, and she totally was.

But did he have to seem so utterly appealing, with his charitable good deeds and his adorable way with children? Now she could add punctuality and good manners to the list, too. Being over him was getting harder by the minute.

Cam dropped his duffel, and it hit the smooth wooden floor of the dance studio with a thud, snapping Jenna back to reality.

You loathe him, remember?

"Does it matter where I stand?" Cam nodded toward the ballet barre where a row of toddlers in fluffy pink tutus had positioned themselves less than an hour ago.

"No standing. We're going to be focusing solely on your upper body today." She pointed at a chair situated in the center of the room, facing the front mirror.

"Oh." Cam's brows rose a fraction as he strode to take a seat. He really had no idea what was coming, did he?

"Dr. Nick mentioned my *Ballet is for Everyone* curriculum, but I'm guessing he didn't tell you anything about it?"

Cam shook his head.

"It's a class I developed for the residents at the senior center so older adults and people with mobility issues can still enjoy ballet." Jenna met so many people who told her how much they loved watching classical dance but either gave up on lessons when they were children or never had the chance to study ballet themselves. Developing a class based on the idea that ballet could truly be for everyone had been one of her primary goals when she'd decided to open her own dance academy. "I teach group classes on-site at the senior center three times a week. Dr. Nick's grandmother is one of my students."

"Wow. That's amazing, Jen." Cam sat down, stretched his long legs out in front of him and glanced around the studio. "And now you're getting involved with pet therapy work."

Jenna's first instinct was to insist that they didn't have time for chitchat. The sooner they got started, the sooner this would be over and done with. But she'd just pointed out his early arrival. *Twice.* Pretending they were pressed for time wasn't going to work.

Besides, she liked talking about Ginger. Most of the time, Jenna couldn't shut up about her dog. "Someone abandoned her at the pet clinic in the middle of the night, and she nearly died."

Jenna went on to tell him about Ginger's puppies and the idea behind Comfort Paws.

"Training a puppy for pet therapy probably would've been easier, but I'm not surprised in the slightest that you wanted to adopt Ginger instead. She's a sweetheart." The corners of his mouth turned up. "And if memory serves, you've always had a heart for underdogs."

"I don't know what you're talking about," she countered, hating the way he still seemed to remember everything about her. Jenna assumed Cam hadn't given her a second thought in years.

"Come on, now. Volunteering at the animal shelter together was all you. I was just along for the ride."

"Says the man who heads up an entire charity devoted to sick children," Jenna said before she could stop herself. "You've always downplayed your softer side, but it's still there."

A silence fell between them, thick with things unsaid. There was still so much Jenna didn't understand, so many things she longed to ask him.

But she was afraid of the answers.

"I always loved the way you saw me. Sometimes it felt like you were the only one who really knew me," he finally said. Then he let out a laugh, but his easy smile no longer reached his eyes. "Did you know my dad once accused me of throwing a game just so you'd feel sorry for me and make those brownies you gave me the time we lost the playoff game junior year?"

Ouch. Jenna knew that Martin Colden had an overbearing streak, especially where sports were concerned, but Cam had never liked talking about it. "I was really sorry to hear about your dad's heart attack."

Cam nodded and said a quiet thank you.

"Also, I didn't actually bake those brownies. Adaline did," she confessed.

"I know. I knew all along." His eyes sparkled. "I could always see you too, you know."

Jenna's knees turned to water. Over the course of their conversation, she'd lost the shaky stage fright feeling without even realizing it. She wished it would come back. Nerves, she could deal with. This heady nostalgia, not so much.

"We were talking about Ginger," she said. A weak attempt at steering the conversation back to safer ground.

"That's right." Cam glanced around the studio. "Where is your little candy striper, anyway?"

"She's sound asleep in my office." Jenna nodded to-ward the open door at the far corner of the room where Ginger was just visible in the attached closet-sized of-fice, snoozing on her pink pouf of a dog bed. "I let her greet my pre-ballet students before class earlier, and then they had a little petting time with her before they left. I think the toddlers wore her out."

His gaze flitted to the ballet barre. "How long have you been teaching?"

"I opened the dance school eight years ago, but I started teaching *Ballet is for Everyone* about a year prior." It felt weird updating him about the past decade of her life when he used to be the first person she wanted to share her hopes and dreams with. "I broke my ankle during my first year in Fort Worth and had to move back to Bluebonnet. I got the idea for an adaptive ballet curriculum while I was rehabbing my injury. By the time I was healed, I'd already studied the traditional arm movements from ten different classical ballet pieces and choreographed enough mate-rial for a six-week modified class for adults with mobility challenges. I taught the program at various assisted-living facilities all over the state, mostly to students in wheel-chairs, until I'd saved enough to open the dance school."

"I shouldn't be surprised. I always knew you'd end up changing the world for the better." Cam smiled, but the softness in his eyes was bittersweet. "I'm sorry you were hurt, though."

It wasn't the apology she'd dreamed about all those years ago, but it still made her want to cry. She didn't even understand why. They were talking about her foot, not her heart.

Weren't they?

His eyes never left hers as he stood and took two tentative steps toward her. When she backed away after the second one, he flexed his hands at his sides, like he was waging a war with some invisible force reminding him of all the reasons why he wasn't supposed to touch her.

Heaven help her if he did.

"Jenna," he said, voice breaking on the last syllable.

Something inside her broke too, and Jenna could only shake her head. She'd thought every last part of her had already been broken a long, long time ago. She was supposed to be invincible now.

Cam's forehead creased. "I wish I'd been there for you."

He wasn't making any sense at all. He *could've* been there. If he regretted his actions on homecoming night, he should just come out and say it. Tiptoeing around the memories was only making being around him that much harder.

You had your chance, Cam Colden. There's nothing left for you here anymore.

"If I didn't know better, I'd think you were trying to put off actually doing any ballet," she said, but the words didn't come out as sharp as she'd intended. Her tone had gone breathy, and before she realized what was happening, she'd closed the distance between them, coming to a stop just a whisper away from his broad, muscular chest.

She lifted her gaze, and her attention snagged on his mouth—so strange and so familiar, all at once. She'd kissed those lips countless times when they'd been in love. But they'd been teenagers back then. Kissing this new grown-up version of Cam Colden might be an entirely new experience. He wasn't a kid anymore. He was a man.

And she was a woman—a woman who was apparently suffering from a very specific case of amnesia, because she suddenly couldn't remember why she was trying so hard to push him away. The details of the past were taking on a dreamy watercolor quality, and what Jenna wanted most of all was to go back…

Back to a time when she knew without a doubt that she was loved. Back to that sweet and tender place where they'd been unstoppable. Back to innocence and dreams and the unshakable belief in happy-ever-after.

Somehow it seemed like they could find all of that again if only she could muster up the courage to touch her lips to his.

"Oh, Jen," he whispered. "Sweetheart."

She rose up on her tiptoes and wound her arms around his neck, breathing deep. He smelled the same way he always had, like warm leather and crisp, clean laundry that had dried under the Texas sun. And when his hands slid into her loose ballerina bun, she wasn't sure if she was falling back into the past or into a new unfathomable future. All she knew was that she was falling…

Her eyes drifted closed, and in the final, breathless moment before her lips touched his, a bundle of fur wedged itself between them.

For a disorienting second, Jenna wasn't sure what happened. Then her gaze landed on Ginger, wagging her tail and pawing at Jenna's shins as if she'd just suffered through the longest sit-stay of her life. The little dog had probably panicked when she woke up in the office all alone, and in her rush to get to Jenna, she'd pried them apart.

Just in the nick of time.

Chapter Seven

Cam spent the remainder of his first ballet lesson dutifully learning the upper body choreography to Swan Lake, which was shockingly difficult. Difficult enough, in fact, that he managed not to think about the near-kiss for the rest of the session.

How ballerinas moved their arms and shoulders like that while also dancing on their toes was a mystery he'd never understand. By the end of class, he was drenched in sweat and his shoulder felt like he'd just quarterbacked three Super Bowls, back-to-back-to-back.

Was Jenna this hard on her elderly students? Cam seriously doubted it. But he was in Bluebonnet to heal, and if a few torture sessions to Tchaikovsky would help do the trick, he was all for it. Even so, he couldn't help but wonder if Jenna was purposefully trying to make him forget that she'd almost kissed him.

He'd felt it coming. A delicious heat had wrapped itself around them while they'd been talking earlier. It had been like old times, only better. They were all grown up now, and while the innocence of young love had been undeniably intense, they could really connect now without worrying about external factors that were hopelessly out of their control. Like parents…college…distance.

For a moment, Cam had thought they might get a second chance. He could see it in her eyes when she wound her willowy arms around his neck, could hear it in the sharp intake of her breath when she decided to kiss him.

As for Cam, the decision had been made a long time ago. He'd always wanted Jenna Walsh, and he always would—yesterday, today, tomorrow. She'd just felt like a far-off dream for such a long time now that he hadn't dared think they could really make their way back to each other. Especially after she'd left him for someone else.

It still cut deep, but time had taken the sharpness out of that particular wound. Cam was no stranger to scar tissue. He'd been beaten up his entire career, and he always got back up again. *Always.* The body was amazing that way—wounds scarred over. It was nature's way of healing, and the heart was a muscle, just like any other. He was ready to leave the past behind him where it belonged.

But once Ginger interrupted them, Cam lost Jenna all over again.

Jenna was all business afterward, and once his private class ended, she roundly dismissed him. He offered to stick around and help her work with Ginger on the dog's sit-stay, but even that wasn't enough to recapture the magic that had slipped so quickly and easily through their fingers.

We'll find it again, he told himself as he left the studio. His shoulder throbbed with fresh intensity, but it was a good kind of ache—the sort Cam recognized as a sign that he'd eventually be back on the field, maybe even sooner than the team trainer had predicted.

The good news stopped there, though. The next day, Jenna and Ginger accompanied him on another hospital visit, and it was back to business as usual. Jenna lavished attention on the children and guided Ginger in how to interact with the patients, but she spoke to him only when it was strictly necessary. Again he offered to help with Ginger's sit-stay practice afterward, and she begged off, citing a pre-pointe ballet class she needed to teach. But when Cam drove past the dance school an hour later on the way to his sister's house from another physical therapy appointment at the rehab center, the windows were dark and Jenna's car was nowhere to be seen.

He was beginning to wonder if he'd only imagined the way she'd looked at him the day before. Maybe he'd dreamt the entire episode, from the way she'd opened up to him and told him about her life to the wonder in her gaze when she'd risen on to her tiptoes to kiss him.

He hoped they could talk about it at his next ballet class, but instead of giving him a private lesson, Jenna texted and asked him to meet her at the senior center. Cam spent the better part of the afternoon learning adapted *Sleeping Beauty* choreography alongside a group of octogenarians in wheelchairs.

On any other day, he would've loved it. The seniors were ready and waiting for him in Rattlers jerseys and waving silver-and-black pompons. It was just the sort of event he loved, and while a part of him was touched that Jenna arranged it, he couldn't help wondering if she'd done so simply to avoid being alone with him again. As it was, they barely had a chance to speak. Cam caught sight of Jenna leading Ginger to her car after class while he posed for selfies with the residents and staff.

"Okay, out with it," Kelsey hissed under her breath

later that night after he'd read the twins another round of bedtime stories.

Cam had returned to the living room to find her perched on the very edge of their father's recliner, like she wasn't sure whether she really wanted to sit in it or not.

"Out with what?" he asked, rolling his shoulder.

"That." She gestured in the direction of the movement he'd just made. "Tell me the truth. It's bad, isn't it? Your shoulder isn't healing the way it's supposed to."

Of course this was about football. What wasn't in this house?

He dropped onto the sofa. "Sis, my shoulder is fine. It's healing right on schedule. Why would you think otherwise?"

The shoulder was doing great, actually. As luck would have it, the Rattlers had a bye this week. Cam was going to give the physical therapy and ballet training a few more days, and on Monday, he was going to contact the team doc and ask to be reevaluated. He might get through this injury without missing a single game.

"Why would I think otherwise?" Kelsey's eyebrows drew together. "Are you serious? Your head has been anywhere but here the past couple nights. At dinner, Hunter asked you how to spell *touchdown* three times before you even heard him."

Guilt pricked Cam's consciousness. Ignoring his nephews was hardly the path to redemption he'd laid out for himself when he'd first come back to town. "I'm sorry. It won't happen again."

"I don't want you to be sorry, Cam." Kelsey scooted closer to the edge of her seat and reached to give his forearm a squeeze. Another inch and she was going to tumble right out of the La-Z-Boy. "I want you to talk to me. You seemed so relaxed a few days ago, and now you're all broody and tense. Something's happened. Is your shoulder really going to be okay?"

"It really is. I promise," Cam said.

He'd probably be tossing footballs until the end of time. Under normal circumstances, Cam would be thrilled. Football…his foundation…that part of his life had always been enough. But things were different now that he'd come home. *He* was different. Or maybe he'd never really changed at all. Maybe deep down he'd always been the same small-town kid who just wanted to play ball on Friday nights, but he'd tried to transform into the person everyone told him he should be once he'd moved away. All he knew was that being back in Bluebonnet made him want things—things that had faded to the background while he'd been gone. Things like family and community and connection.

And Jenna, of course. Always Jenna.

"Because if it's not, everything will be okay. I hope you know that. You can stay here as long as you want." Kelsey's eyes shimmered with unshed tears, and her grip on his forearm tightened. When was the last time they'd had a heart-to-heart like this? Cam couldn't even remember. "There's life after football."

Cam went very still as her words washed over him like a balm to his soul. He wasn't ready to give up the game, but someday he would be. It was nice to know his family wouldn't consider that day a failure. This was a conversation he never would've had with his dad.

"Thank you. I needed to hear that in a big way." Cam reached into his pocket, pulled out a Rattlers bandana and handed it to her. "Now wipe those tears away before the twins wake up and come in here. We don't want them to think someone died."

Someone had, though. And while his presence still loomed large, the Colden siblings were figuring things out. In the long run, they were going to be more of a family than they ever had been.

Kelsey sniffed as she dabbed at the corners of her eyes with the bandana. "You still haven't told me why you've been so quiet lately."

Cam had never really discussed his love life with his little sister. She'd only been in ninth grade when he'd gone off to college, but she'd known Jenna. If they were going to do this close-knit family thing, he may as well tell her how he felt.

"It's Jenna." Just saying her name was enough to make him ache. He closed his eyes and pressed his fingertips against his eyelids. His head was pounding.

"Oh," Kelsey said, and something about her tone made Cam open his eyes. When he did, he found her wide-eyed and gnawing on her bottom lip. "I didn't realize you two were seeing each other again, apart from working together on your therapy."

"We're not, but…" *But I'm in love with her. I always have been.*

"But you wish you were?"

"Something like that." He nodded. "I have feelings for her, and I think she does for me. But there's some baggage there, and I'm not sure we can get past it. I feel like I'm hurting her, just by being here."

And there it was: his worst fear, laid bare. He'd worried that saying it out loud would make it real, but it was a relief to get the truth off his chest. Maybe now he could breathe again the next time he saw her.

If there was a next time.

"It might be time for me to head back to Houston," he said.

"No. That's a terrible idea." Kelsey gave her head a hard shake. "You're not finished healing. If you have feelings for her, why would you leave? Don't you think you should tell her how you feel before you take off again?"

"I don't think she wants to hear it, and I don't want to force her to listen if it makes her uncomfortable." Cam wasn't blind. He'd gotten Jenna's message loud and clear—she regretted their brief moment of intimacy, and she was doing anything and everything in her power to make sure it didn't happen again. What kind of man would Cam be if he didn't respect her boundaries?

"You really need to tell her how you feel," Kelsey said again, this time with more urgency in her voice.

Cam regarded her, and a prickle of unease made its way up his spine. "I'm surprised you feel so strongly about this. You were in middle school when Jenna and I were together. I figured you were probably too young to remember much about her...about *us*."

"I remember more than you think." Kelsey dropped her head in her hands and stayed that way for a long moment—a moment that seemed to stretch backward in time, straight to the past. When she finally looked up, her eyes were puffy and red-rimmed. "I remember more than you even know."

Cam went cold all over, like he'd just plunged into an ice bath. What the hell was going on? "Kelsey?"

"There's something I need to tell you."

Chapter Eight

"Sit." Jenna made the hand signal for the sit command—an upward-facing palm.

Ginger plopped her rump on the floor and gazed up at Jenna expectantly.

"So far, so good," Adaline said from the sidelines. "Now tell her to stay, and I'll walk slowly over so you can hand the leash to me while you go hide behind the gazebo."

It was Thursday evening in the town square, the night before Ginger's therapy dog certification test, and Jenna was trying to get in some last-minute practice on their most challenging training exercise. When Adaline generously offered to help, Jenna had jumped at the chance for a little assistance, despite turning down a similar offer from Cam when they'd been at the senior center this afternoon. And yesterday, as well, if truth be told.

He'd been so great with the *Ballet is for Everyone* group class, charming the elderly women just as easily as he did the kids at the children's hospital. Jenna had been a nervous wreck ahead of time, knowing full well that she was waffling on her promise to give him private lessons. He had every right to be upset with her. But as usual, Cam had been his affable, charismatic self, and despite her best efforts, Jenna couldn't seem to fall out of love with him again.

You are not *in love with Cam Colden. You had a moment of weakness, that's all. Once he leaves Bluebonnet, you'll never even miss him.*

"Jenna?" Adaline prompted. "Are you going to give Ginger the you-know-what command?"

Right. She was supposed to be training her dog, not mooning over her high school sweetheart. *He broke your heart, remember?*

"Sorry. I don't know where my head is tonight," Jenna said. *Liar, liar, tutu on fire.* She knew exactly why she was distracted. Since the interrupted kiss a few days ago, she'd thought of nothing else. "If Ginger doesn't pass tomorrow, it's going to be one hundred percent my fault."

"Of course it is. Training errors are always the handler's fault, never the dog's." Adaline shrugged. "We learned that very thing in the pet therapy training manual."

"True. But I haven't been the best about practicing lately. I'm afraid I'm going to let everyone down tomorrow—you, Belle, and Maple. But mostly, I'm scared I'm going to let my dog down." Jenna glanced down at Ginger, still holding her sit position like a champ. Her tail wagged, swishing across the soft grass of the park that sat in the center of Bluebonnet's historic town square.

Local businesses, including Adaline's bakery, *Cherry on Top*, and Smokin' Joes, everyone's favorite barbecue food truck, surrounded the grassy area. The park was dotted with dogwood trees, but its central feature was the white gazebo, where Jenna was supposed to be hiding from Ginger.

"Now, wait just a minute. No matter what happens tomorrow, you're not going to disappoint anyone. If you don't pass, you can take the test again. You could even wait until Comfort Paws starts its own training class and evaluation process. No one said you had to do this all on your own. You've done wonders with Ginger since you adopted her. This dog *worships* you." As if on cue, the little Cavalier's tail wagged even harder. "Maybe a little too much, which is why she doesn't want to S-T-A-Y."

"I love that you're spelling it out like she has no idea what's coming. We haven't practiced this command much over the past few days, but we've been over this many, many times." Jenna laughed.

It felt good to relax, even if her personal life was still the same hot mess it had been just seconds before.

"Okay, let's do this." She took a deep breath and focused on her sweet dog, always so willing to please. "Ginger, stay."

She held out her hand with her open palm facing forward. Ginger licked her lips, already anticipating Jenna's departure.

She handed her end of the leash to Adaline and walked toward the gazebo without looking back. Maybe if she projected enough confidence, some of it would rub off on the Cavalier and she wouldn't get anxious in Jenna's absence.

One minute. That's all we need. Just sixty short seconds. You can do it, Ginger.

Jenna counted out the time in her head as she hid behind the gazebo, out of sight. For the therapy dog certification test, this exercise wasn't judged as strictly as it would be if they'd been competing in a formal obedience trial. Once Jenna was out of sight, Ginger could technically break her stay and stand up, but she needed to display relaxed behavior. The evaluators would be looking for excessive panting, whining or drooling—anything that indicated distress. Barking was also a no-no.

Ginger never barked, but every time they'd practiced this exercise so far, the poor dog started crying the moment she could no longer see Jenna.

Jenna squeezed her eyes closed and tried to think good thoughts as the seconds wound down. Once they did, she walked back out in the open and walked calmly toward her dog. The best way to handle comings and goings for a pup with separation anxiety was to keep things low-key. But Jenna could already see Ginger pacing at the end of her leash, ears pushed far back on her head.

The little dog was upset.

Jenna's stomach plummeted. The Cavalier had so much love to give, and she was wonderful with people. But she'd been abandoned by the people who'd raised her. A little separation anxiety was totally understandable. Maybe she was pushing her too hard. Maybe she should just cancel tomorrow's exam altogether.

"Adaline, I'm not sure we're ready for—" Jenna stumbled to a halt as her gaze traveled the length of the leash from Ginger to the handler standing at the other end.

It wasn't Adaline.

"Cam." She couldn't seem to move any closer. "What are you doing here?"

"I've been looking everywhere for you, and when I drove past just now, I spotted Ginger." He nodded toward the dog. Now that Jenna was back in her line of vision, she'd calmed down and curled into a contented ball directly between Cam's feet. Too adorable for words.

Jenna's heart closed like a fist.

"W-where's Adaline?" she stammered.

He tipped his head in the direction of Cherry on Top. "She's inside the bakery, where I'm fairly confident she's spying on us through the window. I asked her if you and I could have a few minutes of privacy."

Jenna looked him up and down. For once, he didn't seem like the cool, confident quarterback, Bluebonnet's conquering hero. He looked more tired than she'd ever seen him before. Lines creased his face, and both his shoulders sagged—not just the injured one—as if the weight of the entire world rested on them.

An ache formed in the back of Jenna's throat. "Cam, are you okay? Has something happened?"

She'd thought he'd come to find her so they could finally talk about the fact that she'd almost kissed him the other day, but this seemed far more dire.

"No, I'm not okay. And yes, something happened." A muscle flexed in his jaw. "Something happened ten years ago, and I just learned the full extent of it tonight."

Ten years ago? A chill coursed through her. Surely he didn't mean…

"Homecoming." The word came out as a pained whisper. He shook his head. "Jen, I had no idea. I'm so, so sorry."

What was he saying? None of this made sense. "You had no idea that you stood me up? How is that even possible?"

He flinched at the sharpness in her tone.

Good, she thought. If he was going to force her to relive that terrible experience after all this time, let him see just how much it had hurt.

"My father." He took a ragged inhale, and his eyes glittered in the twilight.

If Jenna didn't know better, she might've thought he was on the verge of tears.

"He told me you'd found someone else. The morning of the game, he called and told me you'd gone to the homecoming bonfire the night before with your new boyfriend. He said the entire town knew about it, and no one wanted to tell me because they knew how upset I'd be."

Jenna felt like she might pass out. This couldn't be happening. Not now…not after all this time.

"And you believed him?" It caused her physical pain to ask the question. The words themselves felt like nails against the back of her throat.

Cam held up his hands. "He was my dad, Jen."

What was she supposed to say to that? His father was gone now. In a way, none of this should matter anymore.

Then why does it hurt so much?

A sob escaped her, and Ginger immediately sat up. The dog's furry little brow scrunched in concern.

Jenna pressed a hand to her mouth to stop herself from crying. She wasn't going to fall apart over this. Not again.

Cam must've sensed what she needed most right then, because he bent to gather Ginger into his strong arms, walked slowly toward her and gently handed the Cavalier over to her. Jenna hugged the dog as if her life depended on it. Right then, it felt like the truth. Ginger's soft, warm fur and the comfort of her beating heart were the only things holding her together.

"You knew my father. You knew how overbearing he could be, especially about football. He probably thought keeping me away from you was the only way to make sure I'd fully commit myself to my career. And like an idiot, I never saw it. Looking back, it all makes sense. He never wanted me to set foot in Bluebonnet again—not even for his funeral. If I'd come back, I might've learned what he'd done. Until Kelsey told me the truth tonight, I had no idea." His eyes were overly bright, and his voice shook, like he was in a panic to try and explain how he could've believed something so out of character for her.

But the sad truth was that Jenna understood. They'd been so young. If Cam's father hadn't come between them, something else eventually would've done them in. Real life wasn't a fairy tale. First love never lasted. Everyone knew that.

Cam took a deep breath. "I should've known, though. I blame myself, not my dad. I should've had more faith in you. I'm sorry I didn't. Believing what he told me was the biggest mistake of my life."

"It's okay," Jenna said, because she really wanted it to be. She wanted that more than anything…

But things couldn't truly be that easy, could they? History was stacked against them. She couldn't just let it all go.

Could she?

"I'm in love with you," Cam said, and the glimmer of hope she saw in his eyes broke her heart all over again. "I want us to be together, and I know you want that too. Please tell me we can start over."

Jenna clung to Ginger as she shook her head. "You don't love me, Cam. You just think you do. You feel bad about what happened, and you're caught up in the nostalgia of homecoming, and—"

"I do love you, sweetheart. I never stopped." He lifted

a hand toward her and then let it drop slowly to his side as he took in her expression.

Her fear must've been written all over her face. Because that was her overriding emotion as he poured his heart out to her: stone-cold fear.

You love him too, and you know it.

Of course she loved Cam Colden. She loved him so much that it terrified her to her core.

This was too much, too fast. They didn't even live in the same city. He was on television every week, and she taught ballet to preschoolers and senior citizens. The past few days had been magic, but magic wasn't real. Magic couldn't be trusted. Magic didn't last. How were they supposed to pretend that the past decade had never happened?

"I think you should go back to Houston." She couldn't even look him in the eye as she said it. If she did, she might accidentally say what she really wanted most of all.

Stay. Just...stay.

Cam dipped his head and tried to force her to meet his gaze. "I know you don't mean that, Jen."

She hadn't realized she'd started to cry until Ginger licked a tear from the side of her face.

"But I do," she said. More lies. Would they ever stop?

The front door to Cherry on Top swung open, and Adaline marched outside with her arms crossed. "I know I should be minding my own business right now, but I can't. Not when Jenna's out here in tears. Is everything okay?"

"It's fine." Jenna nodded and finally forced herself to fix her gaze on the man she loved. "Cam was just leaving."

Chapter Nine

Jenna woke the next morning to a relentless pounding in her head. She'd cried herself to sleep the night before, and the result was a horrendous headache. She wasn't sure what time it was, but sunlight streamed through her bedroom window, burning her puffy eyes. When she tried to swallow, her mouth was as dry as a bone.

Great. She'd managed to sob herself into a state of dehydration.

She pulled the covers over her head and wished that instead of working so hard on therapy dog training, she'd had the forethought to teach Ginger how to fetch a bottle of water instead. As it was, the Cavalier remained curled next to Jenna's side, snoring while her tiny paws twitched in her sleep.

Jenna envied the dog. She wanted nothing more than to close her eyes and fall back into oblivion. She tried, but the pounding started up again.

Louder this time.

Jenna threw the covers off and sat up. The racket wasn't in her head, after all. Someone was knocking at her front door.

Her gaze flew to Ginger in alarm. "You don't think it's him, do you?"

The dog's small jaws opened, and she released a squeaky yawn.

At least someone around here is relaxed. Jenna's entire body tensed as she braced for another round of pounding.

"Jenna, it's me. I know you're in there. Open up," Adaline called from the front porch.

So it wasn't Cam, after all. Relief coursed through Jenna. She was certain that's what the feeling was, except it felt oddly like disappointment.

Ignore that thought. Cam Colden is probably half-way to Houston by now. Jenna climbed out of bed and headed toward the front door. *As he should be.*

Ginger shook herself off, hopped down from the mattress and pranced after Jenna.

"Good morning," Jenna said as she opened the door and pretended she currently didn't look like death on a cracker. "Thank you for checking on me, but I'm fine. I told you last night I was okay, and it's the truth."

Ginger wagged her entire back end as if Adaline's arrival was the best thing that had ever happened to her. The dog was truly a people person.

"Yeah, you look fine." Adaline snorted. *Ouch.* She shoved a pie box at Jenna as she breezed past her and entered the small cottage, uninvited. "I'm not here to check on you. I'm here to feed you pie for breakfast and to give you and Ginger a ride to your therapy dog certification exam."

Right. That.

Jenna carried the pie to the kitchen, carefully avoiding Adaline's gaze. "We're not going. I thought I mentioned that to you last night."

Adaline heaved a massive sigh. "Don't take this the wrong way, hon. But you said a lot of things last night, and most of them were really dumb."

Jenna regarded her through narrowed, puffy eyes. "If you're going to hit me with those kind of truth bombs right now, this pie better be cherry crumble."

Adaline opened the pie box and waved at her creation with a flourish. "Tada! Of course it is. Cherry crumble is your favorite. Why would I bring anything else?"

"You know me so well." Jenna opened a drawer and removed two forks. The temptation to plunge one of them directly into the pie and eat the entire thing straight out of the pan was very, *very* real.

Adaline gathered plates from a nearby cabinet. "I do, and that's why I'm here. You and Ginger are going to that exam. You've worked too hard for this. If you give up without even trying, you're going to regret it."

Ginger's head cocked to one side at the sound of her name.

"See? Your dog is totally on board." Adaline set the plates down on the counter and bent down to dote on the Cavalier. "Aren't you, you sweet thing? Who's going to pass their therapy dog test today? You are!"

"We're not ready," Jenna said.

"Stop. You're totally ready, and I'm going with you for moral support. Austin isn't exactly close, so we need to eat fast. It might take you a bit longer than usual to get yourself put together." Adaline stood back up and pulled a face as she gave Jenna a once-over. "No offense."

"Lots taken," she said with a laugh. She couldn't even pretend she didn't look like a mess.

Her entire *life* was a mess of epic proportions.

"Should we talk about Cam now or on the drive?" Adaline asked as she set a generous slice of pie onto one of the plates and pushed it toward Jenna.

"Neither." She took a bite, but her throat closed up at the mention of Cam and she could barely choke it down. "There's nothing left to say. I told him to go back to Houston."

Adaline pointed a fork at her. "You neglected to mention that last night."

"I did?"

"Yes." Adaline frowned, but she looked more confused than upset. "You made a point to tell me you definitely weren't in love with him. Several times, actually. But you never said you told him to leave town."

Jenna could barely remember what she'd said. Once Cam had done what she asked and left, everything else became a blur. The sight of his broad back as he walked away had nearly made her crumble. It had taken every last shred of her self-control not to scream out loud and beg him to turn around.

"Thank you for listening last night." Jenna smiled at her friend. She'd told her all about the bombshell news of Cam's father's betrayal and about their almost-kiss at the dance studio, among other things. She wasn't sure how she'd failed to mention the bit about urging Cam to go back to Houston. "And thank you for the pie. I'm just not ready to talk about him yet. All I can say about that is that Ginger was right all along."

Adaline glanced down at the dog, who was staring up at the kitchen counter with laser focus, waiting for a stray crumb to drop. "I'm not following."

"She was right about the kiss. Ginger knew it was

a terrible idea, so she put a stop to it," Jenna said. The Cavalier was worth her weight in gold, but of course she'd known that much already.

"I think we can chalk that incident up to coincidence. Ginger woke up and wanted to find you, plain and simple. She reacted the same way she does whenever you practice her sit-stay. It had nothing at all to do with Cam." Adaline's eyes narrowed. "Furthermore, if you truly want to learn something from your dog, you should pay much closer attention."

What was that supposed to mean? The Cavalier was practically glued to her side twenty-four seven. "Now I'm the one not following."

"Hon, think about it. Ginger has every reason in the world not to trust people, but she's trying her best. That little dog is full to bursting with love, and despite everything she's been through, she lavishes it on you freely. Don't you think fear gets the better of her sometimes? Don't you think she's scared you might leave her, like the terrible person who dumped her at the vet's office when she almost died?"

Jenna's heart plummeted. Adaline was right. That's why the stay command was so difficult for Ginger.

But still the dog tried. Still she loved...without abandon.

"Maybe what Ginger is trying to teach you is the last thing you ever expected." Adaline gave her a hopeful smile.

"It's too late." Jenna shook her head. Cam was gone, and this time, she'd been the one to send him away. She couldn't blame him or his father. This time the heartbreak had been her own doing. "Anyway, you were right about the time. If I don't feed Ginger, let her out and get dressed soon, we'll never make it in time for the test."

Two hours later, Jenna was standing in front of the therapy dog certification exam evaluator with Ginger sitting politely by her side. As expected, the Cavalier passed the basic obedience portion of the exam with flying colors. The second part of the test consisted of various role-playing scenarios like the ones a therapy dog team might encounter in various health-care settings. Jenna guided Ginger on a mock visit with a patient in a makeshift hospital bed, as well as a walker and a wheelchair. Ginger didn't even flinch. After all the practice she'd had at the children's hospital, the senior center and the rehab facility, she was a pro.

"Outstanding work." The evaluator looked up from his clipboard. "You two work really well together. You're going to make a great team out in the field. This little dog of yours is going to make a big difference in the lives of a great number of people."

"She already has," Jenna said with a lump in her throat. *Most of all, she's made a difference in mine.*

Adopting Ginger had changed her. Maybe it had changed her in ways Jenna hadn't even realized yet. Hope stirred deep inside her soul…

Until the evaluator made a note on his clipboard and said the words she'd been dreading since the start of the test.

"Time for the sit-stay portion of your exam." He motioned toward the spot where he wanted Ginger to sit. "This is your final exercise. Best of luck."

"Thank you." Jenna turned her attention toward Ginger and gave her the proper hand signal. "Ginger, sit."

The dog obeyed, and her big, melting eyes never left Jenna's as she executed a beautiful sit.

Jenna took a deep breath. It was time to give her the stay command. *Project confidence*, she told herself.

But then she thought about all the things that Adaline had said earlier about what lessons she could learn from Ginger, and she changed her inner monologue. This wasn't about Jenna's confidence. It was about Ginger and all the ways she'd grown. It was about their relationship.

It was about the power of love to conquer fear.

"Ginger." Jenna made a stop-sign motion with her hand. "Stay."

She handed the leash to the evaluator and walked out of the room with a calm she'd never felt before when practicing this exercise. Her heartbeat remained steady, and more than anything, she felt pure joy at what she and her dog had accomplished together. If they didn't pass the test this time around, that was okay. One day, they would.

"Miss Walsh, you can return now," the evaluator called.

Jenna squared her shoulders, strode back inside the exam room and nearly burst into tears. If she hadn't already cried so much in the past twenty-four hours, she surely would have. Ginger, her sweet, brave little dog, was still sitting exactly where Jenna had left her. She hadn't moved a muscle. Better yet, she seemed perfectly relaxed and content.

She knew I'd come back. That's why she stayed.

"Good girl, Ginger." Jenna heaped praise on the dog. Forget keeping things low-key. This moment deserved a proper celebration. "Good girl."

"Congratulations, Miss Walsh." The evaluator extended his hand. "You and Ginger are an official therapy dog team."

Jenna could hardly believe her ears. "Thank you. Thank you so much."

"You're both excused. I'm sure you're probably eager to share the good news with someone special." He winked at her. "Have a safe trip back to Bluebonnet, Miss Walsh."

She nodded. Jenna didn't need to think about who she wanted to tell first—after Adaline, of course. She knew…she'd always known. Now she just needed to find him. That shouldn't be too hard, right? It wasn't as if Texas was big or anything.

She glanced down at Ginger as they exited the building. "How do you think Adaline might feel about a quick trip to Houston?"

"Houston? Why on earth would anybody want to go there?"

Jenna gasped.

"Cam. You're here." He was right there, in the flesh, waiting for her. Never in her wildest dreams had she allowed herself to believe he might show up today. She'd never even told him where the evaluations were taking place.

"I'm here." He searched her gaze for permission before moving closer, and when she offered him a smile and a nod, he reached for her free hand and wove his fingers through hers.

Then he lifted their intertwined fingertips and pressed a tender kiss to the back of her hand.

She couldn't stop staring at him. Was this really happening? She'd rejected him last night. He'd told her he loved her, and she'd sent him away. And still, here he was, offering that love again. Trusting her to accept it. "*How* are you here?"

"A little birdie might've given me some inside information." He cast a glance over her shoulder where Adaline waved from the other side of the parking lot. No wonder she'd looked confused when Jenna had mentioned she'd told Cam to go back to Houston. She'd probably already known where he was all along. "Might some congratulations be in order?"

Jenna nodded. "We passed."

He squeezed her hand and flashed one of his famous touchdown smiles. "I knew it."

"How could you possibly have known? Ginger only learned how to stay this morning."

"Because I had faith in my two favorite girls." He leaned closer and lowered his voice to a whisper that danced across the sensitive skin on the curve of her neck. "Do you want to hear a secret?"

She nodded, not fully trusting herself to speak. The reality of the moment was finally settling over her, and it was lovelier than a dream.

"Ginger's not the only one who's learned how to stay." Cam's eyes turned serious. "I know there's a lot to figure out, but I'm committed to splitting my time between Houston and Bluebonnet. I've already talked to my coach about it. I'm going to sell the River Oaks house and find a place at home so I can spend the entire off-season there. We can take things at your pace, sweetheart. If you want to go slow, we'll go slow."

A giggle burst from her mouth before she could stop it. Cam tilted his head. "What was that for?"

"You just called Bluebonnet your home." She grinned from ear to ear. "I like the sound of that, Cam Colden."

"Good, because I have an important question to ask you." His eyes danced. "Would you do me the honor of being my date to the homecoming football game tonight?"

At long last, they'd come full circle. They were right back where they'd started, but they were different people now—and still head over heels in love. It was a homecoming in the truest sense of the word, and it had never tasted sweeter.

"It's a date."

* * * * *

HARLEQUIN
Reader Service

Enjoyed your book?

Try the perfect subscription for Romance readers and get more great books like this delivered right to your door.

See why over 10+ million readers have tried Harlequin Reader Service.

Start with a Free Welcome Collection with free books and a gift—valued over $20.

Choose any series in print or ebook. See website for details and order today:

TryReaderService.com/subscriptions